BETWEEN SAND
AND STARDUST

By the Author

Stealing Sunshine

In Every Cloud

Venus in Love

Between Sand and Stardust

Visit us at www.boldstrokesbooks.com

BETWEEN SAND AND STARDUST

by

Tina Michele

2018

BETWEEN SAND AND STARDUST
© 2018 By Tina Michele. All Rights Reserved.

ISBN 13: 978-1-62639-940-2

This Trade Paperback Original Is Published By
Bold Strokes Books, Inc.
P.O. Box 249
Valley Falls, NY 12185

First Edition: January 2018

Credits
Editor: Cindy Cresap
Production Design: Stacia Seaman
Cover Design: Sheri (graphicartist2020@hotmail.com) and Tina Michele

Acknowledgments

First of all, thank you to my tribe. My merry band of misfits, and the renegades of the river. You are the magic that makes this book what it is. I told you I'd write about you all one day, and I kept my promise. All my love to Caitlyn, Chad, Chris, Colin, Garland, Gianna, Jen, Katie, Lyle, Matt, Nancy, Rebecca, and Stephanie.

Thank you to Epic Experience and Renaissance Adventure Guides for providing an environment of love and adventure for thrivers, survivors, and caregivers to "Live Beyond Cancer." You changed my life.

As always, Cindy, this book would not be what it is without your keen eye and talent. Of course, thanks to BSB, Sandy, and Rad for understanding that sometimes life gets in the way of art.

Finally, this finished project would be less than it is without the help, guidance, and "show"manship of my dear friend Kim.

Acknowledgments

For my soul friends and caregiver companions,
James, Wendy, and Shannon.

CHAPTER ONE

Willa Bennette surveyed the freshly turned field that was bordered by a mix of green cypress and pine trees. It was the last thing to check off her to-do list before leaving on this trip. She could smell the fresh soil as it began to warm under the midmorning sun, and it was a scent Willa could never get enough of. She stepped over the primitive border log that edged the field. It was no more than a foot high, yet Willa managed to catch the toe of her boot when she misjudged the height. She stumbled several steps forward into the soft dirt as she recovered her balance, but not without a zing of frustration.

As much as she tried to ignore it, or pretend it wasn't happening, there was no denying that Willa's vision was progressively getting worse, and it was now to the point that it was affecting her depth perception. Eventually, the sight in her right eye would blur, darken, and fade into complete darkness. Willa closed her bad eye and peered out over the field wondering how she was ever going to get used to the fact that one day she would be partially blind. She crouched down and took a handful of soil in her hand, then brought it to her face and closed both eyes. Willa inhaled the earthy scent of the land. Her land. The smells around her gave her a sense of peace and tranquility, and she could feel the tension in her muscles fade away. Feelings she once thought she'd never have again. Willa wondered if her other senses would heighten as her vision faded away. She let the dirt filter through her fingers and paused in the moment trying to slow the passage of time. She took a deep, satisfying breath and let it out slowly. It was times like this, when she was alone with nature, that she had no desire to be anywhere else. She stood, clapped the dust from her hands, and made her way back toward the house.

She had always dreamed of having her own farm. It was one of several dreams that she gave up the moment Dr. Carter sat her down and uttered the unexpected word, cancer. As soon as the word was spoken, Willa had set a plan into motion that would ensure those around her would be sheltered from the process and the outcome, good or bad. While the diagnosis and its aftermath had devastated Willa's life in nearly every way, she had survived.

Willa never discussed the "C-word" with anyone, not even her brother and business partner, Kyle. He had no idea the effects that the chemotherapy and radiation had on her physically or emotionally, and he most certainly didn't know that she was steadily going blind as a result of her treatment. Her treatment had no visible effects on her. There were no scars, no hair loss, and no uncontrollable nausea. All in all, the worst of it was the surgery to implant the radioactive plaque directly onto her eyeball over the tumor inside the eye. Then she spent five days in quarantine in the hospital wearing leaded safety glasses. She had no computer, no cell phone, and no visitors outside of the hospital staff.

Willa didn't want sympathy or sad looks. She didn't want anyone going out of their way or changing their life to help her, and she refused to have anyone treat her differently because of it. Yet, as much as she avoided discussing it with others, she had a constant reminder she could never escape. Willa had done what she needed to do each step of the way. She received the diagnosis, began treatment, and got scanned every six weeks. But even now she hadn't truly processed everything that had happened over the last three years of her life, at least not in the way everyone else thought she should.

Until she began to lose her vision, she had been able to compartmentalize the events surrounding her illness. She tried to keep it separate from her life. If she didn't, she was afraid that she would be too scared to move on for fear of it returning or spreading within her body. Willa couldn't live like that. How could anyone live with a constant fear of death looming over them every moment of the day and night? It was bad enough she had such a reminder every four months when she went to Miami for her routine scans and the inescapable anxiety that accompanied them.

One of the ways Kyle thought she should deal with things was to attend a group camp in the Colorado Rockies. He had come to her a few months earlier with an acceptance letter from Valiant Adventures for her to attend a cancer survivor camp. She appreciated that he cared enough to submit an application on her behalf, but she was also annoyed by his audacity at taking it upon himself to sign her up for six days of misery in the mountains. How could commiserating with a group of cancer patients in the middle of nowhere be anyone's idea of a good time? She had combated the disease and won, that's all that had mattered to her.

Kyle heaved the duffel into the back of the black pickup. It landed with a booming thud. "What on earth do you have in this thing, Will?"

"I don't know, everything. The list of crap was damn near two pages long." Willa might have overcompensated and packed an extra this or that just in case. Her entire body was awhirl with anxiety and anticipation and not in a good way. She hadn't slept at all the night before thinking about the coming days. When Kyle had come to her with this idea, she had no intention of actually going on this trip. That was until she had some time to think about it and go over the packet of materials they had included with her acceptance letter. The brochures and pamphlets were filled with images of smiling campers on horseback on a beautiful, historic ranch surrounded by whitewater rivers and mountain lakes. There wouldn't be enough time to even think about cancer with all the activities that were planned for the week. And that, Willa was more than okay with. Even still, a part of her felt guilty leaving her brother to tend to their farm on his own. "I don't have to go, Kyle. There are a ton of things we could be doing around here instead of—"

Though she was still a bit hesitant with the idea of spending a week with complete strangers, Willa was excited about her trip. It had been years since Willa had taken any time to step away from life. Truthfully, the last major adventure she'd been on was to

Wyoming and the Grand Tetons with her ex-girlfriend, Haven. It had been their last trip as a couple and the most memorable time in her life. Less than a month after they returned, her world imploded, and Willa chose to make the most painful decision in her life. She left Haven. Without reason or explanation, Willa walked out on her, the life they had built, and the future they had planned together. As soon as the doctor uttered the word cancer, Willa vowed that she would not put Haven through the agony of seeing her suffer, becoming her caregiver, or God forbid, watching her die.

Her chest tightened and she tried to swallow around the lump in her throat known as guilt and regret as she remembered the painful months following her diagnosis and the devastating heartbreak she inflicted not only on Haven, but on herself as well. Her life had changed in such a short time. Willa still had days where she wondered what would've happened had she not made the decision she had. There was no use worrying about such things now. It had been three years since all that, and she wouldn't be where she was had it not all gone down the way it had. The way she had arranged it.

"Enough, Will. You're going. For once, take some time for yourself. You need it."

Willa hopped into the rusty pickup, and the engine sputtered to life. She was going to cancer camp. The best she could hope for was a week of fun and adventure, trying new things, and doing as little talking about her cancer as possible. Although she knew that was almost as unlikely as Kyle making it a week without cutting off a finger doing something stupid.

Willa looked back toward the farm as they bumped down the gravel drive to the road and she felt her chest swell with pride. She could still hardly believe that what she was looking at was hers. Well, hers and Kyle's. Three years earlier, every hope and dream she had seemed lost, either snatched from her or tossed away. But then came the day when she heard Dr. Carter tell her that the treatment had worked. However, with the good news came the bad. He warned her that due to its proximity to her retinal nerve it was possible that she could lose some or even all of the sight in that eye. He didn't seem overly concerned until her first scan and vision test. The tumor had maintained its size, but they were already seeing a slight reduction in clarity of her vision. It seemed that she would in fact lose sight in her left eye. She didn't feel the need to tell anyone, including Kyle. Willa never talked about her treatment or prognosis with him, and he knew her well enough never to ask.

With the tumor under control, Willa began to work toward gathering the pieces of her life back together. She had closed herself off from everyone, except for Kyle, and that was only due to his unyielding commitment to always be around. Even if she never told him, she was glad for his companionship. When Willa had the idea to move forward with her dream of buying a piece of land to start a farm, there was no question that she would want Kyle to be her partner. Besides Haven, he was the only person she could make it work with. She might not have been able to salvage the wreckage of her previous life from the choices she had made, and cancer might have taken everything else from her, but if she could make this venture work she would ask for nothing more from the time she had left on this earth.

As they got closer to the airport, Willa got more and more reluctant about getting on the flight. With these memories bombarding her, she started to feel uneasy about the trip. She wasn't afraid of flying as much as she was uncomfortable with the unknown. Plus, she was leaving Kyle on his own to tend to her responsibilities. She had grown used to having very few people around her on a daily basis, and she wasn't going to know a single person on this trip. Willa felt her stomach churn and her breathing quicken at the thought of having to talk about herself, about her cancer in front of a bunch of strangers. Hell, she hardly knew the person she had become over the last few years, and now she would have to talk about herself? She had a sudden desire to jump out of the moving truck and run in the opposite direction of the airport. She rubbed her temples, trying to ease the headache that was now threatening to take over her entire head. This was going to be a long week.

❖

Haven Thorne closed her eyes and steeled herself before the reverend called her to the pulpit. It wasn't the first time that she'd been called before the congregation and guests to express her deepest condolences for the loss of their friend. "Thank you all for being here to celebrate the life of our dear friend, Falsey Daniels. A beautiful soul whisked away from us by the bane that is cancer. So many times I have been asked why I choose to fight alongside these brave men and women as they battle whatever comes at them. My answer is simple, because I am one of them." Haven finished her eulogy and dabbed the tears that clung to her lashes.

In what seemed like a lifetime ago, Haven had been a victim of cancer. She had been diagnosed when she was seventeen after a rapidly growing mass was discovered on her thyroid. Within months, what had started as a small lump had grown to the size of a golf ball. As a self-conscious teen in her senior year of high school, Haven had simply done what she could to hide the growth and pretend it would just go away on its own. It hadn't.

"Haven, what is that?" Willa asked.

Haven covered the large lump at the base of throat. "It's nothing. Just a knot."

Willa grabbed Have's hand and moved it out of the way to expose the knot on her neck. "This isn't nothing, Haven. Do your parents know about this?" Willa's face flushed white.

That was all it had taken before all hell broke loose in her life. The next few weeks were a buzz with doctor visits, waiting, biopsies, waiting, CT scan, bone scans, blood tests, always followed by more waiting. She could still recall the fear in everyone's eyes when the results determined that it was in fact cancer. She had cancer. How could this be happening? She was only seventeen.

The whole time, Willa had never left her side. She was there with her on the day of her surgery, holding her hand and talking about everything they still had yet to do in their lives.

"We could take a gap year and backpack across Europe. Or we could move out to Colorado and work as ranch hands for minimum

wage." Willa did whatever she could to keep Haven's mind on the future.

"You've been my rock through all of this." She knew that there wasn't anyone else she wanted to spend her future with. "I love you, Willa." Somewhere in the middle of the worst days of her life, she had fallen in love with her best friend. The last thing she remembered before they took her to the operating room were the soft, warm lips pressed against hers.

In the end, Haven had been lucky. The tumor was centralized to her thyroid, and she was able to avoid both chemotherapy and radiation. Of course, she was now forced to take daily medications to compensate for hormones her body could no longer produce. For years, it had become the only reminder of her cancer battle, and in her mind, she got off far easier than so many others.

Haven returned to her seat and sat next to Bianca Nathan and let her own hand be held in Bianca's lap. She wasn't always opposed to public displays of affection. Sometimes, Haven felt that Bianca's constant adorations and declarations were a bit over the top, but she always knew when Haven needed a little external support, whether it was a hand or a hug, or even a boost of confidence when she was feeling low on self-esteem. Their relationship was still quite new to Haven, both personally and professionally. She was just getting used to the directions her life was taking, but she was thankful to have someone like Bianca supporting her as she explored this life she was making for herself.

Her road out to Colorado was an interesting one. For Haven, her cancer had always been just a blip on the radar. Save for her anxiety disorder, it wasn't an issue that came up often or affected her in any significant way. As strange as it was, most of the time she actually forgot that she'd had it unless some stranger noticed the scar on her throat and asked her about it. Which, awkwardly enough, was how she eventually found herself on a plane to Colorado to attend Valiant Adventures. As fate would have it, she met a fellow cancer survivor, Caitlyn, when she began dating one of her friends back home. It was her experience with melanoma that led her to Valiant as a means of meeting others dealing with cancer and learning how to keep living in spite of it. While Haven had thought she was doing a fine job of living beyond cancer, she had no idea just how much it had truly affected the decisions she made every day. Caitlyn helped her see that no cancer is easy, and that Haven still found herself obsessing over every odd bump or pain wondering if it might be the disease making its return to her life.

Once she made the decision to attend the camp, she learned so much in just six days with ten survivors on the rivers of Colorado. It changed her life, but more than that, it gave her life back. She could help others the way Caitlyn had helped her. She found a family and they filled her with hope and purpose. Haven was now dedicated to Valiant and helping other cancer patients find their new normal and the strength to keep up the fight. Unfortunately, there were times when that also included saying a final good-bye to them when they were too weak to go on.

After the service, everyone flowed out of the church. Haven and Bianca mixed and mingled briefly on the steps outside of the church before saying good-bye and heading to the car. "I still don't understand how you do it," Bianca said, holding the passenger door open for Haven.

"Because it makes such a difference in their lives. Before it's too late."

"But they always die. You make friends and then they die." Bianca closed the door and circled around to the driver's side.

Haven had answered this question before. Not just from Bianca, but from just about everyone she'd ever talked to about her dedication to the nonprofit camp she volunteered with. She took a deep breath as Bianca slipped into the car. "They don't always die. And if they do lose the battle, I know that for a time they lived. Truly lived, and I get to be a part of that. I get to see them in their happiest moments, living in spite of the disease that is trying its damndest to kill them."

"It just seems like a lot of loss to purposely set yourself up for, you know?"

"None of us are getting out of here alive, Bianca. Valiant gives them a chance to experience life, even for a short time. It gives them hope. It gave me hope."

"And it brought you to me, and for that I am thankful. You're an amazing woman, Haven. I love you." Haven smiled as Bianca reached once again for her hand and rested them on the console between them.

As they approached the next intersection, Haven blurted out, "Wait, turn here!"

"What? You're not coming home with me?" Bianca asked.

"I can't, hon. I'm leaving for camp in the morning, and I haven't gotten any of my stuff together yet," Haven said.

"You do this every time." Bianca laughed. "Are you serious? I don't know how you manage to get anything done sometimes."

"That's what I have you for, remember? At least that's what you constantly tell me. You can always come stay with me and leave in the morning when I do."

"Do you have to go away to camp this time? I'd like us to spend some actual time together."

Haven sensed what was coming next. They were minutes from her apartment, but she didn't think they were going to get there before Bianca would get to ask her question. No matter how hard she pressed her foot into the floorboard, the car wouldn't go any faster.

"Why don't you just move in with me? Then we don't have to spend half our time arranging our relationship around all our commitments." Bianca pulled into the parking spot but made no move to exit the vehicle, which meant neither could Haven.

"Bianca, you know I'm not ready for that. We've only known each other a short while and have dated barely half that time. I just don't think it's a good idea."

"It's a fine idea if you think about it. We could combine our professional and personal relationship into one perfect package. And I wouldn't have to keep asking you how your portraits are coming along. I could see it for myself."

Haven always felt that the moment she would make art her

career that it would no longer be fun for her. She didn't like to be told what to do, and she certainly did not like being hovered over. Whether it was in her life, love, or career, she had always found it difficult to meet any sort of deadline. The best way to get her *not* to do something was to tell her she had to. And that hadn't changed just because she had moved to Colorado and gotten involved with Bianca, her artist agent. She decided that she wasn't going to think about that right now.

"Oh, wow. Um. How about we go inside?" There was nothing Haven wanted less than someone standing over her shoulder watching her work. The idea almost made her never want to pick up a brush ever again. Haven headed into the house.

"So, is that a yes?" Bianca asked, following Haven inside and closing the door behind her.

Haven took a deep breath and strode toward Bianca. She wrapped her arms around her shoulders. "Bianca, I like things the way they are right now, and I can think of several different things I'd much rather be doing than talking about this, again." Haven traced a finger along Bianca's collarbone. Haven dipped her head and ran her tongue along the taut muscle leading up to her ear. Bianca purred.

"Now? We just got back from—ahhh." Haven flicked open a button and slid her hand into Bianca's shirt. She cupped a full breast in her palm and pinched a nipple roughly between her fingers until it rose in response. Bianca sucked a quick breath through her teeth.

"Everyone has sex after a funeral. Plus, I leave tomorrow for an entire week. A whole week without sex is the worst part about these trips." Haven quickly worked the buttons of Bianca's shirt open. This was just one of the things she'd rather do than discuss a question she had no intention of answering. She slipped Bianca's shirt down off her shoulders and dug her nails into her soft and supple skin. Goose bumps rose over her own body as Bianca groaned from the sting.

"Mm, somebody wants to play rough, I see," Bianca said.

Haven stepped back and feigned innocence before Bianca lurched forward and took a handful of Haven's long hair and wrapped it around her wrist. Haven gasped at the jolt of electricity and heat that flooded her body. Bianca controlled Haven's movements and pulled her close, tilting her head to the side and exposing Haven's neck.

"Take me," Haven demanded as she offered herself to Bianca. As Bianca leaned in to lick Haven's delicate skin, Haven ran her hand down to the zippered seam of Bianca's tight pants. She felt an unexpected yet familiar bulge and her heart raced with anticipation. "You naughty girl." To think that Bianca had packed for a funeral with every intention of taking Haven whenever and wherever she'd asked sent waves of need through her.

Bianca held all the control with one hand wrapped tightly in Haven's hair. She spun her around and bent her over the back of the couch. She tossed up Haven's skirt and squeezed her ass. Haven moaned with desire. Bianca pushed her panties down and ran her fingers through Haven's wet folds.

Bianca released Haven's hair and freed her silicone cock from the boxer briefs. Once free, she slid inside Haven with a commanding thrust. Bianca gripped Haven's hips and pushed deep inside her, claiming her, taking her. Haven opened herself up and let Bianca take everything she wanted. Everything except for her heart.

❖

Haven pulled into the driveway and honked the horn. As she waited, she connected her cell phone via Bluetooth so she could access her music files on the drive. This was one of her favorite parts of camp week, the drive up into the majestic Rocky Mountains. To make it even better, her dear friend Wendy was coming along for the ride. She had met Wendy just a year earlier when Haven attended camp as a camper.

Haven looked up as Wendy lugged her duffel to the SUV. Her modern black and blond hair was pulled up in a short, simple ponytail. Haven hopped out and opened the back so Wendy could toss her things in. "Hey there!"

"Hey, hey!" Wendy said before she grunted and tossed her bag into the truck.

"Are we ready to go?"

"Giddyup!" Wendy said, tapping on the dashboard.

Haven still found herself in awe each time she headed west on I-70. The earth dipped and then rose suddenly toward the sky. It kept rising with each curve and turn along the way. The red rock cliffs transformed into steel gray rock face covered with evergreens and splashes of yellow from the early changing aspens. Remnants of the Old West dotted the mountainsides with abandoned gold mines, vacant tunnels, and dilapidated ore mining rails jutting out and dropping off the hillside. The Colorado River rushed alongside the highway, and Haven couldn't wait to get back on the water. The river roared between the colossal range and surged over the boulders and obstacles in its way, and her heart raced with it.

CHAPTER TWO

Haven and Wendy met up with two other volunteers, Caliente and Diego, on the patio of the main lodge. Haven was excited about the week already. She'd met them when she was once a camper at Valiant. They had each changed her life in the most unique and unexpected way. Prior to her experience as a camper Haven had never considered herself a cancer survivor in the grand sense of the term. In her eyes, her personal experience with the disease had been brief. In her mind, she had barely had time to absorb her diagnosis before she was declared disease free.

Haven rubbed lightly at the scar on her throat. Her heart skipped, a rush of adrenaline surged through her, and her thighs tingled with pins and needles. She took several deep breaths and fought back the sudden onslaught of panic. She could rappel from a three-hundred-foot waterfall, kayak a Class IV rapid, or zip line over a thousand-foot gorge, but when her thoughts centered around her health, it sent her anxiety into full tilt. She always became hyperaware of each and every pang and pain in her body.

It was when she attended the camp that she finally confronted those repressed fears, irrational thoughts, and the uncertainty about her future if the cancer ever returned. As much as she told herself that she'd escaped the worst of the cancer, ultimately, her mental and emotional battle was like that of so many others regardless of severity or prognosis. It was worse every twelve months when she went in for her routine scans. Fortunately, this anxious episode was brief and she pulled herself back into reality and the excitement of the day and the week ahead.

Besides Wendy, Diego was one of her best friends. His heart was as big as he was, and a single hug from him wrapped Haven in more love than she thought possible. During their first camp together, he and Wendy became her people instantly. They were the three musketeers and forged a bond that would last a lifetime. They were the reason she packed up her life in Florida and moved eighteen hundred miles across the country. Of course, a devastating breakup had its own significant role in the decision as well.

Everything always came back around to Willa Bennette, the woman who broke her heart into a million tiny shards. The woman who stuck by her through her diagnosis, surgery, and recovery. The woman she'd known nearly all her life, and the one who almost killed her the day she walked out of her life without reason or explanation. Haven almost didn't make it to that first camp to meet Diego, Wendy, and so many strangers who she now considered her family, her tribe. It was in her darkest and scariest months afterward, when Haven found it just about impossible to deal with life, that she found Valiant. It was a cancer camp, but she found more solace and hope for life in one week than she ever thought possible. She owed them her life, in more ways than one.

As the black SUVs rounded the long driveway, Haven grew even more excited. She couldn't wait to meet the newest members of the Valiant family and experience so many amazing moments with another group of fighters and thrivers. Haven hoped there was a mixture of young and old, men and women, as it made things so much more interesting. The way such an environment could bring together a thirty-five-year-old mother from Tennessee with a seventy-six-year-old gay man from Boston and spark a connection that would last a lifetime.

Haven stretched her back from side to side in preparation for the hardest part of the guests' arrival. The luggage. She was thankful to have Diego and his mass of muscles to help out with this part. Her belly grumbled as the trucks pulled up to the lodge, and she wished she'd eaten the energy bar she knew was still sitting on the counter between the kitchen and dining room.

As soon as the vehicles came to a stop, the doors popped open at once. And just like that, people and bags were spilling out of every opening. It was a cool afternoon at 13,000 feet in the Colorado Rockies, so it was easy to tell who her fellow thin-skinned Southerners were as they smiled and laughed between gasps of surprise and the weird fishy mouth movements they made trying to see their breath in the air. There were hugs and cheek kisses all around as the volunteers greeted the guests as well as the other volunteers just arriving. Everyone introduced themselves.

The commotion was exhilarating, and Haven moved amongst the crowd making her way toward the rear of the truck. She stopped when a large black duffel came flying out of the backseat and landed with a heavy thud on her feet. "Whoa, shit!" Haven shouted at almost being knocked out by a sixty-pound sack chucked at her.

"Sorry!" the voice shouted from inside the vehicle.

She had expected a deep, male voice in response to her, but what she heard was not deep, nor was it male, but it was all too familiar. Her stomach leapt into her throat and her heart slammed to a stop. She peered into the truck as a figure emerged. Her head was tucked, and Haven couldn't see her face. Her heart started again but in triple time. The woman stepped out onto the ground with a crunch of gravel beneath her worn brown Justin work boots. Her jeans hung loose around the calf but worked up to a snug fit around strong thighs. Haven's gaze traced up from the boots up, and her heart felt like it would burst from her chest. Her head told her it couldn't be, but everything else inside said her otherwise. She could feel her ears burning, and the whooshing of her blood deafened her. The T-shirt, front-tucked to show a statement buckle that Haven had once purchased as a gift. Haven watched the woman's hand as it reached up to the bill of her ball cap as she straightened it and then looked with dark brown eyes straight into her own.

"What the fuck?" Haven said without any ability to do otherwise. Her hands turned into ice, her blood ran cold in her veins, and she struggled to keep her legs beneath her. Haven had no idea where she was. For all she knew, she had just been hit by a bus and was in the throes of death on her way to the hospital. "I...I need..." Haven stumbled backward, pulling her feet from beneath the heavy bag. She held up her hand and mumbled something about nothing. She blinked in confusion, trying to make sense of what, or rather who, she was seeing. She turned away and headed through the crowd into the lodge. Someone had handed her a backpack and a bag of cups and napkins as she passed, so she set them down on the table as she made her way through the dining room in a daze.

She finally let her legs give out, and she fell into a large blue denim chair. She sank down and prayed that it would swallow her whole. Haven tried to convince herself that she was seeing things. She'd heard many times about doppelgangers; it could be that. There could be another woman on Earth who looked, dressed, and smelled just like Willa. She knew it wasn't a doppelganger, or a long lost twin situation. She knew there was not another woman in the world with eyes that could see into her soul. The world had one Willa Bennette, and she was here.

Haven's heart was beating double-time. She clenched her fists, closed her eyes, and jammed the pads of her thumbs into the sockets at the bridge of her nose. *This can't be happening. This can't be happening.* Her entire body was ablaze. Not with arousal or desire, but with a building fire of anger that she hadn't felt since the day Willa had given her some bullshit excuse for why "the relationship was no longer working for her." Haven had replayed the moment in her head a thousand times, but suddenly with the rushing of blood in her ears, and the beads of sweat forming on her lip, she couldn't recall the exact words Willa had used. The last words she thought she'd ever hear her say, before today.

❖

Willa could only stare in disbelief as she watched Haven disappear into the lodge. The awe and wonder that she had experienced driving up into the mountains was gone in an instant.

Her mind swirled with a thousand disconnected words, her ears hummed with the buzz of muffled voices, and her body stood frozen in place. How was it even possible? Willa couldn't even begin to fathom what the odds could be that she would come face-to-face with Haven after three years, eighteen hundred miles, and thirteen thousand feet.

Her hair was blonder, more of a bleach blond versus her once natural golden color. It was a wild style sticking out in various uncontrolled directions with a vibrant headband doing nothing to hold the unruly strands in place. Willa couldn't help but notice how natural it looked on her, but also how uncharacteristic it was for Haven. Add that to her capri length, roughed-up boyfriend jeans, and what Willa could describe as a sort of long, crocheted, hippie sweater vest. Anyone else might not have recognized her. Hell, had it not been for her steel blue eyes and the familiar way her lips puckered up as she silently mouthed her name, Willa would've missed it, too.

A tap on her shoulder zapped Willa out of her haze. She blinked and focused on Diego, who stood next to her motioning to her bags.

"Hey there," Diego said. "Is this all we have for you?"

"Uh. Yeah. That's it." Willa stooped to pick up her duffel, but he was faster.

He scooped her bag up and slung it over his shoulder in one smooth motion. "Follow me," he called to her, heading off and away from the main lodge.

Willa glanced one more time toward the door where Haven had disappeared before she jogged along after Diego. "We've got you in cabin two with your bunkmate, Corey."

Just then, Corey popped her head out the front door of the cabin and smiled.

"Willa! Sweet."

"Hey there. It looks like we're roomies." Willa was pleasantly content with her roommate lottery. She and Corey had actually met in the airport earlier that day as they sat and waited for the other campers' flights to arrive. She was eleven years younger than Willa but mature beyond her twenty years. Cancer did that to people, it seemed, but Corey had an undeniable love for life, and it showed on her face with a constant toothy grin. Willa expected such a perky attitude to grate on her nerves, but so far so good.

Diego bid his farewell. They had just enough time to freshen up and change for dinner. Willa heaved her duffel onto the bottom bunk, and to her relief, the younger and smaller Corey had opted for the top bed before Willa had to beg. The cabin was small and old. The floors creaked with each step and sloped more than a little to one side. She leaned down to take a look out the window, and she could feel the draft from the outside. She had a feeling it was going to get a bit cooler both inside and out as night moved in.

Willa rummaged through her bag looking for something to change into. She was kicking herself that she hadn't brought a single nice thing to wear. She was prepared with an assortment of water-friendly attire made of the less-than-flattering spandex. As she removed each item from her bag, she thought she might have under packed. She growled and threw a wad of undergarments back into her duffel.

Corey peeked down over the railing of the top bunk. "What's up, Willa?"

"Would you believe it if I told you that I didn't bring anything to wear?"

"No. Your bag weighs a million pounds. I'd say you brought everything to wear. Why does it matter?"

"I don't know. It doesn't." Willa picked out a pair of jeans and a T-shirt from the pile and wrapped them up together. An image of Haven flashed through her mind. While her chance at a first impression was out the window, she thought she could make it up by changing into something a bit nicer for her.

"You don't have to impress me if that matters any. I met you after a six-hour flight and two-hour time change, so it's all downhill from here." Corey reached out for Willa instead of taking the ladder at the end of the bed.

Willa chuckled and helped Corey off the top bunk. She was a small girl, made even smaller by the effects of chemo. Willa imagined that if she had to, she could carry Corey around on her back. "Don't get used to this, miss."

"Too late," she said as Willa set her down onto the floor. "Now, why are you so concerned over your clothes?"

"Nothing. No reason. I just like to be presentable. You never know." Willa dismissed her and picked up her change of clothes.

"Oh. You're gonna be a fun nut to crack. Don't worry, I'll figure you out." Before she even finished her threat, Corey disappeared into the bathroom.

"Hey, not cool," Willa called out before she smiled and sat on her bed. Willa liked her. She was fun, and she had no doubt that the kid was going to be able to ferret out everything sooner rather than later. Though she would prefer it be later. Much later. "Hurry up. I have to pee!"

Oh yeah. Just like having a little sister.

❖

Haven stood at the sink as the cold water hissed from the tap. She stared down at the lettuce she turned over and over in her hands.

"Haven. Hello, anybody home?" Wendy reached over and took the world's cleanest vegetable from Haven's hands. "You've nearly washed the green right off this lettuce. Where are you right now?"

"What? Oh, here. I'm here." Haven was sure her body was where she thought it was, but her mind was most definitely somewhere else. "Sorry," she said as she turned off the running water.

"It's okay. But you've been acting like a weirdo since the campers got here. Weird as in it's not like you to run off and hide while we are trying to get everyone's stuff unloaded." Wendy ripped the leaves of lettuce into small shreds and dropped them into the bowl beside her. "Cut those avocados," she said as she motioned with her head toward the bowl of wrinkled fruit.

Haven hated avocados, but everyone always insisted that she was the best at cutting them up. *Everybody has something.* Willa loved avocados. She would eat them any way they were served—

cubed, sliced, mashed, or guaced. Her first thought was to cut an extra or two just for Willa, but then she came to her senses. She didn't need avocados; she needed to get the hell out of Haven's space.

Her beautiful, new, heartache-free space. She didn't move eighteen hundred miles across the fucking country to have Willa just stroll into her new life and start screwing shit up. Haven had spent three years trying everything she could to get her out of her mind and memory. How was it even possible that after all that Willa would find the one place on earth where Haven was at peace and ruin it? Haven heaved the chef's knife down into the pit of an avocado and hacked straight through it. She stared at the murdered fruit with shock. She had no idea how much force it should take to split an avocado pit in one swoop, but she just did it. She set the knife down and backed up a step from the counter. Out of the corner of her eye, she saw Wendy, who was just as surprised and a little paler than usual.

"What the hell?" Wendy said as she grabbed Haven by the shoulders and maneuvered her away from the instruments of death. "Okay. Spill. Something is going on with you. You could have cut your entire hand off. What gives?"

"Willa," Haven whispered.

"Your ex? What in the world does she have to do with anything?"

"Shhh." Haven's eyes darted around them as the campers started to gather in the lodge.

"Why?" Wendy's eyes followed Haven's. "Is she here? Ha." Wendy's laugh was truncated when Haven looked her in the eyes with certainty.

"Yes."

"What. The. Fuck. You're shitting me."

"Oh, how I wish I was."

"I didn't know she had cancer, too."

"She doesn't." It wasn't until Wendy said it that it hit Haven, and it hit her like a ton of bricks. "Oh." She felt her lungs tighten and her stomach turn. Why else would she be at a cancer retreat?

Seeing Willa get out of the SUV had been a jolt, but the realization that Willa had cancer was paralyzing. How did she not know? When was she diagnosed? Why hadn't she called? A million questions flooded her mind. The thought of Willa fighting the disease alone was devastating to Haven. Although, as far as she knew Willa wasn't alone. A selfish streak flashed as she imagined someone else holding Willa's hand through her battle. Guilt overtook the jealousy as she admonished herself for even thinking it. "I'm going to be sick."

Wendy slid her hand under Haven's arm just as her legs began to shake. "Come on." Wendy and Haven slid out the back door of the lodge into the cool evening air. She took several deep breaths and grounded herself. So many thoughts and emotions swirled inside her mind and body, each one being replaced by another as quickly as they came. "Look at me," Haven said as she held out her trembling hands.

"I'm speechless, Haven. I don't have any idea what to say. I should say something, but, yeah, I've got nothing." Wendy rested a comforting hand on Haven's.

"You and me both," Haven said as the dinner bell rang out.

"I've got to go, but I think you should stay here. Go back to the bunkhouse for a bit. I'll bring you a plate."

"Nah. I'm just gonna sit here for a minute. Till I get my legs back, plus I'm not all that hungry anymore."

"Okay. I'll be back to check on you once everyone is all set." Wendy gave Haven a couple of quick swipes on her back before she disappeared back into the house.

As soon as Wendy was gone, Haven pulled herself up and wandered off the porch into the dusky night. She followed the stone path around the lodge to the clearing between the main house and the cabins. They led her back to the fence line of the north pasture just beyond a stand of evergreens. Several large boulders made for an elevated perch above the damp grass. She hoisted herself up onto the flattest one and crossed her legs.

The ridgeline was barely visible as the last of the evening sun set beyond the mountains. Soon the sky would dance with a million diamonds, so spectacular it would make her dizzy if she hadn't been already with the arrival of Willa and the subsequent whirlwind of emotions.

"Three years." So much had happened in just three years. Haven had lost the love of her life when Willa walked out on her. Haven spent month after month holding out hope that a lifetime of friendship and love was enough to bring Willa back. She avoided familiar places and painful memories. And when none of that worked, Haven said good-bye to the sand and sun of her hometown and moved to Colorado. She found a new life in the mountains, a new career as a professional artist, and a new romance with Bianca. But it had always been Willa Bennette. From their childhood days on the kindergarten playground, they had been inseparable. First as friends and then as lovers. They had experienced every moment of life together, good, bad, or indifferent. They had grown up together, grown into each other, and the day Willa left, Haven felt that her body had been torn in two, like a tree struck down the middle by a bolt of lightning. It was a deep scar, ripped open once again by those dark brown eyes.

Chapter Three

Willa and Corey sat together at the long, rustic table made from a solid plank of wood. Silverware clanked on plates and laughter filled the room as campers and volunteers got to know one another. Willa tried to pay attention to everyone as they introduced themselves, but her mind was somewhere else. Her attention was caught by every movement beyond the dining room as she searched for Haven. She wasn't at the dinner table, and Willa hadn't seen her since she arrived. She was starting to think that maybe she truly didn't see her, and it had been some bizarre hallucination. She felt someone looking at her and scanned the room for Haven, but it wasn't her. Diego and another one of the volunteers, a woman, smiled and waved at Willa from the end of the table. Willa returned their greeting with a nod. As she smiled in return, she watched the woman's focus shift beyond Willa and her eyes widen with surprise.

Without needing to turn around, Willa felt Haven's presence behind her. Diego looked from Willa to Haven and back again, before standing and calling out to her, "Haven, over here."

Haven made her way over to Diego without ever looking in Willa's direction. Haven smiled and greeted everyone she passed except for Willa, but she wasn't surprised. She got to Diego and rubbed his broad shoulder with her petite hands. Willa didn't recall Haven's hands being so small, but she did remember how soft they were. It was when Haven leaned down to the woman beside Diego and put a gentle kiss on her lips that Willa looked away.

The unexpected expression of affection hit Willa in the gut and left her breathless. She crumpled her dinner napkin and dropped it onto her unfinished plate. She was becoming anxious and suffocated by the warm air and chattering people in the shrinking dining room. Willa looked over at Corey in a panic. "Excuse me. I need to get out." Willa barely waited for Corey to move over before she shifted to stand and swung her leg out over the bench.

Just as she'd gotten both legs onto the other side, Mama Lu called everyone's attention. Willa groaned with an unexpected volume. Corey looked at Willa with wide questioning eyes. Willa made an attempt to cover it up by clearing her throat and then taking a large sip of her beverage. "I'm so sorry. That came out wrong. Please, continue." Willa hung her head, embarrassed, and she had no doubt everyone in the room stared in her direction, including Haven. Willa wished for nothing more than for the entire room to shrink down into a speck with her in it and implode into a little poof of smoke.

Willa sat with her back against the table as Mama Lu announced the plans for the remainder of the evening, which involved the first group evening meeting to be spent by the campfire. Willa had hoped that after dinner she could escape to her cabin and figure out what she was going to do about Haven for a week. The group was dismissed with just enough time to go and gather sweatshirts or other items for warmth since the temperature had dropped.

Willa beelined toward her cabin with Corey close on her heels. "Willa, wait up," she called after her. Willa didn't slow down, so Corey sped up. "Dude. For real, your legs are longer than my entire body."

Willa heard the breathlessness in Corey's voice, so she slowed down enough for her to catch up. "Sorry."

Once they were alone inside their cabin, Corey grabbed her by the arm. "What the hell was that all about?"

Willa tucked and rolled into the bottom bunk and let out an exasperated sigh. "My ex is here."

"What? Bullshit! Who?" Corey asked as she invited herself into Willa's bunk and crossed her legs.

"Haven."

"Nooo!"

"Yesss," Willa hissed as she flung her arm over her eyes.

"Okay. Okay. Good grief. You have so many questions. Okay. Wow." Willa could feel the bed vibrating with Corey's unrestrained excitement.

"This is so exciting!"

Willa uncovered her eyes and stared at Corey. "This is anything but."

"Oh, ended badly, did it?"

"You could say that."

"Was it your fault or hers?"

For Willa, "fault" implied that she or Haven had done something specific to lead to the demise of their relationship. It wasn't like Willa gave herself cancer as an excuse to bail on Haven and their life together. In fact, Willa felt that she had ultimately done Haven a favor. "Let's just say that she had no choice. I ended it, and I didn't give her any other option."

"You cheated on her, didn't you? Not cool, Willa."

"No, I didn't cheat on her. But I may as well have. It would be a better story than the truth."

"You chased her away. You got cancer, and you chased her away."

Willa sat up so quickly that she bumped her head on the slats of the top bunk. "How the fuck could you know that?"

"I have cancer, too, remember? You aren't the first person diagnosed who's shut everyone out or chased everyone away. It's easier than when they leave you, I suppose."

"You know, I never even told her I had cancer. I just decided that I didn't want her to be responsible for taking care of me. She'd already fought her own battle. She didn't need me putting her through that again."

"Oh, wow."

Willa had never told anyone that, not even her brother. "I never thought I'd see her again or have her find out. And now here I am eighteen hundred miles from home at a cancer camp with her."

"You didn't know she'd be here?"

"No fucking idea. None. I'd never even heard about Valiant until my brother signed me up a few months ago."

"Fate."

"What?" Fate. Willa didn't believe in fate. Not anymore. Once upon a time she had, back when she and Haven first met in elementary school. In high school, they'd both struggled with their feelings for years, as life pushed them together and pulled them apart. It wasn't until college that they decided to stop denying themselves a chance at true love. "Fate is crap."

"I don't think so. But either way, something brought you both here together."

"You did see her kiss that other chick, right?"

"What? No! Who? The other blonde, Wendy? Ha! No way. She's married to a jujitsu instructor in Denver."

"How the hell do you know that?"

"At dinner, when I was talking to Scrat, the kayak instructor who was sitting next to you."

"Who? Kayaking?" Willa hadn't heard any of the conversation held right under her nose, literally.

"Oh my, let's go. I'll fill you in on the way to campfire." Corey crawled out of the bunk, grabbed the large hoodie hanging on the post, and tossed it to Willa.

❖

Haven and Wendy picked their log at the campfire and scooted close to each other. Each of them had layered up in comfy sweats and coats with a thick wool blanket across their laps. After they were settled and warm, Diego strolled up looking to get in. Haven took one look at his flip-flopped feet and flung the edge over his bare legs.

Once they were settled, Diego leaned over Haven. "What was with the kiss at dinner, ladies?"

Wendy leaned toward him, until Haven was squeezed in the middle. "That's what I want to know," she whispered.

"I'm so sorry about that. I was feeling a little overconfident after spending twenty minutes psyching myself up."

"And part of that was to use me to make her jealous? Not that I mind. I've had worse offers," Wendy said.

"No. Not at all. I just...I don't know. Maybe?"

"Yeah, I don't know what you're going to do the rest of the week, because if you keep kissing me it's going to start all kinds of rumors around here. Not that I mind. I could use a sharper edge."

"You don't need any more edge, Wendy," Diego said.

"Don't worry. I won't do it again. I'm just going to avoid her, that's all. Kitchen duty for me." Haven despised kitchen duty, and washing dishes make her sick to her stomach. But it was a sacrifice she was willing to make in order to avoid seeing, hearing, or interacting with Willa.

"Um, I doubt Mama Lu is going to let you do that. Plus, you won't be able to hide in the kitchen all the time."

"I can try like hell."

"Then you better get going," Diego said as he sat back and looked out across the fire.

"What?" Haven asked as she spotted Willa and her bunkmate. She couldn't see the detail in her eyes through the flickers from the flames, but she knew Willa was looking straight at her. "Shit."

Haven's stomach turned. She tried to look everywhere except at Willa, who had decided to sit across from her. She looked stiff and frozen already, and Haven remembered just how much Willa hated being cold. She refrained from suggesting that she choose a chair where she could move closer to the fire in order to be warmer. She told herself that she couldn't care less if Willa froze her ass off. She wrapped her hands into the heavy quilt, not caring.

Mama Lu and her son, Wingman, welcomed everyone and began the round robin tradition of introductions, beginning with themselves. As they moved around the circle, Haven grew more and more anxious to hear Willa speak. She hadn't heard her voice in about three years before that afternoon. Haven was dreading the moment she would hear Willa say that she had cancer. She wouldn't wish the disease in any of its forms on her worst enemy, and now she was going to hear the woman she loved say it. Well, the woman she used to love, before she walked out on her and stomped her heart into dust.

Why was she feeling sorry for Willa? Haven was the one who was left heartbroken when she left. It wasn't her concern that she had cancer. If Willa had wanted her to know, she'd have called or texted or emailed. She could've sent a damn carrier pigeon, for fuck's sake. If Willa didn't care, Haven didn't care. Simple as that.

When it was Willa's turn, Haven looked anywhere but at her. As soon as she spoke, Haven could hear the nervous rattle in her voice.

"Hey. Uh, I'm Willa Bennette. I'm from Florida, and I was diagnosed with stage one intraocular melanoma about three years ago."

The words and meanings flashed through Haven's brain. Ocular melanoma—cancer of the eye. *Three years?* She looked up and across the fire at Willa, who was staring back at her. Willa nodded just enough for Haven to know that what she was thinking was correct. The timing could have been a coincidence, but it seemed that Willa had left not long before she was diagnosed. *Or was it after?* The thought that Willa knew she had cancer before she broke up with Haven made her stomach harden. Willa wouldn't have done that to her—to them. She had to have known that Haven would have helped her fight, just as Willa had done when Haven had been diagnosed. Haven's hurt quickly turned to anger when she thought of Willa not even giving her the chance to help take care of her during that time. She had managed to tune the other campers out, and she felt heat flushing through her body that wasn't from the campfire. She suppressed her anger long enough to catch the end of the introductions.

Haven's rear was starting to go numb from sitting and she knew they still had a couple more hours of cleaning and prepping to go before the volunteers were let go. Thankfully, Mama Lu gave the announcements for the next day's activities. Haven loved this part because it got the campers all worked up with ideas and excitement since they didn't tell them what they'd be doing, just how they needed to dress.

The day before, Haven had been overjoyed about getting back on the river. In addition to the river guides, Haven, Wendy, and Diego were always the extra boats on the water to help with whatever situations might arise. Haven was always the designated photographer of camp, so she went everywhere the campers went. But not this time, there was no way she was going to be able to spend six days following Willa around the damn Rockies. She was going to have to give up her spot to another volunteer. Haven felt a small pang of disappointment that she wouldn't be in the water this time around, but there would always be other camps. She just knew that she needed to stay as far away from Willa as possible for the next six days.

❖

Before Willa even had the chance to get up, Haven had disappeared. She had no idea what she was going to say to Haven if she ever stood still long enough to get the chance. A part of her felt a sense of relief at having told Haven, and complete strangers, about her cancer. She rarely, if ever, said it aloud or told anyone outside of her very small social circle. Willa never had any intention of telling Haven, mostly because she never anticipated coming face-to-face with her again.

She only had herself to blame. Their relationship might not have crashed and burned if she had been honest with Haven about why she had ended things. If Willa had believed in fate she would've thought that this was fate making an obvious opportunity for her to come clean with Haven about everything. She just didn't think it would benefit Haven to learn the truth after all the time that had passed. She had moved and begun a new life far from their old one.

"Oh, I'm so excited! What do you think we're doing tomorrow?" Corey asked as she bounced up next to Willa.

"I don't know. Hopefully, it doesn't involve talking." Corey looked rebuffed by Willa's statement. "I didn't mean it like that. I'm just not a 'let's talk about our feelings' type of person, that's all."

"Yeah, I get that about you."

"I'm not that obvious."

"Really? You literally introduced yourself in fifteen words or less. And that was it. No story, no quirky jokes, not even a window for questions had anyone dared to have one to ask."

No, she didn't. Sure, she could've given them backstory. She could've told them that she was single and running a farm in Florida with her brother. She could've gone into detail about the life-changing decision she made when she walked out on her partner to undergo cancer treatment alone. She could've opened up about how that woman was sitting across from her now, but she didn't. "Yeah, not my thing, I suppose."

"I'm sure that having Haven sitting across from you didn't make it any easier."

Corey was beginning to creep Willa out with her uncanny ability to read both her thoughts and postures. "How do you do that?"

"Do what?" Corey smiled. "I'm gonna go get some cookies. Wanna come?"

Willa was about to say no but then figured what the hell. She liked cookies. "Fine." Willa followed along after Corey, who skipped along the path to the lodge. In spite of their differences, Willa found herself connecting with Corey's bright and positive energy. She wasn't the type of person Willa would normally be friends with, but she liked her nonetheless. Willa could be herself and, hell, even a little childish. "Race ya!" Willa called as she took off at a sprint and passed Corey on her left.

"What? No fair!" Corey squealed and took off after Willa up onto the front porch of the lodge.

Willa reached the door first and swung it open as she looked back at Corey and laughed victoriously. "I beat y—" Her triumph was cut short when she almost smacked right into Haven. Willa stopped, their faces mere inches apart. Willa's heart pounded, and her chest burned for air. She found herself breathless from the horseplay, but paralyzed before Haven's eyes. Her mind flashed to one of the last times she had been this close to her. Haven had kissed her and asked her what she had felt. In that moment, Willa had felt heartbreak and guilt, because she had slowly been pulling away and Haven felt it.

Willa was jolted from the moment as Corey slammed into her. "What the hell?" she asked before peeking around and spotting Haven. "Oh. Um."

When Willa could find her voice she said, "We came to get cookies." She never imagined that those would be the first words she would say to Haven after years apart.

"Right. They're in the kitchen. Help yourself."

Haven's voice wasn't bitter or harsh. It was soft and sweet and unexpected. "Thanks. Uh. Would you like one?" she asked before she could stop herself.

"Oh, no thanks. I made them."

"Peanut butter?"

"Of course," Haven said.

"My favorite."

"I know," Haven said as she slipped past Willa and out the door.

Willa had no words. She had even forgotten what she was doing before that had led her to this spot. "Cookies," Corey said as she grabbed her by the arm and led her into the dining room.

Chapter Four

Five o'clock came early for Haven. She wasn't a morning person, except for the weeks she was at camp. Each day always brought such excitement she hardly noticed that she was running on five or six hours of sleep. Now that Willa had dropped in to destroy everything she held dear, it shouldn't have surprised her that her sleep would also suffer. She crawled out of bed and stumbled into the bathroom before anyone else woke up.

Although in all honesty Haven hadn't slept well since the last night she and Willa had shared a bed. Her nights were spent staying up too late, waking up every hour to calculate her remaining sleep time, and then getting up frustrated after nine snooze slaps at the world's most obnoxious alarm clock. She did find that the nights Bianca stayed over were less restless, yet she didn't know if that was from exhaustive sex sessions or just the comfort of a body lying next to her. She didn't so much *miss* Bianca when she was gone, but there was a part of her that liked the warmth she provided when she was there.

Haven started the shower but sat on the edge of the tub staring into the water in a sleepy haze. Her relationship with Bianca was fine. She enjoyed the time they spent together, and she'd discovered just how much she enjoyed the sex. She had definitely learned a thing or two about herself when it came to fulfilling her desires in the bedroom, or wherever else. When she was with Willa their lovemaking had been just that—perfect, passionate, and full of love. With Bianca, Haven had discovered a whole new side of intimacy that involved more eroticism and less affection. It allowed her to explore her own desires without fear of being misunderstood. Her sexual relationship with Willa had always been skin to skin, fingers and tongues, with kisses filled with promises. Bianca had introduced her to the world of lascivious accessories and matter-of-fact fucking.

Haven tried to imagine what *making love* to Bianca would be like. Would their kisses linger with tangling tongues and teasing fingers? Would it all start with a romantic home-cooked dinner and wine? The first time she'd made love with Willa that's how the evening had begun. *They'd enjoyed a quiet dinner before Willa started a hot shower for two. They teased and touched, building the passion and anticipation with each passing moment beneath the spray. Haven could recall the crisp taste of water combined with Willa's salty skin. But it was beneath the silver satin sheets that Willa and Haven had connected. Their bodies pressed together and—*

A loud bang on the bathroom door jolted Haven from her unexpected memory. "Yeah?"

"Don't waste all the hot water. There's three of us that need to get in there."

"I'm not," Haven said as she pulled the lever and the shower switched on.

"Are you in the shower? I've gotta pee."

Haven stepped out of her shorts and into the tub, closing the curtain. "Yeah, come in," she hollered back. She was going to have to make it quick because the water was starting to turn cold. It was a good thing; she needed it.

Once everyone was up, showered, and dressed, and Haven was adequately admonished for wasting all the hot water doing "God only knows," they trudged across the dewy lawn to the main house. The sun had yet to break above the ridges, but the orange horizon had begun to fight back the dark blue night speckled with stardust. The Colorado sky never ceased to amaze her. It was her favorite place on earth. She wondered if Willa had spent any time the night before looking up at the sky but then reminded herself once again that she didn't care.

Mama Lu and Wingman were sitting at the table sipping their

coffee and reviewing camp paperwork. Haven needed to make sure she told him not to put her with the groups this week, but her need for coffee came first. She took her first sip and her eyes flung open. Yes! Mama Lu made it, and that stuff could run heavy machinery. She sat next to Wingman and leaned her head on his shoulder.

"Good morning, Haven. Ready for another week?"

"For sure. Could I ask you a favor, though?"

"Yeah, what's up?"

"I'd like to stay at camp this week. Help around the kitchen and stuff."

Wingman pulled back and turned to look at her. "What? Why?"

"No reason, really. I just thought someone else might want to be on the water with y'all."

Caliente and the other volunteer, Dunkin', both spoke up with an "I'm good" and a "Nah, that's all right."

"Are you for real? I need you on the water with the cameras," Wingman whined at her.

"But I—"

Wendy cut her off. "Oh no. You're coming with us. Don't let her…Don't be a dolt. You're coming." She looked around Haven at Wingman. "She's coming."

Haven looked at Wendy, but she got the look that told her she would lose any fight she started. "Fine."

Mama Lu called them all to the kitchen to start breakfast. For some reason Haven enjoyed cracking two dozen eggs and whisking them for scrambling. Each of them had their task to assist Mama at the stove. She did all the cooking; the volunteers did all the dirty work. The smell of bacon had Haven's mouth watering. As if her stomach knew that her body was going to need the energy for the day, it began to growl to be fed. She resisted the urge to sneak strips of salty goodness off the tray and into her mouth. However, she wasn't a barbarian and could wait until the campers were served first.

The smell of breakfast drew in the campers right on time. More than half of them were bleary-eyed with sleep. Those were the younger ones. The older, wiser ones hadn't stayed up all night chattering with excitement. It was typical. No matter how much they emphasized the need for sleep, the first morning was always the hardest. By the end of the week even the youngest ones would be tucking in early.

While she should have expected it, Haven was still taken aback when Willa walked in the door. For the briefest moment, as she enjoyed everyone's mumbled morning greetings, she'd forgotten about her. But there she was, bright and bushy just as Haven remembered. They always had different ideas about morning. Haven liked the sun to be up before she was, whereas Willa would rather beat it. It seemed that hadn't changed over the last three years, but it was probably the only thing.

Haven pushed the trays of food through the service window and went in search of her coffee cup. She waited for a couple of campers to make their own before she slid in and grabbed the carafe. There was just enough for a cup's worth. "Save some for the fishes."

Haven had heard that line before at least fifteen years earlier. She'd said the same thing to Willa during band class as Willa drank from the water fountain. "Fish don't drink coffee," she said as she looked up at Willa standing next to her.

"But I do." Willa's smile was contagious in spite of Haven's attempt to resist.

She could have poured that last cup for herself and then made fresh, forcing Willa to wait the ten extra minutes as it brewed. But she didn't. She poured the coffee into a clean cup and slid it over in front of Willa. And before she could ask, Haven set out two packs of Sugar in the Raw and the nondairy creamer just as she had done a thousand times before. Without refilling her cup, brewing another pot, or saying another word, Haven walked away.

❖

Willa glanced from the creamer to Haven as she walked away. She wasn't sure if the gesture was out of kindness or habit, so Willa was uncertain about how to feel. As she added the ingredients to her coffee she analyzed the meaning. *Did she do it to be nice or was it involuntary? Certainly that would mean that Haven still remembers how I like my coffee, or does it? Most of all, why does it matter?* Willa grabbed her mug and set it on the table before getting in line for the buffet. Willa's attention was drawn to Haven. She could recall a handful of times that she'd seen her out of bed before the sun was well over the horizon.

Haven was engrossed in a conversation with the other volunteers at the far end of the table as they waited their turn for food. As the line inched forward, Willa stared across the room at the cheerful glow of Haven's face. Her platinum hair was as surprising as it was stunning. She never would've imagined Haven having the guts to do something so drastic even if she wanted to. But beyond the hair and more defined figure, there was an air of confidence in her. There was an obvious pride and comfort in her that Willa hadn't seen since they were kids.

When they were kids, no one could tie Haven down. She was loud, creative, full of confidence, and went through handfuls of boyfriends. None of them made it more than a few weeks once they tried to get anything other than a kiss from her. Willa had been the complete opposite. She could see a little bit of that fun and fickle young Haven showing through. She wondered what else had changed in the last three years. What brought her to this camp in Colorado? If she wasn't dating Wendy, was she dating anyone else? Had she moved on entirely and gotten married? The thought made her stomach knot, and a lump formed in her throat. She hadn't seen any sign of a ring, but that wasn't unusual since they were at an adventure camp.

Willa had made it to the serving table and piled her plate high. She turned toward the table and heard the pleasant familiar ring of Haven's laugh. Caught off guard, her feet tangled in the turn and she tripped herself, lunging forward. She managed to catch herself with one hand and keep hold of her plate with the other.

Willa was off her game. She'd never been one to trip over her own feet, and not in front of a room full of people. She took a deep breath and stepped into her seat trying to ignore the silence and stares. The attention didn't last long when the volunteers got the all clear for their go at the food, and the clattering of dinnerware and conversations resumed. As everyone talked and picked up with introductions from the night before, Willa focused on her plate. Doubt crept into her mind, and she wondered if it would be better for her to leave.

With everyone now fully invested in eating, the discussions had dwindled and Mama Lu took the opportunity to address the group. "While everyone finishes breakfast, I want to say a couple of things and then hand it over to Master Chief to explain today's adventure."

Willa was looking forward to learning what sort of fun was waiting to be had, and then Mama Lu dropped the bomb. She explained that they'd be broken up into small groups for morning discussions of topics related to living beyond cancer. And then they'd discuss their achievements and breakthroughs during the evening campfire. *What the fuck?* She had no desire to discuss her feelings and emotions with complete strangers. It had been hard enough for her to even open up about the type of cancer she had, especially in front of Haven. *Great.* Now Haven was going to be there to witness her forced therapy. That tiny seed of doubt in her mind grew larger. Willa hadn't heard whatever came after, at least not until Master Chief, known to everyone simply as MC, got up in front of everyone.

He introduced himself as MC in his brief and comical introduction and gave them the surprise. They were going to be learning how to kayak. But not just any kayaking, whitewater kayaking.

Okay. Sweet! I know how to kayak. Maybe not whitewater, but the techniques are the same. Right? MC dismissed them and gave them just twenty minutes to get changed and be ready to get on the bus out front.

He hadn't been kidding either. It was a bus. It was short and bright yellow just like they were in elementary school. Everyone loaded in and picked seats. Colorful drawings, stickers, and graffiti covered every surface of the bus. Willa recognized several of the volunteers among the tags and signatures. Willa chose the front while everyone else filled up the rear seats first. It must have been an instinctual move recalled from their early years of school transportation, but Willa had always preferred the view and quiet of the front. She imagined that was the opposite of what this particular group was attempting to accomplish, but it was too late to move even if she'd wanted to. Not only were the backseats now taken, but Haven, Diego, and Wendy had hopped up into the back. The last few seats had been removed for an equipment area, and a bench put longways against the side. As luck would have it, Willa chose the seat on the opposite side, which gave her an unobstructed angle to where Haven was sitting. Thankfully, she was soon distracted by views outside the bus as they headed toward their destination.

❖

Haven sat between Wendy and Diego. Most times they'd spend this hour-long ride chatting about their lives outside of camp and shaming themselves for never getting together as often as they talked about. Camp was their time together; as much as it was an opportunity for campers to escape life, it was theirs as well. This time things were different. In addition to Haven's world being disrupted, so was their routine, all because she couldn't keep her mind or eyes off Willa.

Haven was glad that Willa had decided to look out the window rather than sit sideways and make awkward eye contact every few seconds for an hour. Plus, it gave Haven an opportunity to see Willa for the first time in so many years. Her presence caused a long forgotten tingle in her belly. Her hair was the same dirty blond, although the cut was a little different. Haven had always cut her hair on a stool in their kitchen whenever she had asked, which was like clockwork every two months. She imagined she hadn't found anyone to cut it the same way.

Willa wore the same red, white, and black rash guard swim shirt that she had when they were together. It hugged her strong body in all the best places and emphasized her full breasts and hourglass figure. She was tall and solid, but still had the smooth curves of a woman. It might have shaded her skin from the sun, but Haven had no problem remembering in great detail what was hidden beneath.

"I'm afraid if she doesn't blink soon her eyes might shrivel up and fall out of her head," Diego said to Wendy.

"No worries. She needs them to stare down Willa like she's on a turkey farm at Thanksgiving."

"I can hear you guys. I'm not deaf."

"Well, look at that! It's a miracle. She's finally out of the coma." Wendy chortled. "Really though, what are you going to do about that? You can't go all week avoiding her."

"Sure I can."

"Haven, you moved all the way across the country because you couldn't handle being in the same state as she was. Now you're on the same bus, literally ten feet apart."

They were. Willa was within a few feet of touching her, but that was it. "We are much further apart than that." It was an odd feeling being so close to Willa, yet so disconnected. There were dreams she had where she felt closer to her than she did at that moment. "That's a good thing, right? It means I'm moving on. I've moved on."

Wendy and Diego looked over at Haven and raised their eyebrows at each other. "Um, I don't think that's it," Wendy said. "You are a fantasist and a hopeless romantic. This is your very own awkward romance novel."

Diego offered his own disturbing and awkward book titles. "*Colorado Courtship*. No! *Mountains of Love*. Oh wait, no. *Camp Lady Lovin'*?"

Wendy and Haven both stared at him in disbelief. "You're kidding, right?" Wendy said.

"What?"

"This is not a romance novel. You do realize the shit in those books doesn't actually happen. Yeah, I read them, but it's not like I believe that garbage."

"Wait. What? No. I'm the one that doesn't believe in that second chances, soul mates, long lost lovers garbage. You do," Wendy said.

Sure, she had, once upon a time. But Haven had long dismissed the idea that she would ever get a second chance with Willa. She'd watched every rom-com and read every sappy novel trying to make sense of her situation. She used the stories and fictions as strings of hope keeping hold of the idea that maybe she could have that second chance with Willa. But time passed and the distance grew, and with each passing day Haven lost that hope and let that string slip from her hand. "Not anymore. I've got a new life now. A fresh start."

Before Wendy or Diego could say anything to make the situation more uncomfortable, they had arrived at their destination. As the campers disembarked at the front of the bus, the three of them hopped out the back and unloaded the cargo. Today was an easy day as the campers learned the basic of kayaks and paddling. Volunteers were there to hand out lunch, and with any luck they'd get some time in the boat during the afternoon lessons on the lake.

Wendy and Haven lugged the giant Yeti cooler from the bus to the pool area. The campers shuffled along, no doubt wondering why they were at a pool in the middle of a subdivision. But once they were inside the gate, everyone's eyes widened with excitement, including Willa's.

The campers gathered around MC and Scrat for their kayak assignments as the three of them hung the wet suits and kayak skirts on the fence and laid out the many pairs of water shoes for those without their own. Haven found herself looking forward to watching Willa get fitted for her wet suit. If anyone could look good in skintight neoprene it was Willa. Her strong legs and muscular ass were meant to be accentuated by the body-hugging garment. Haven's body heated in spite of the cool mountain air of the foothills. If she kept up this unexpected admiration of Willa's figure, she would need to jump into the pool herself. She forced herself to focus on the cooler of food and bags of supplies to bring her out of the spiraling fantasy.

CHAPTER FIVE

Willa gathered around MC and Scrat, and more than a dozen brightly colored kayaks. Scrat was MC's right-hand woman. All of his jumping, bouncing, and whistling was equalized by Scrat's subdued, focused, yet cordial demeanor.

Haven had her hair split into two uneven halves with each side massed into its own little nest. Her polarized sunglasses were pushed up onto her head as she bent over a rubber tote and rummaged through it. It was a full rear view, but Haven's body was angled enough for Willa to get a good enough look at the sleek and toned legs she'd always been so fond of. They were her favorite part of Haven's body save for a few others she remembered.

She'd known Haven for so long that at one time they'd been convinced if one of them hurt the other could feel the pain as her own. They were merely high schoolers then, oblivious of the feelings bubbling below the surface. But now, she barely knew the woman adjusting the camera mounted on what was more than likely her own personal sport helmet. The giant University of Central Florida knight insignia emblazoned the back of the black helmet along with a variety of other Haven-esque stickers. Willa wondered how long Haven had been doing this to have invested in her own gear. The Haven she knew just three years earlier didn't even know how to swim. Haven had almost drowned her on no less than four occasions, including one time during a snorkeling trip to the Keys. Thank God for the mandatory life vest that kept her afloat enough to kick around in her flippers. Willa never was sure why all of their adventures involved water, except that Haven always ended up with her smooth, wet legs wrapped around some part of Willa's body. So there was a slight benefit.

When Scrat got to her, Willa started to feel a twinge of anxiety. She pointed to a bright yellow boat just to her right and told her to take a seat. Scrat crouched down and wrote Willa's name onto the white duct tape stuck across the bow. Willa looked down at the tiny boat and wondered if Scrat had been mistaken. "Um. Are you sure about this?"

"Yeah, why?"

"I'm taller than this boat is long. I think that defies some concrete rule of physics or something." Willa instantly knew that this was not going to be like kayaking in a flatwater boat down a lazy Florida river, and her anxiety rose. She paced the length of the kayak and shook out her hands in an attempt to relieve the twitching in her muscles.

Scrat laughed. "It's fine. Slide down in there and you'll see." Scrat held the boat with her foot as Willa hesitantly did as she was told.

Willa wiggled into the seat and found it roomier than it looked, although her knees rammed into the underside of the cockpit. Scrat made a few quick adjustments to the levers and straps, and before she knew it, Willa felt as though the kayak had been tailor-made to fit her bottom. When Scrat engaged the tension levers on each side, Willa felt a bit trapped. They could pick her up and the boat would come with her. "Am I supposed to feel, uh…"

"Snug?"

"Yeah. That's one word for it."

"Sort of. You should feel secure and comfortable. Keep your knees here and your feet there." Scrat pointed and moved Willa's legs into position. "The boat should move with you. Rock your hips back and forth, like this." Scrat did the hula for example, and Willa copied her. "Remember that."

"The hula?"

"Sure. If that helps." Scrat smiled and moved on to the next camper.

"Does it look like I'm built to hula?" Willa asked as she released herself from the boat and climbed out.

"Willa, if you're comfortable you can go over to MC and he'll explain what's next."

Before Willa got to MC he had thrown himself ceremoniously into the pool with a big flourish. She was certain she'd heard him whistle the iconic six note fanfare "Charge" on his way in.

MC explained that the next step in their introduction to kayaking involved something called a roll and a wet exit. Willa imagined that if her brother had been there he'd have made some obscene pun about the term. But she chuckled at one or two possible one-night stand jokes that might work. MC asked for volunteers, and since Willa had been too busy making childish double entendres she wasn't quick enough to hide behind the rest of the group before he pointed to her.

"Willa, you're up!"

She slid into a kayak perched at the edge of the pool. As soon as she was seated, Diego gave a quick push and into the water she splashed. She had been prepared for the jolt forward, but that was the least of her concerns when the frigid water rolled up over the front and down into the cockpit. She took a ragged breath and squawked in surprise as the water soaked into her trunks. She felt everyone staring in her direction, and unfortunately that included Haven. *No problem. You got this.* Willa repeated to herself. She'd been kayaking a hundred times back home. She could swim, and she was in a pool no more than four feet deep. *Relax. Do not make a fool of yourself in front of...everyone.*

MC proceeded to explain the definition of wet exit, although this time Willa was too preoccupied with everything else he was saying to make jokes. He told her several steps that she would perform after she went over. "Over?" she said, her voice an octave higher than normal.

"Yes. That's where we get the wet part of the exit." Everyone laughed. Nervousness made her search the crowd for a familiar face for comfort, and she found Haven. Haven gave just the slightest hint of a smile, and Willa sat up straighter.

"Okay." She could do this. She didn't need a confidence boost or a nostalgic look from an ex-lover. All she needed was herself and her natural instincts. "Now what?" MC explained each step in detail and she repeated them. *Flip, wave, tap, and flip.* "Easy stuff! Let's do it."

Willa leaned far to her right and the boat began to tip. She took a deep breath and went under. As soon as the cold water penetrated her shirt, her memory faltered. *Flip. Flip. What? Oh, wave!* She stuck both arms up out of the water and waved them along the length of the capsized boat. *Tap.* She tapped the bottom of the boat three times fast. MC flipped the kayak back upright, and she emerged from the pool soaked and disoriented. She gasped for air and choked on the gallon of water she had inhaled before she was all the way out of the water. She coughed as water came up and out of her mouth and nose. Her hair was stuck to her face as water and who knows what else dripped down her chin.

"Nice job. You all right?" MC asked, unfazed by her spasms and snot.

Willa wiped her face and pushed back her hair, and the thought of everyone, especially Haven, laughing at Willa's unfortunate first attempt. She had been cold, but a fire erupted within her. Willa looked over at Haven, who was in fact watching her flounder like an idiot. "I'm fine." She scoffed at his concern. "Can we do it again?" She needed to get it right.

"Yes. This time slow your taps."

That was all he said before she leaned to the right and sent herself back under the water on her own terms. Her breath was deep and her taps were slow. On the way up she blew air from her nose and rose to the surface like a pro. She searched for Haven, hoping to see that pretentious smile wiped off her face, but she was no longer standing there.

❖

Haven couldn't watch Willa go through that again. She knew just how difficult it was when she had to do the same training, and there were very few newbies who didn't suck a pool full of water up their nose the first time over. Actually, Haven still choked on water when she went in for a swim on the river. But it was different with Willa, as failure meant embarrassment. When they had been together, she often believed that Willa would rather not try something than fail at it. Which didn't appear to have changed in their years apart. Haven didn't want to add to any turmoil that was already brewing inside Willa, so she made busy with setting out cups and snacks away from the pool.

To Haven, it seemed that Willa hadn't changed a bit. She was still stubborn, witty, and liked her coffee more beige than black. Her presence was commanding, yet she always preferred to look unassuming. Haven had always adored her shortcomings. They were what made Haven feel needed and helpful in their relationship, like she made Willa a better or more complete person. But Haven had grown comfortable in being taken care of. Willa could do anything she set her mind to. She could cook, clean, and fix the spark plugs on her pickup all at the same time. She didn't need Haven, or so it seemed. She'd felt like that had been one of the catalysts to Willa leaving her, and as clichéd as it was, Haven had spent the last three years doing everything she could to change that. She learned to be independent, take care of herself, and never said no to learning something new, so maybe if Willa ever did come home she would see that Haven was able to be equal partners. It seemed that Willa had only grown more comfortable in her ability to take care of herself.

Haven wondered what Willa's new partner was like. Did she stand next to Willa after dinner and dry the dishes Willa washed? Did they make that dinner together, chopping vegetables in unison on color-coded boards? Or worse, did they sit up until four a.m. wrapped in each other's arms planning a cancer-free future together as Haven and Willa had once done? Haven was curious to know how long after Willa had left that she met someone new.

It didn't matter, though. Haven had moved on, too. Hell, she had moved in order to move on. Granted, she'd done it begrudgingly after years of putting her life on hold hoping that Willa's leaving was just a bad dream. "I'm in a good place, dammit!"

"Uh, oookay," Wendy said.

Haven restacked the cups that she'd been manhandling for at least twenty minutes now. "I'm happy. I have a girlfriend, a career, and great friends. I don't need her. Or this."

"That's great, sweetie. But if that's the case, why has it got you so turned around?"

"It doesn't. Maybe it does. A little. I don't know. I reckon I just never expected to see her again. And here of all places. What does that mean?"

"What does it mean for you or what does it mean in real life? Because those are two different things, ya know."

Haven didn't even pretend to protest. Wendy was right. She was a dreamer in a world of realists. "There has to be a reason, Wendy. Things like this don't just happen." Haven straightened the napkin stack again.

"You know I don't believe in all that fate and destiny bullshit. But it is curious nonetheless. I mean, what are the odds?"

Both of them looked over at the crowd gathered around the pool. Willa stood out from the crowd not just because of her height, but somewhere she'd gotten a flashy silver emergency blanket and had it wrapped around her shoulders. They couldn't help but laugh at the sight of Willa shivering as if she were a couple degrees shy of hypothermia.

"I feel so bad for her. She hates being cold."

"Obviously. I didn't think anyone could be less cold tolerant than you were a couple of years ago. But it seems I was wrong."

"It's almost lunch. The soup should help her...eh, them."

As the last camper climbed out of the pool, Haven and Wendy set up the lunches of soup and sandwiches, each thermos and bag marked with the camper's name in their own handwriting. Willa had also taken an extra minute to draw an image of a prideful rooster on her baggie.

Haven's imagination flashed to a cocky Willa surrounded by a flock of women. To Haven, Willa implied a freedom to come and go without the trappings of a cage or relationship. Maybe she didn't have a girlfriend; maybe she had several. The thought that Willa was involved with one woman, let alone several, sent a wave of unexpected jealousy through her. Haven looked up and saw Willa headed straight toward her, but before she was forced to have yet another awkward encounter with Willa, she stepped away from the table to where the other volunteers gathered together for lunch.

After everyone had finished eating and had time to rest and digest, they were fitted for wet suits, water shoes, and PFDs. Haven had been looking forward to this moment when she could get back in the water. In spite of her conclusions regarding Willa's newfound freedoms, Haven allowed herself a brief minute to admire just how well that wet suit fit. Once everyone had hopped, skipped, and stretched themselves into their new skin, MC led the entire group down to the lake.

They lugged their boats out of the pool enclosure and down toward the shore. With the overcast day, Haven knew that it was going to be a cold one in the mountain water and it excited her. Not because of the cold, but because this was her favorite part of the week and she always got the greatest pictures and reactions from campers on their first time in.

As MC and Scrat gathered everyone around and gave them the rundown on the next lesson, Haven shimmied into her suit. It hugged her in all the wrong places. There wasn't a suit out there that didn't seem to cut her right up the middle of her lady business. She pulled her kayak skirt up around her waist, which would at least hide her most unflattering features until she got into her boat. After Haven strapped on her helmet and adjusted the camera mount, she picked up her kayak and waded into the water in front of the others.

A sharp, frigid sting ran up her legs. *Oh yeah. Willa is going to shit herself.* She looked for Willa so that she could give her a kind warning, but she was caught off guard to see that her eyes were already trained on her. She shied away from her stare and, without giving her any acknowledgment, slipped into her boat, engaged the tension, and secured the skirt from back to front. With three strong strokes, Haven was out into the deep waters of the lake.

She maneuvered her boat pointing back toward the shore so that she could capture everyone's initial reactions to both the temperature and the instability of the kayaks. It was almost guaranteed that at least half of them would swim within the first six feet of the shoreline.

She had her waterproof digital at the ready and pressed record on the helmet cam as the first of camper entered the water. She was curious about everyone's initial reaction, but it was Willa's that she was most anxious to witness. Haven was a mix of excitement and trepidation as she watched Willa approach the water's edge. She couldn't wait for her to experience something Haven was so passionate about, but she also feared that she would be too anxious about the moment to enjoy the beauty of it. Haven gave a murmur of encouragement. Even if Willa couldn't hear it, maybe she could at least sense it.

CHAPTER SIX

Willa crept up to the water as Scrat held her kayak steady. Although she doubted that if she started to wobble over, Scrat would be able to do anything to stop her from going in. She looked at the dark water with hesitation. Every alarm bell in her head rang with warning. She was from Florida, and no one in their right or sane mind got within five feet of an unknown body of water without expecting a fourteen-foot alligator to take their face off. She stepped back. Her head knew that gators didn't frequent the mountain lakes of Colorado, but a country girl from the South had inherent instincts to the contrary. She looked out to where Haven floated looking back at her. She wasn't sure, but Willa felt a sense of encouragement in her face that helped to ease her fear.

As soon as she entered the lake, a freezing bolt of electricity shot through her. "Whaa! Holy shit!" At that moment, Willa resigned herself to never being warm again. All thoughts of alligators and water monsters fled from her mind. Hypothermia would kill her today. She sucked air in and out through her teeth with a loud hissing sound. It did nothing to slow the numbness already working its way up her legs.

Willa slid herself into the boat and adjusted the seat before securing the skirt around the cockpit. She hoped the body heat from her lower half would defrost her legs while she was tucked inside. Scrat gave the kayak a push and she was off. The boat teetered from side to side as Willa struggled to remain upright. The more she fought the wobble, the more unstable she became. She slapped her paddles wildly to each side hoping to use the momentum and support of them to keep from tipping over. But she soon discovered that the blades did nothing except cut through the water instead of offering a solid surface to brace against.

Scrat was soon by her side offering a firm anchor and words of advice. "Keep your hips loose and don't fight it." She demonstrated with a quick hip wiggle and the boat responded. "Stay centered and use your legs for support."

Willa spread her legs and pushed her knees against the sides. She could feel the change as her center of gravity shifted. She was no longer struggling against herself and fighting to stay upright. "Much better. Thank you."

"Excellent. Now, let's have some fun." Scrat took several big strokes and sped away.

"Fun. That'll be nice," Willa said. So far her existing skills had been useless, and she hoped at least the paddling part would be familiar.

MC called the entire group into the middle of the enormous lake. Willa managed to make it the hundred yards without toppling over. Her strokes were smooth although she couldn't seem to get the boat to keep in a straight line no matter how hard she tried. It could've had a mind of its own. Once she reached the group it was clear that she wasn't the only one with the issue. It made her feel better and a little worse. Willa had no problem trying new things, however she didn't like *trying* to be good at them.

MC paddled into the center of the circled group and held up a ball the size of a grapefruit. It was neon green and squishy like a Nerf toy. He dunked it into the cold water and slung it at an unprepared Wendy. She dropped her paddle into her lap, reached out to her left, and caught it with an expert's ease. Willa was impressed by the skillful maneuver as there wasn't even a rock in her boat.

MC explained the "game," which seemed to her like much more of a skills assessment than just a fun time. If Willa had the rules correct, they were about to play a soaking wet and precarious game of keep away. "I should just toss myself into the water now."

"Come on, roomie. You've got this. Hell, you made it farther than I did." Corey was already drenched through, and Willa wondered how in the world she missed that.

"What the hell happened?" she asked, trying to suppress a laugh.

"It's fine. You can laugh. I did. I wasn't six feet from the launch before I leaned over to look down in the water and bloop, in I went."

This time Willa did laugh out loud. It was just the thing she hadn't wanted to happen to her.

"Laugh it up, buttercup. Just remember that when you go swimming."

"Ugh." Willa dreaded the moment that would happen. And she knew it was going to happen.

When the game began it turned out to be much less like keep-away and much more like bumper cars with the addition of a sopping wet projectile and death paddles. If she wasn't getting slapped by an errant oar, she was being rammed from all sides by the other players. It was kill or be killed, and Willa was done playing nice. Confident in her boat, she joined in the fray. As long as she was moving and engaged in the play, she didn't think about going over. It was then that Willa grasped the true point of the game.

Another camper they called Shark zinged the ball straight at Willa, but before she could react it smacked her square between the eyes. The sting of the ball was intensified by the cold water it held. The collective gasp of the group brought the whole game to a halt. It was a shocking hit, but it sounded worse than it was. Willa took the opportunity to claim the ball and race away from the other team before they collected themselves.

Once they were all sufficiently drenched and exhausted, MC called the game. Willa still had the ball, but she didn't even think there were points, let alone a winning team. Although it hadn't mattered to any of them anyway.

Willa took the opportunity during the downtime to take in the beautiful scenery. It was a picturesque landscape painted by Mother Nature herself. The cloudy sky had opened up for a backdrop of blue against the unspoiled range speckled yellow from the aspens. Wildflowers and reeds lined the lake that doubled the beauty in its mirrored surface. And in all of that artistry was Haven, like a wild columbine at home in the mountains and valleys of Colorado. The Haven she'd known her whole life was almost unrecognizable in this new place. The distance between them now was more than just the number of miles. It was perhaps for the best. After all, so much had changed in both of their lives. Despite the memories and familiarities that seeing her brought, the truth was that they weren't the women who'd been both lovers and friends all those years ago.

❖

For the first time since she arrived, Haven saw Willa smiling. It wasn't the polite smile she plastered on when she was uncomfortable or the strained smile she mustered up for pictures, but a real and true smile. The kind of smile that Willa would try to cover with her hand if she knew anyone was watching. It was a bright, wide grin that extended past her mouth up to her eyes. Beyond any of Willa's other features, this was by far Haven's favorite. It was pure and spoke more than words.

In reality, Haven didn't know anything about Willa or her life, and she didn't know how or if she'd been coping with her cancer. It was obvious by her succinct introduction around the fire the night before that she wasn't used to talking it about it. And knowing Willa as she once had, it wasn't something she was willing to talk about to others or herself. Haven wondered if that would've been different had she been diagnosed while they were still together.

Haven looked on as MC taught them one final lesson for the day—bow rescues. Haven hated them, for no reason beyond the fact that she had zero core strength. And without even a two-pack of abs Haven had about a hundred failed attempts under her flabby belt. Willa lined up perpendicular to Corey's boat as instructed, and Haven raised her camera.

Willa leaned to the side with both hands on the bow of Corey's kayak. She lowered herself into the water, and Haven laughed when she heard Willa holler, "Fuck," as her left side from waist to shoulder entered the water. It looked good. She had hold of the other boat with both hands and a parallel position with the water. All she had to do was snap her hips and push herself upright. Haven's own hips flicked a bit as she encouraged Willa telepathically. But the longer Willa hesitated, the farther away Corey's boat drifted backward. Haven grew concerned. Willa stretched with her long arms to keep hold of the slippery boat. Her left arm lost contact and Willa scratched with the nails on her right hand to keep balance.

"Snap," Haven said under her breath. She leaned forward in her kayak willing the other to move for Willa.

Corey paddled forward for Willa to grab onto, but she had already over tipped and was now struggling to keep her head above water as the boat turned over.

"Shit." Haven's heart pounded. "Wet exit!" she shouted. Willa needed to give up and go all the way over, but if she didn't stop fighting it she wouldn't get a good breath before going under. "Shit!" Haven dropped the camera around her neck and rushed over with a few strokes. When she reached Willa, her face was a panic. Haven leaned over and cupped Willa's face. Looking into her eyes, she said, "Take a deep breath and go under. Release the skirt and push out. I'm right here."

Willa nodded and took a deep breath and let the boat turn all the way over. In just a few seconds she popped up at the rear of the capsized boat and took several deep breaths as she bobbed on the surface.

"Great job, Will. Relax." Haven braced herself and heaved the kayak up over the bow of her own. She tipped it back and forth a few times to empty the water before turning it over and setting it back into the lake. "You okay?" she asked Willa, who looked less frightened and more embarrassed.

"I'm fine."

Willa's lips were bluish, and she was very much done with the day. "It happens to the best of us. I still can't do it." Haven smiled and tried to make light of what had happened. Scrat floated up and assessed the situation before taking over. Haven backed out of the way so that Scrat could help Willa back into the kayak.

Willa was much better at getting back in the boat than Haven was. Scrat pulled the boats together and Willa lay back into the water and swung her legs up into the boat. While Scrat held the kayak steady, Willa pulled her body up and into it. She made it look so damn easy that Haven wanted to give her shit. First of all, for scaring her to death, and then for making that move look so easy. But this wasn't the time or place, as the once friendly rapport they shared was nothing more than a distant memory. Haven felt a sudden sadness fill her body.

Her racing heart slowed back to a steady beat once Willa was safe and back in her boat. She went back to catch a few shots of everyone else's progress before MC called it a day and herded them all back to shore.

Wendy, Diego, and Haven met up and waited in the lake for the campers to get out of the water. "So, what was that all about?" Diego asked.

"What?" Haven wasn't stupid. She knew what.

"That life or death rescue situation you got yourself into."

"It wasn't…I was there, and she needed help. I couldn't just watch her drowning and not help."

"Okay. Okay. Sorry. I didn't realize how bad it was. What happened?" he asked.

"She was fighting going under and got herself too exhausted to correct it and then she panicked."

"Didn't you do the exact same thing with me our first time out here?" Wendy asked.

"Yes. Which is why I…I knew it was going to happen. I know her."

"Obviously. Well, I'm sure she's grateful that you were there."

Haven knew Willa; she wasn't. "Don't count on that. She isn't one to rely on other people for help. Even if it means killing herself trying."

"Some people change, Haven."

"She's not 'some people.' Believe me," Haven said.

❖

After they were all safe and back on dry land, Corey pulled Willa off to the side for a private conversation. For the first time since they'd met, Corey had lost her happy-go-lucky grin. "Next time you try to drown please pick someone else's boat to hold on to."

"I wasn't trying to drown. I was fine." Willa had no intention of admitting that she had lost control of herself in that moment.

"Give me a break." Corey rolled her eyes at Willa.

"What?"

"I saw your face, Willa. You were not fine. I didn't know what to do. If Haven hadn't come when she did, I—"

"Enough. Fine. I had some trouble with getting myself back up with this life vest. Can we just keep the other details here, between us?"

"Of course. But you know they don't expect us to be pros. You're allowed to make mistakes."

"It wasn't a mistake. It was—"

"Just stop, Willa. You don't have to impress me. We are all in this together. Nobody else has done this before either."

"You're right. Let's just leave it at that, okay." Willa hated that she was so transparent, especially with someone she didn't even know.

"That's not what I wanted. I just want you to know that you don't have to be good at everything."

"I'm trying," Willa admitted.

Once they were out of their suits and back on the bus, everyone's energy level picked back up. On the way back to the ranch, they shared their mishaps and moments and harassed each other. Willa played along but left out the part where she'd been paralyzed with panic and unable to save herself from drowning.

The bus had gotten quiet as the excitement of the day wore off and exhaustion set in. She closed her left eye and looked around. Things seemed clear and normal. She did the same with her right eye, and the difference was shocking. Or at least it would've been had Willa not expected for her vision to be dark and blurry.

Although it seemed much darker these days. She blinked back and forth observing the difference.

"What are you doing?" Corey asked.

"Are you always this—"

"Annoying? Nosy? Attentive?"

"Yeah, actually."

"I don't know. I just notice stuff, I guess. Are you having trouble seeing?"

Willa knew that there was no use in trying to avoid answering Corey's questions, so she just gave in. "Yes. Well, not any more than usual, I don't think. It's a side effect of the radiation."

"You're blind?"

"No. Not yet anyway. It's been pretty hazy since treatment, but it seems to be getting worse, darker it seems."

"In both eyes?"

"No, just the one. They said it might happen. I reckon it's a good thing I've got two." Willa laughed, but it hadn't been sincere.

"So sooner or later you'll lose all sight in that eye? Wow. How is that gonna work out?"

"Eh. It's just an eye."

"Why do you do that?" Corey asked in a huff.

There wasn't a person on earth, save for Willa's oncologist, who knew Willa was losing her sight. She hadn't even told her brother. This girl figured it out after a single day, and now she wanted to know how it affected her. "I don't know. Maybe because I haven't figured it all out myself, even two years after my last treatment."

"Why do you always think that you need to have everything figured out? Do you talk to anyone?"

"Fuck no, I don't talk to anyone." Willa's voice was louder than she meant it to be. "What am I going to talk about? My feelings about getting eye cancer and going blind? Had I known there was going to be mandatory therapy here, I wouldn't have come."

"You don't have anyone that you talk to about this stuff? Family? Friends?"

"No. My brother is as close as I have to real friends, and I purposely arranged my life when I was diagnosed so that I had to depend as little as possible on anyone other than myself. It's worked out just fine."

"It's not always about needing people to help. Sometimes it's just about having someone to listen, someone who understands."

"Yeah, well, I managed to shit on that real good, too. Which seems to be coming back to kick me in the ass something fierce."

"I don't know about that. She did go out of her way to rescue you today."

"I was waiting for that," Willa said as she looked out the window, remembering the touch of Haven's hand on her cheek. She had been so in control, so calm. Haven had reached in through the fear to help her. There was no one else on earth who could pierce through Willa's very being the way she did. "She was just doing her job," Willa said.

"No. She was watching you. How else do you think she got to you so fast? Hell, she beat Scrat, and she's a trained lifesaver."

"I'm surprised she didn't let me drown."

"Maybe you should take advantage of this situation and start making some changes, Willa. If I've learned anything in my short and hectic twenty years, it's that you don't always get a second chance."

Willa knew that Corey was being sincere in spite of the cliché. Willa pressed her forehead to the seat in front of her and looked over at Corey. "Do you honestly believe that this is something more than a coincidence?"

Corey leaned forward and stared into Willa's eyes. "Absolutely."

"I knew you'd say that."

Chapter Seven

After breakfast, Willa and the rest of her small morning group made their way to the staff bunkhouse for their meeting. Mama Lu had broken up the ten-person group and the volunteers into three smaller ones. Willa was not looking forward to their first gathering and the sharing of emotions. She had already had her fill of that crap and there had only been two campfires and one bus ride with the ever-observant Corey.

As it turned out, they'd arranged for Willa and Corey to be assigned to different groups. While it should've made Willa relieved to have a reprieve from her, she would rather not have to add more people into her personal bubble. She needed to resign herself to the fact that it was part of the camp experience and escaping it was impossible.

As luck would have it, she got stuck with the one camper she thought was a complete tool. His nickname was Spartan, but she preferred to call him "Mr. Douche in Boots." He wasn't the only member of her group, but he thought he was. He'd had every job imaginable, done everything she had but better, and loved 'Merica.

In addition to Spartan, there was Survivor, Blue Ridge, and Miss Fitt, along with Wingman, and the volunteer, Diego. Willa hoped that their energy and personalities would overpower most of his douchey ignorance.

The bunkhouse was just that. It was a large open space with two sets of bunks and a mix of other bed styles and sizes squeezed into the space without design. There were bags, duffels, clothes, and equipment strewn about over all of the furniture. It was a colorful and chaotic mess, and Willa wondered just how much of it was Haven's. She spied several mismatched socks thrown across one of the single beds in the corner of the room. It was the only bed that someone had taken the time to make before they dumped a heaping pile of clothes on top. Willa was certain that someone was Haven.

The group sat at the rustic table in the middle of the eat-in kitchen. Wingman explained the purpose behind the small morning gatherings which Willa interpreted as, "Blah, blah, blah, more therapy." He gave them a philosophical topic with a quotation and corresponding visualization. The one for their first mini group was something about life, wind, and adjusting your own sails. There was nothing like cancer to force change upon someone's life, and now she was going to be forced to talk about it.

Wingman told the story of his brother's cancer journey and how it had changed more than the way his brother lived, but also those around him. When he mentioned that they were going to go around the table, Willa regretted sitting next to him as there was a fifty-fifty shot of her being selected as first to share. However, it didn't turn out that way. Wingman wasn't going to force anyone to talk. It was a free-flowing discussion dictated by the individual's desire to participate and share. Willa breathed a sigh of relief. She would be glad to sit for the next thirty minutes and not say a thing about herself.

It wasn't a surprise that Spartan chose to speak up first. As soon as he opened his mouth, Willa changed her mind about how long she'd be able to do anything in the same room with this tool. His first words were, "Cancer was the best thing that ever happened to me." Every eye around the room widened with surprise, including Willa's. *What the actual fuck?* He continued for what seemed like days, droning on about how it brought him the love of his life—a woman who'd left him years earlier for someone else but who he managed to get back by using his "cancer card." Willa felt sick to her stomach, then she felt her body start to shake with rage. When she stood, she knocked her chair back and it skittered across the floor. She closed her eyes and held up her hand.

"Wait, stop. I can't. I had every intention of sitting here in silence until this was over, but I can't."

To her surprise, Wingman encouraged her outburst. "What is it, Willa?"

"Ugh. You can't be serious. How can you sit over there and thank God for giving you cancer? Okay, it brought back your ex, but how could you use that as collateral to win her back? It's... it's...abhorrent. No one deserves to be stuck with you while you slowly waste away. Cleaning up your mess when you throw up on yourself or piss on your own legs before you can make it to the toilet. No one deserves that. Especially not someone you love." Willa was disgusted and livid. Her eyes welled with tears of anger as she spoke.

"She wanted to help. She wanted to be there for me during those difficult times," Spartan explained.

"Bullshit, Spartan. That is pure selfishness."

"There are many types of people, Willa. Some are caregivers and find solace in taking care of others," Wingman said.

"Nurses and doctors. Not lovers or partners. You have to let them go. You have to do what is necessary to make sure they move on and don't stick around just to watch you die. That's how you adjust your sails. And you make sure that no one else is on your boat when it smashes into the rocks and disappears below the surf." Willa retrieved her chair and sat down. She cleared her throat and wiped away the tears that stained her cheeks.

The room sat in silence for several minutes until Survivor spoke. Her voice was soft and quiet. "I met my husband two weeks before I was in a crash that put me in a coma for thirty days. He came every day to see me even though I didn't know he was there. He helped me through physical therapy and learning how to walk again. Three months after we got married, I was diagnosed with lung cancer, and again, he never left my side. I don't know if I could've done it without him."

"Sometimes it's about more than having someone there with me," Blue Ridge said.

It was obvious that few people agreed with Willa's thoughts on the idea, although it didn't change how she felt about it. "I did what I had to do. For her."

As soon as she'd said it she regretted it. It was the very thing Willa had not wanted to do, and she didn't want to be such an asshole either. She didn't say another word for the remaining time they had. Instead of listening to the others discuss their life changes and sails metaphors, Willa was lost in her mind reliving the moment she chose to alter her entire life.

Willa sat in the hot truck as it idled in the parking lot of her doctor's office. Her hands rested in her lap clutching her cell phone. She needed to call Haven, but she couldn't. Cancer. Fucking eyeball cancer. They'd thrown so many numbers and statistics at her in the last thirty minutes that her head spun. "Two thousand five hundred cases annually. Fifty percent chance of metastasis within ten to fifteen years with a smaller percentage of twenty-five to thirty years before it spread." She wasn't even thirty years old yet, and they gave her a window the size of her lifetime to live or die. How was she going to tell Haven that all of their plans for life now had an expiration date? They had made it through Haven's disease by the grace of God. There was no chemotherapy and no radiation. It wouldn't be the same for Willa, plus there was a great chance that she would lose her vision and quite possibly her eye itself. She couldn't expect Haven to go through that. She wouldn't. Her decision was made.

Willa just wanted this part of the day to be over already; however, Spartan was once again speaking about some vain and asinine factoid of his life. Before Willa could care too much about whatever he was saying, an alarm chirped on Wingman's watch. He apologized for the interruption and encouraged any additional comments from the group, but thankfully, Spartan had lost his momentum. When no one else made a move to speak, Wingman dismissed them to load up on the bus for their first day on the Colorado River.

As soon as they were on the bus, MC wasted no time getting on the road. Today the bus took them down the mountain and along the river. The cliffs shot straight up into the sky beyond what Willa could see without sticking her head out the windows, which was not recommended while traveling at seventy miles an hour through the narrow passes and tunnels, especially if she wanted to keep her head attached to her shoulders.

The water below was swift as it tumbled up and over enormous boulders hidden beneath the waves. An Amtrak train hugged the side of the mountain face on the other side of the river and sped away in the opposite direction. The entire bus squeaked and squealed when they spotted a small herd of bleach white goats balanced on a precarious ledge above the highway. Willa was beginning to feel nauseous from the constant dancing back and forth of her eyes as she tried to take it all in. She'd never seen anything as vast or diverse. It was a stark contrast to the flat lands of Central Florida, or any part of Florida, for that matter.

Willa gave her eyes a rest and turned her attention to the conversations of her fellow campers. Corey was entertaining the bus with her sing-along performance to whatever "DJ" Scrat played on the radio. At the moment it was "Brick House" by the Commodores, complete with awkward sexual dance moves. Corey's wild childishness reminded her so much of a young Haven, who was laughing, singing, and dancing in her seat along with everyone else.

Diego leaned over and whispered something to Haven and Willa's stomach dropped. She remembered that he was in her small group from earlier that morning and had been a front row witness for her outburst with Spartan. She had no doubt that Haven had told Diego about their relationship, and now he was probably relaying everything she'd said. That's all she needed to turn her day into complete shit before it was even nine in the morning. The best she could hope for now was if she fell out of her boat and hit her head on a boulder. Willa was exhausted by the constant ups and downs that this week was causing, and they were just two and a half days into it.

She just wanted to get to the river and get off the bus. As if MC had read her mind, he pulled off the road into a primitive gravel parking lot on the banks of the Colorado. They unloaded the bus and gathered around the boats that had already been lined up along the shore. Scrat introduced a new river guide, Mateo, who was joining them for the rest of the week. He called names and tossed them their gear out of the back of a large box truck. Willa caught hers with a slap of cold, wet neoprene against her face. The wet suit she'd worn the day before hadn't dried out overnight. She was disturbed by the idea of squeezing herself into something a hundred times worse than a soggy swimsuit. Willa, along with everyone else, shrieked and snarled as they forced themselves into their wet suits.

Once she was outfitted from head to toe, Willa wandered down to the water's edge. The river stretched a hundred yards at the widest point where it split around an island just upstream. As if a line was drawn down the center, a calm area of water was separated from a swift-moving current several feet offshore. Downstream, the river turned to the left and disappeared between a massive cliff face and a gigantic boulder. Her stomach knotted with anxiety of the unknown.

MC called the group together and then separated them all into three groups. One guide and one volunteer was assigned per group. As luck would have it, both Spartan and Haven were in her group. The one plus was that Corey, Dunkin, and Shark had gotten tossed into the mix with them. Mateo directed the group to the water and launched them each into the frigid mountain flow.

The water grabbed Willa's boat and directed it downstream. Mateo instructed them to paddle from one calm area to the next, or ferry as it was called, and then wait for the rest of their group. "Okay. I can do this," Willa whispered to herself. The current pushed her as she struggled to paddle against the rushing water. She felt as if she'd been tossed into the deep end of a pool without knowing how to swim. All her confidence and everything she had learned the day before seemed to have shot clean out of her head.

She heard Mateo whistle and yell, "River right!"

"Right." Willa glanced to the right and saw the calm eddy she needed to reach. She aimed her kayak and paddled with determined force straight toward the still waters. As she crossed over that invisible line, her boat tipped to the right, and Willa's heart stopped. "No!" she screamed, slapping the water with her paddle and jerking herself to the left. She had never been so relieved when she grabbed onto the stable branch that hung out over the water. "This is going to be such a long day," she said.

❖

Haven coasted into the eddy behind the group and heard Spartan call out to Willa. "Looks like I'm the only one who doesn't plan on swimming today!"

So far, no one had fallen out, but a couple of them, including Willa, had weebled and wobbled a bit. It was nothing out of the ordinary for a first time on flowing water. There was always one douche in the group, and she had a feeling that Spartan was going to be it. "Everybody looks great! Let's have some fun." Haven wasn't going to acknowledge his comment, but Mateo would.

"Five bucks says you're the first one in," he said.

Everyone, including Haven, laughed. Mateo had no problem calling out the ones whose verbal skills were better than their physical ones. Haven had hoped he was right, and she found herself looking forward to it. If for no other reason than just an attitude adjustment, as she knew that there wasn't a single camper in the bunch who'd ever done whitewater. All she had to do was wait, and her cameras would be ready.

Haven felt so good to be on the river again. It was as exhilarating as it was magical. The weather could change in an instant and they could find themselves floating downriver in a rainstorm. Next to one with crystal-clear blue skyline above the cliffs of Glenwood Canyon, that was her favorite kind of day. The levels were high, and the flow was swift. It was going to be a great day.

Mateo gathered the boats around in the calm pool at the bend of the river. They would spend no less than half an hour here learning how to enter and exit the eddies without tossing themselves into the water. Except for the actual rapids, this was the most common reason anyone went for a swim. Mateo gave them a demonstration of how to ferry across the river and pull in and out. He called for the first volunteer, and they all turned to Spartan. It was clear to Haven that he had no intention of going first, but instead of backing down he stuck his chest out and pulled out for the other side. Whether it was beginner's luck, or actual skill, he made it to the other side without incident.

Shark was next, and he met the eddy at the worst possible angle and it knocked him out. He popped out of the water like a bobber. "Swim for shore," Mateo hollered once Shark signaled with a helmet tap that he was all right. While Mateo took off for the kayak, Haven went for the paddle. Once they had him back in his boat, Mateo resumed the lesson.

One by one, they crossed the river, and with the exception of Shark, everyone else had made it across. They repeated the crisscrossing several more times until they were comfortable with the process. Haven was glad to see that Willa was having very little trouble with the technique, although still a little stiff in her seat. Willa glanced over to Haven and smiled. The gesture was unexpected considering that she'd just been caught looking at her. Haven's ears warmed, and she smiled back.

MC's and Scrat's groups merged before meeting up with Mateo's and they all headed downriver together. MC called for an eddy out on river right about a hundred yards downstream so he could evaluate their new skills. He had them line up, paddle out facing upstream, then turn and eddy out at the end of the line. Each of them did just as they were instructed without anyone going overboard. They all whooped and cheered when MC gave them the all clear to press on.

Haven loved the variety of facial expressions she got as each of them paddled out and followed behind MC. Willa paused beside Haven. Her heart stalled and a butterfly danced in her gut. She cleared her throat. "Are you ready?"

"As I'll ever be."

"You're doing great, Will. Loose hips." Haven demonstrated by rocking her boat side to side.

"Okay." Encouraged by Haven, Willa took a deep breath and paddled forward.

Willa crossed the line and joined the pack. After the rest were out, Scrat and Haven brought up the rear. Haven was surprised that Willa had opted to push toward the front of the group with MC,

Spartan, and Diego. It wasn't because they were all men; she just thought that maybe Willa would've tried to hang back instead. She hadn't realized that was something she'd have wanted until it didn't happen. "Great. That's exactly what I don't need right now," she mumbled and slapped her paddle onto the surface of the water.

"Did I miss that part of the lesson?" Corey asked as she drifted up next to Haven.

"What? Oh, no. Just working out the kinks is all."

"Kinks, huh? More like a big giant knot named Willa, I'd bet."

Haven didn't know anything about Corey save for her diagnosis, her sparkling personality, and that she was Willa's roommate. It seemed very doubtful that she would've told Corey anything about them, yet here she was making statements like she was in the know.

"Uh, no. I don't even know Wi—"

"Ha! That's what I thought," Corey cut her off mid-denial. "Well, if it's any consolation, she slaps a lot of shit around after encounters with you, too."

"I...no, what?"

"For two people who've known each other their entire lives, you don't act like it. It's cute. And weird, but mostly cute."

"I don't know what you're talking about." Haven couldn't believe that Willa had opened up to someone she just met, and about their relationship of all things. She had no intention of confirming or denying the nonsense Corey was blabbering.

"Right. It took some convincing for Willa, too. No worries."

To Haven's relief, the subject changed when Scrat called out the instructions for their first rapid of the day. It was a mild Class I and everyone conquered it with ease. They listened to MC's direction and followed the flow right through the waves. The next two miles were smooth flats that gave everyone the opportunity to take in the surroundings and get comfortable in their boats. MC showed off his many skills doing rolls and boofing over the boulders that dotted the river.

The group split and merged into different formations as they floated along. It was another opportunity for campers to get to know each other and deepen connections. Sharing the life-changing experience created a bond between each other away from the pressure of their real lives. Haven was blessed to have the chance to capture those moments forever. She needed to make her way toward the front of the pack so that she could set up for pictures as they came over the bigger rapids up ahead.

Wendy dropped back as Haven moved forward. "Getting a closer look, huh?"

"What? No. I need to—"

"Check out her technique?"

"You're worse than Diego, Wendy." Haven could hear Wendy's laughter behind her as she raced away from her and the conversation. "What is with everyone today?"

CHAPTER EIGHT

Willa watched in awe as Haven paddled her boat up to the front of the group. Haven didn't even bat an eye when a traffic jam of boats forced her to paddle straight toward a large rock that rose from the river. Water rushed up and over the rock, pouring over into a swirl of boiling white foam. Willa's eyes darted back and forth from Haven to the pour-over as she made no attempt to avoid it. Haven did just the opposite, digging in with her paddles and aiming straight for it. Just as Willa was about to shout out to her, Haven hit the rock and took a long final stroke before sailing over the hole and landing with an audible "boof" on the other side.

Willa found herself speechless, but the hoots and hollers from the other campers rose above the sound of both the water and Willa's racing heartbeat. She didn't know if she was impressed or aroused by the sheer dominance that Haven had over her kayak and the river. It was a side that in all their years as friends and lovers Willa had never seen. This went beyond a "head high and shoulders back" attitude because it took more than that to conquer Mother Nature.

MC whooped and cheered at Haven's successful display of skill and used her impromptu demonstration as a teaching point. What they had just witnessed was called a boof, so named by the sound the hollow kayak makes on a successful landing. Even if MC hadn't told them so, Willa and everyone else could have guessed that Haven's demo was just that. They spent several minutes in an eddy as MC taught them the different occasions and methods for performing a proper boof. He tossed around a few alternative definitions of the term, one of which involved illicit drugs in a rectum, and that she could've gone without knowing.

Willa was trying to keep her attention on MC and Scrat as they ran a few demonstrations of the lessons, albeit none of them as dramatic or exciting as the one Haven had given them, but she couldn't keep herself from stealing glances at her. Willa was mystified by this new woman she'd become, and long-forgotten feelings were beginning to bubble below the surface. She felt so drawn to her, not just with distant memories of their years together but more with new feelings of curiosity and desire. Haven was a powerful force, and it aroused Willa in an unexpected way.

As she stared at Haven, her boat drifted from the calm eddy and into the current. Her kayak slipped away from the bank that she'd docked herself against. Instinctively, she slapped her paddle at the shore, hoping to get a hold and pull herself back in. One of the worst side effects to losing sight was her lack of depth perception. Unfortunately, she was already too far, and her paddle sliced through the mud as her reach stretched to its max. She leaned over just a touch hoping to give herself that extra inch she needed to keep from being washed out of the eddy, but it was one inch too far. She lost the grip on her paddle as she and her boat went over. Willa gave out a sharp screech and a "fuck me" before going under.

Without a paddle, she was forced to wet exit in the three-foot-deep water, brushing her back along the riverbed as she pushed out of the boat. She kept hold of her kayak and resurfaced to a roar of laughs and whistles. MC declared it the most dramatic swim so far, a record Willa feared she would always hold. Her face burned bright red, and in spite of the frigid water, she could feel the heat on her ears and cheeks. Here Haven was jumping boulders and she tipped herself over trying to reach for the shore. *What's done is done.* She gave her audience a quick bow.

So much for the heat that was beginning to churn in her belly thinking of Haven. She just threw an entire river of freezing water onto every part of her body. That was a good thing considering that she had zero chance of making an impression on Haven anytime they were in the water.

"Well, that was an easy win." As he had predicted, Spartan had been the only one of their group not to turn over that day. While it wasn't a competition, it was clear that Spartan made everything a game that he needed to win. As Willa climbed back into her boat, she decided that she was done playing around. She might not be able to impress Haven with her skills, but she knew she could beat Spartan at his own game. They were just about done on the water for the day, so Haven decided she would be ready to make him eat his words tomorrow.

Willa's stomach growled as she hauled herself and the boat up the ramp to the truck. The breeze was crisp and cut through her wet suit, making her nipples sharpen against the fabric. She didn't know what she wanted more, to be dry or fed. She handed her gear over to Mateo and climbed onto the bus that had been commandeered by the females as a temporary changing room. Towels hung from the seats along the aisle in makeshift changing cubicles as the women shimmied out of their wet clothes and into dry ones. Willa hesitated at first, making sure that Haven wasn't on the bus. She was not in a place to see or be seen by Haven in all their naked glory. With Haven's location by the supply truck noted, Willa peeled off her rash guard and swim trunks before slipping on a tank top, T-shirt, and jeans. She skipped over the bra and panties to save herself the awkward struggle of wrestling a tight sports bra over wet skin like Ross in the leather pants episode of *Friends*. She was just shy of six feet tall, and there was no way to make that graceful in the small space of the bus.

Thankfully, she had just slipped into her sweatshirt before the men and volunteers had enough of waiting and bounded onto the bus. Unlike the other ladies, she'd have changed with the guys without problem; it was just Haven that she wanted to avoid. Willa had done so successfully, and so had Haven because she was no longer in her suit but in a pair of black yoga pants and a long, flowing tunic top. Her short blond hair was still wet and slicked back on the sides with an edgy top poof.

The sight of her took her breath away, and a shiver ran through Willa when they made eye contact. She was thankful for the sweatshirt that hid her unexpected goose bumps and hardened nipples. What was happening to her? She turned her attention away and slunk down into the seat. She was determined to stay that way for the entire ride back to the ranch.

❖

To Willa's surprise, they didn't head straight back to the ranch. Instead they pulled into a crowded parking lot and up to a massive redstone building. She hadn't been paying attention to her surroundings so she was at a complete loss as to where they could be. Corey tugged on Willa's arm and squealed, "Hot springs!"

Hot springs? Willa couldn't help the disappointment that she felt that they weren't returning to the ranch. She just wanted to stuff her face with home-cooked comfort food and disappear into her bunk for some alone time. All the camaraderie and group togetherness was making her a bit claustrophobic. After a few moments and a chance to think about it, she decided that a nice hot soak wouldn't be so bad. She could warm up, relax, and have a quiet moment in nature's hot tub.

They unloaded from the bus with their bags in hand and filed into the building. Willa was surprised by the commercialization of the space, complete with ticket counter and a gift shop. The group threaded through a theme park turnstile and back toward the locker rooms. So far Willa felt this was anything but nature's intended presentation. She was becoming discouraged and uncomfortable, and was once again wishing they had just gone right back to the ranch. The men and women split off into their separate areas, and Willa's heart stopped when she entered the large open room. Women of all shapes and sizes changed in and out of swimwear or toweled off their naked bodies. *Great.* She has just avoided this a half hour earlier on the bus and here she was again.

The ladies set down their bags on benches in front of their chosen lockers and began to strip down. Willa hesitated and clutched her bag, looking around for a curtain or stall or wall she could hide behind to change. As she glanced around, she saw Haven, who was also looking distressed in the moment. They stared at each other in silence for several moments, until Willa spied an open shower stall. "I'm just gonna…" she said as she motioned in its direction. Haven acknowledged her move and gave an awkward smile before looking down at her own bag. It made Willa feel better to know that both she and Haven were uneasy about the intimacy issues involved with changing in front of each other. It did seem strange, considering their history.

Willa pulled her swim gear from her bag and was a little disappointed that she had to choose between her sporty two-piece or her rash guard. There was no way she could just wear her bathing suit, but her other top would be like wearing a business suit in a hot tub. When she held it up to put it on it was cold as ice, and she ripped it off her skin. "Nope." *Two-piece it is.* It was still wet and cold, but the large towel she wrapped around herself helped. She slipped out of the shower and shoved her bag into the nearest open locker. Even with the towel, her shoulders were bare and she felt exposed. Willa pulled the bind tighter around her chest and held on to it tightly. At least she hadn't been the only one using their towel for that temporary extra warmth before getting into the water. With the entire group changed and ready to go, they headed out to the pools.

Once again, Willa was greeted by the unexpected. Two enormous pools spanned the length of what looked like two city blocks. The shorter was a hundred feet long. A sign indicated that the temperature of the water was a balmy 104 degrees. Older patrons bobbed and relaxed in the pool, and Willa wanted what they were having. In contrast, the long pool on the far end was filled with splashing children and families. A lifeguard guarded the deep end and the diving board. She wasn't in the mind-set for that pool just yet. As if reading her mind, the group moved and claimed a row of lounge chairs near them. They shed their towels, exposing a variety of different body types. Stoma scars, missing breasts, and chest ports made each of them unique and reminded Willa that they all fought and won major battles. An unexpected sense of pride sparked within her.

She unwrapped herself and dropped her towel onto the lounge to follow the others into the pool. Willa eased herself inch by inch into the scalding-hot water. The scent of sulfur and minerals rose with the steam from the surface of the pool. It was an encapsulating sensory experience. Each of her senses was on high alert as she closed her eyes and sank to her neck in the water, absorbing the elements and energy.

After a few minutes of her Zen-like experience, her mind flashed to Haven and she opened her eyes. Willa realized that she hadn't seen Haven since she disappeared into the shower to change. While Willa had floated off in her moment of meditation, the rest of the group gathered at the steps at the opposite side of the pool. In the center of them was Haven kneeling at the edge holding an orange mesh bag.

Willa couldn't hear what she was staying; however, had she been within earshot she'd have heard nothing except the rushing of blood through her ears. Haven was exquisite. Her body was gorgeous, pale, and smooth. She was rounded in all the best places, from breasts to belly. Willa had always thought she had her entire feminine landscape memorized, but Haven had new features Willa didn't recall. She used Haven's preoccupation and her own distance to take several minutes to rake her eyes over each inch of Haven's exposed flesh. It didn't take long for the heat of the pool and the fire burning in her gut to overheat Willa. She needed to cool off in every way.

The one way out of the pool was via the steps that had been commandeered by the Valiant group or the ladder just to her left. She figured it would be easier and faster to avoid Haven and get out of the pool using the ladder. She climbed up easily enough and wrung out the ends of her hair while enjoying the cool breeze on her overheated body. She reached down for her towel and turned toward the pool to see if everyone was still powwowing on the steps. She began to bring the towel to her face but was stopped cold when she saw everyone's eyes trained on her. Her heart stopped and she felt the blood rush from her face. *Oh, God. What are they looking at?* She looked down at herself and made sure her tits and bits were still covered, and they were. She breathed an audible sigh of relief. "What? What's wrong?"

No one said anything. They just responded with darted looks back and forth from her to Haven. It was then she saw Haven's face. It was red and her expression couldn't hide the look of bewilderment. Willa must be mistaken. "She can't possibly be looking at me like that," she mumbled.

Corey broke the tension. "Are we gonna play this game or what?" She grabbed the orange bag from Haven, which snapped her out of her haze, and Willa was grateful. Corey bounced through the pool and climbed up the ladder to Willa.

"You're welcome," she said as she stood up next to Willa.

"Thanks. I think. Why was everyone staring at me?"

"Come on! Games are afoot!" Corey pulled Willa along toward the larger, cooler pool used for games and activities. "She was talking about the game when all of a sudden her face turned red as a beet, and she forgot all of her words. It took us a minute to figure out what had struck her dumb, but then we saw it was you."

"Me?"

"Yes, you. With your rock solid thighs and back muscles for days. No one could blame her. It was quite a sight, actually."

"Please, tell me you're kidding."

"Nope. Not kidding. Haven could've choked on her own tongue panting over you."

"Corey!"

"What? For real. It was adorable and sooo obvious."

"Oh, Christ."

"It's fine. Relax. It's not like you weren't doing the exact same thing to her while she wasn't watching."

"Wha—"

"Shut it. I saw you. Now, moving on. It's time for games. You're on my team."

"But I don't—" Willa tried to protest, but Corey gave her a look with a smirk and raised eyebrow, and Willa relented. "Fine. What are we playing?"

❖

Haven couldn't believe that she had just lost all sense of control and the ability to talk. When she looked across the pool and saw Willa climbing out of the water, her heart seized and her breath stuck in her chest. It was only in their most private moments that Haven had seen Willa in anything less than a sports bra and swim trunks, yet here she was dripping wet in a fitted contour halter and matching bottoms of yellow and blue. Her stomach was flat but soft, and her breasts were full with an enticing space down the center where they teased to be touched. The muscles in her arms were tight as she pulled herself up the ladder before exposing a tight-fitting pair of boy short bottoms. The space where her thighs met her ass taunted Haven for a longer look as her mind flashed back through a slideshow of similar instances, each one enjoyable for its own intimate reason or memory.

Haven remembered a time Willa had picked her up and held her against a wall during sex. The memory aroused Haven as if she had returned in time to their bed as she caressed Willa's soft thigh from the knee to her ass and ran her fingers over the taut mound before she'd grasped it firmly in her palm.

Corey had to pry Haven's white-knuckled fingers from the mesh bags, because she'd found herself paralyzed in this unexpected fantasy. And it was just her luck that there wasn't a single person who'd missed the awkward public flashback she just had. The one thing she could hope for was that each of them had some sense of kindness and wouldn't drag her through the mud for it. When they split the teams, Haven left herself out of the game. She needed a little time to sit and come up with a plan to deal with the next four days. After counting through the players, they needed another body and wouldn't let it go until Haven was in the water. Seeing as she wasn't on Willa's team, she could manage to keep far enough away from her in a pool a hundred feet wide. She was the last holdout, so as soon as she jumped into the water the game began.

The game was a combination of keep-away and water polo. The rules—if they could've been called rules—were ambiguous. It was nothing more than a game that involved sopping wet Nerf balls being thrown as hard and fast as possible at each other. The one thing that made any sense was that the person with ball had to throw the ball, and everyone wanted a ball.

Foam balls zinged and whizzed past Haven, and she leapt for them. Being as short as she was, it was difficult to leap high enough from the water to catch the ones that flew over her head. But that didn't keep her from trying. Diego's entire torso was out of the water standing flat-footed, so Haven used him as a human scaffold to catch the balls.

The game was heating up, with balls flying in from every direction. Wingman eyed her with an evil brow as he cocked back his arm for a direct shot at her. As he released the ball, she shrieked and ducked below the surface of the water. While he missed her face, she felt the ball skip over her head. She bounced back up, spun around, and lunged for the ball she knew was behind her. Someone else already had it. Before Haven could stop her momentum, her body slammed into them with an audible slap and splash. Two arms wrapped around her as her body conformed to the soft and smooth surface. Though tall and solid like Diego, this person was most definitely female. Haven's face was mere inches from a most familiar chest, complete with triple set of freckles where the voluptuous curves of Willa's breasts met. Haven's body fought to melt into the embrace while her mind urged her to recoil. She raised her face to Willa, who stared down at her with an outward expression that mimicked her own inner feelings of surprise and desire.

As Willa stared into her eyes, Haven was very much aware of each inch of skin that connected with hers. Their warm thighs, breasts, and bellies pressed together beneath the water as Willa held Haven against her. Haven was holding her breath, hypnotized by Willa's gaze and embrace. The splashing of water and the laughter of children faded into the background, and the one thing Haven could comprehend was the infinite depth of Willa's eyes. A sharp sting struck her between her shoulder blades, and Haven pushed back against Willa's chest and out of her arms. Her body was on fire, not from the burning of a hit from the ball, but from being held so close to Willa. She was certain the water temperature also played a role. She pushed herself to the farthest end of the pool before climbing out and heading for the locker room. She'd had enough for the day. Enough water, enough heat, and enough Willa.

Chapter Nine

The ride back to the ranch was near silent, and the hour of free time before dinner had most campers spread over every available soft surface. Those who couldn't find a couch or chair in the main lodge opted for their bunk to catch a few minutes of rest. In spite of the relaxing soak in the hot springs, the day had been an exhausting one. If anything, it was the warm water that contributed to the need for a group nap.

Willa had opted for her bunk, slipping under the blankets as soon as she was out of her wet clothes. She'd spent eight hours in water and she just wanted a few minutes to be warm and dry. Willa fluffed the pillow just right, pulled the covers up to her chin, and closed her eyes. She should've expected the image that popped into her mind the instant her eyes were shut. It was Haven. Her pink lips were a breath away from her own and there was even less space between their bodies. When Willa heard the door to the cabin open and shut, she fought against opening her eyes. She could either spend an hour with her eyes closed reliving every arousing moment she was pressed against Haven, or she could do it with Corey asking a thousand questions. It was a crapshoot because she wasn't particularly interested in either.

"Are you pretending to be asleep so you don't have to discuss that interesting situation between you and Haven this afternoon?"

The voice was soft but also awkwardly close to Willa's ear. *This girl is unreal.* She still didn't open her eyes and hoped Corey would go away, but she knew damn well she wouldn't. "Yes," Willa said.

"Ha! Too bad." Corey pulled back the blankets and crawled under them with Willa. "Holy crap, it's so nice under here. I thought I'd never be warm again," she said as she snuggled in.

Corey had a lot of traits and qualities, but boundaries and a sense personal space were not included in them. Corey rolled over and curled up against Willa's back, making Willa the little spoon in their disproportionate cuddle session. "Comfy?" Willa asked once she had finished burrowing herself against her.

"Yes."

"Good." Willa closed her eyes hoping that Corey would do the same, but her hopes were short-lived.

"Soooo..."

Willa didn't open her eyes when she grumbled her response. "So what?"

"You know what. I saw you and Haven all smooshed into each other like two suction cups stuck together."

Willa laughed. "Where do you come up with this crap?"

"I dunno. So tell me, how'd it feel? And before you say 'how did what feel,' you know damn well what I'm talking about. The suction cupping." Corey made slurping noises as she formed her hand into a claw and latched onto Willa's shoulder.

It must have been her relaxed state or the innocence of their snuggling, but Willa felt strangely at ease with talking to Corey about it at that moment, like sisters having a heart-to-heart about their teenage drama. She didn't turn to face Corey. She might be feeling sisterly, but that was outside of Willa's comfort zone. "It was weird but familiar." She remembered how their bodies had somehow fit together just as they always had. "I didn't want to let her go, and she wasn't exactly in a hurry to pull away."

"Yeah. I noticed that much. Did she say anything? Did you?"

"No, neither of us said a word. I don't even think I had a single thought in my head except for—"

"Sex?"

"No. Well…" Willa thought about it and answered again. "No." It wasn't the sex that she'd thought about in those moments. It was something less physical. "I felt like a part of me that I'd been missing sort of, I don't know, snapped back into place. Like two pieces of broken pottery or a torn photo."

Corey adjusted her pillow and wrapped her feet into the blankets. "I once read about this thing called a twin flame, and how each of us has that one person in the universe who we are connected to for all eternity. Maybe she is yours."

"Now you sound like her. Haven always had these crazy ideas of destiny and fate, true love and overcoming obstacles to live happily ever after. Although we do seem to have a history of losing and finding each other. This is like the third time we've somehow managed to find our way back in the each other's lives."

"Wait, what? Three times this has happened, and you don't think that's a little more than coincidence?" Corey grabbed Willa's arm and rolled her back toward her. "Seriously?"

Willa cursed at herself. This was what she didn't want to get into. Some fun banter about an awkward, half-naked encounter was one thing; this subject was something different. "I'd prefer if we didn't—"

"Come on. It's obvious you don't talk about this with anyone, but maybe you should. It beats doing it in front of fifteen people during a campfire."

"I can safely say that this topic would never come up with anyone. Except you, it seems."

"You talk. I'll listen. How did you guys meet?"

Willa smiled at the image of an old class photo that popped into her head. Willa stood in the back with the taller students. She had a wide gap-toothed grin, sporting her stringy long blond hair and wearing a Care Bear shirt. In the front row was Haven in her Strawberry Shortcake tee, teal corduroy pants, and suede Velcro sneakers. "We met in kindergarten, nearly twenty-five years ago."

Willa couldn't help but smile at the memories she had shared with Haven growing up. It had been countless years since she had thought about their childhood together, and it warmed her heart. At least it did until Willa recalled the moment she watched Haven's face in the back window of her parents' car as they pulled away. Willa's father got a new job in Texas and it was the first time she had lost her best friend. The first time she felt heartbreak.

The second time happened after her family had returned to Florida and they found themselves in the same beginning band class. It hadn't taken long for their friendship to re-blossom. They were inseparable once again, until Willa was forced to change schools after some stupid district rezoning. Thankfully, their parents had been friends, but she could recall the disappointment she felt when she realized how different they were becoming. Willa was having curious feelings of attraction to Haven, while Haven was busy chasing every boy that crossed her path. When Haven finally picked one, Willa learned about a whole other type of heartache when Haven discovered the excitement of the catch and release game. Willa never could sit by and watch with hurt and jealousy as Haven toyed with everyone but her.

But when Willa began the story of when they finally reconnected during high school, her whole body hummed with joy. It was the best years of her life, of their life, together. They had spent their lives getting to know everything there was to know about each other, and slowly they learned that their feelings went beyond mere friendship. They were in love. Willa's heart had never felt such fullness as it had during those ten years together. They conquered fear, discrimination, and even cancer to be with each other. Cold sadness and guilt replaced the warmth of happiness in her veins. She had learned that the worst heartache of all was when you failed someone you love. It was a pain she still carried with her.

❖

As soon as they returned to the ranch, the campers headed off on their own until dinner. The volunteers headed to the kitchen to start preparing it. Haven chose to set out the dinnerware and took the first opportunity to get out of the lodge when Diego asked for help gathering wood for the evening's fire.

Haven grabbed the log cart from the side of the lodge and pulled it along the gravel walk behind him. The large stockpile of wood was kept near the western pasture fence past the hot tub, fire circle, and the old homestead which was nothing more than a leaning stone chimney. Its distance from pretty much everything made it a well-known hiding place for volunteers. Haven liked to use the space to sneak away and stargaze, since the wood formed a makeshift wall that defended against both wind and any light from the lodge and cabins. Diego used it as his place to sneak away for a hit or two from a joint he carried in the recycled Altoids tin that he kept in his pocket.

Pot was very much legal in Colorado with or without cancer, so you'd be hard-pressed to find anyone who lived there who didn't partake. Haven was still new to the rules and always got that feeling she was breaking the law even though she wasn't. Diego found a comfort from so many of cancer's side effects from marijuana. It increased his appetite, counteracted nausea from chemo, and reduced his anxiety. And while Haven rarely, if ever, smoked, she was a big proponent of the drug and its benefits for people with life-threatening disease.

The two of them sat on the ground behind the wall of wood. Diego took a few hits from his joint, and Haven fidgeted with a few blades of grass near her feet. They sat in silence for several minutes. Haven was enjoying the quiet time away from the group and the constant chattering of people, but she was having a harder time escaping from her own mind, which was just as busy.

"Is it weird seeing her after all this time?" Diego asked.

Haven plucked the grass from the ground. "I don't know if it's weird seeing her. The weird part is how…I don't know how to explain it."

"How normal it is?"

"Yeah. Maybe? It's just that so many things seem so familiar. Instinctual. I think it was harder to learn how to adjust to life without her than it's been to have her just show up here."

"Well, I don't know about that. I mean, I didn't know you then, but you most definitely aren't yourself this week."

"What do you mean? I'm doing everything I normally do. Nothing's different."

Diego packed up his goods into the tin and lay back in the soft grass. "Okay. If you say so." He slipped his sunglasses down over his eyes and clasped his hands behind his head. It was clear that he had no intention of pressing the issue.

"I do. I haven't changed a thing." She hadn't. She was still the group photographer. Granted she tried to get out of it, but that was nothing. She helped in the kitchen, except for this time, and the night before when Wendy made her put down the knife. "Ugh. Whatever." It was just a few things, but there could've been a hundred reasons for them.

"Mmkay."

"What?" Haven screeched and threw a tuft of grass at him that caught in the breeze and blew back into her lap.

He turned his head toward her, and while she couldn't see his eyes, Haven noticed his raised eyebrow. "Boofing rocks, rescuing guests, kissing Wendy, and slinking off to help me haul wood."

"I needed to…she was…Wendy…I hate you."

"Me? I didn't do it. You're the one going above and beyond for, what exactly?"

"I don't know. It didn't start out that way. I just wanted to show her that I was fine. No, better than fine. Better than I was. It sort of just got out of hand. When I saw the way she looked at me. She seemed surprised, maybe even impressed, and I may have let it go to my head."

"So you wanted to make her jealous by kissing Wendy and impress her with your prowess on the water. Okay. How's that working out?" He pushed himself up off the ground and stood.

"It's not, I suppose. I mean, I don't even know what I'm trying to accomplish with all this nonsense. As awful as it sounds, I want to make her jealous, I guess."

"Eh, I don't think it's jealousy you want. I've seen the way you look at each other when neither of you know it."

"How's that?" Haven's need to know surprised her. Diego began loading the cart with logs, and Haven got up to help.

"Like you're both waiting for that one moment to bring you together against your will and force you to acknowledge the other's existence."

"Oh, gimme a break. We've already established that I'm doing the exact opposite of that."

"Right, it's called building the romantic tension, Haven."

"That is not what I'm doing. There may be tension, but it's far from romantic. She broke my heart, Diego. She destroyed me. There's no coming back from that."

"It seems you came back from that just fine. People make mistakes. Rash, emotional, confusing mistakes even with the purest of intentions. As clichéd as it sounds, there's always two sides."

There wasn't any explanation on the planet that could make Haven forgive Willa for what she had done. Haven swung a heavy trunk onto the cart with a heave, and her knuckles rasped against the bark of another before it was slammed between the two logs. "Shit!" She pulled back her hand and saw the grated skin along the length of each one of her fingers. The blood started to rise to the freshly skinned surface, and she was nauseated by the sight. "Fuck me," she said, covering the injury with her other hand.

"Lemme see," Diego demanded as he grabbed her arm and pulled it toward him.

"Ow. No, no, no." Her knees were beginning to shake beneath her as she fought to pull her hand back.

"Stop it." She relented and let him look at the damage. "Damn, girl. We need to get you to Shannon and get the bark out of this."

She glanced at her bloody, mangled fingers and felt the cool sweat bead on her forehead. He tugged at the hem of her shirt and wrapped it up and over her injured hand. "I'm fine. I can go myself."

"No. Let's go." He put his arm around her and led her back to the lodge.

Her hand throbbed with each pound of her heart. She prayed that it wasn't broken. Haven could feel the sting of the open wounds with the slightest movement of her knuckles. She was already dreading the searing pain of whatever it was going to take to clean it out, and the thought had her knees shaking again. "Stupid. So fucking stupid."

"It was an accident."

They were nearly to the lodge when Haven heard the dinner bell, and the campers began making their way across the lawn toward them. As luck would have it, one of them was Willa, and as soon as their eyes met Haven could see the concern in them. "Hurry. Let's go," Haven said as her pace grew quicker. She beat the group into the house and made a beeline for the office. "Tell Shannon I'm in here," she told Diego before closing the door behind her. There was no need to get everyone worked up over her or make a big scene about what she'd done. Haven sat in the chair and began to unwrap her hand when the door opened. She quickly recovered it before looking up at the train of people who followed Shannon into the room. "Oh, for heaven's sake," she said when Diego, Wendy, Mama Lu, and Shannon gathered around her. "It's fine."

"Really?" Shannon gestured toward the bloody shirt Haven was clutching to her belly.

When Shannon reached out for her injured hand, Haven looked up at Wendy. She couldn't look at it. Maybe it wasn't as bad as it felt, but she couldn't bring herself to look at it without getting light-headed. As if reading it in her eyes, Wendy knelt at Haven's side and drew her attention away from what was going to happen next. She grimaced and sucked air through her teeth as Shannon peeled the fabric from her wounds. A chorus of gasps and groans confirmed that it looked as bad as it felt. She felt the blood wash from her face, and cold sweat slithered down the backs of her thighs as the light danced in the room.

"Look at me, sweetie," Wendy said.

Haven stared at Wendy, focusing on her comforting gaze. "It's bad, huh?" The voices around her were muffled by the swishing of blood pumping through her ears. When she heard Shannon say that they needed to clean it out, Haven's stomach jolted.

Shannon and Wendy led her to the adjoining bathroom and sat her on the toilet with her hand draped over into the sink. Wendy stroked Haven's hair, which always did wonders for her in stressful situations. When Shannon turned on the faucet, Haven flinched. Mama Lu stood in the doorway with a worried look. Diego leaned into the room, grabbed a towel from the rack, and handed it to Haven. "When you scream, scream into this."

❖

A muffled, groaning cry from the bathroom stopped everyone in their spots. Willa's stomach lurched in recognition of Haven's voice. While everyone else had been oblivious of Haven and Diego on their way to the lodge, Willa had seen the pained look on Haven's face. Haven had disappeared into the office, but Willa heard the whispers from the kitchen just before four of them had rushed through the house to the office.

Willa stood in line for the buffet, but each time it nudged forward she allowed the person behind her to go ahead. Her place in line was the best position to see the office door without making it obvious.

Willa met Mama Lu halfway to the dining room. "Is Haven all right?"

"Yes, she's okay. Just a little accident with the fire logs. Nothing to worry about."

Willa could feel that she was being brushed off with the same generalized information she was about to share with the rest of the group. But Willa deserved more than that. After all, she was Haven's…nothing, actually. She was nothing. She had no more right to knowledge than the room full of strangers in the next room. But they had history; they had a connection, and Willa wanted more. "I know Haven. I know the kind of situations that make her cry like that. What happened?"

Willa didn't know what caused Mama Lu's expression to soften, but it had. "They're cleaning it out now. Shannon doesn't think it's broken. Thank goodness. It's banged up and bloody."

"Oh no. Did she pass out?" It made sense to her now why Diego had such a hold on her and why Haven's face was drained of color.

"I don't believe so."

Willa tried to imagine how much pain Haven was in and wondered how she was coping with the blood. If she hadn't passed out then she might have been just as fine as Mama Lu had said. Plus, for all Willa knew it could just be one other thing about Haven that had changed. With her dangerous new adventure hobbies, it might have just been a normal thing for her now. Although that didn't explain the look on Haven's face earlier. Willa looked around Mama Lu toward the office and wondered how she'd be received if she just popped her head in the room.

"It's probably not a good idea," said a low voice from behind her. Mama Lu smiled softly and excused herself. Wingman slid around her into the spot his mother had just occupied.

"I just wanted—"

"I know. But no. One, from what I know about Haven, she's probably embarrassed as shit. And two, if she didn't pass out I'd be surprised."

"She still passes out at blood, huh?"

"Oh yeah. She's tough as nails on the water, but don't squash a mosquito around her or down she goes."

Willa found it somewhat endearing that as tough as she'd seemed to have become, she still held on to a part of her old self. And from the story Mama Lu relayed about the incident, Haven also appeared to have kept her clumsiness, too. "Okay," Willa said hesitantly.

"I'm headed in to check on things, so I'll make sure everything's okay and let you know."

"I'd appreciate that. You know, we all would."

"Of course."

Willa tried to catch a glimpse of anything when he opened the door to the office, but there was nothing to see. She waited just a few seconds to see if he would return right away, but he hadn't returned before Corey summoned her to the table for dinner.

"I fixed you a plate," Corey said as Willa slid onto the bench.

"Thanks."

"So she smashed her hand between two logs, huh? Damn!"

"Yeah." Willa picked at the salad with her fork.

"Do you think she'll still be able to kayak?"

Willa hadn't even thought about it being so bad that Haven couldn't be in her boat the rest of the week. "Shit. I don't know." As distracting as Haven was, Willa hated the idea that she wouldn't get to see her all day on the river. She couldn't help but think things might be easier for her out there without Haven, but this most certainly wasn't the way she'd have it.

"We'll have to wait and see, I guess."

As soon as the words were out of her mouth, Willa heard the sound of a door and chattering of voices from the other room. She set her fork down and stared waiting for Haven to come into the room. She needed to see that she was okay. By this time everyone else was positioning themselves to see Haven, and Willa was craning her neck around the others and not even attempting to be discreet. Wingman came through first. His eyes met Willa's and he nodded at her. While his affirmation eased a knot in her stomach, she waited for Haven, who followed in behind Diego. Willa stood up to see over everyone else. She breathed a sigh of relief when Haven smiled, but the last of it caught in her throat at the sight of Haven's bandaged hand.

"Haven, my gosh!" Willa heard Corey call out.

Haven stopped when Corey spoke. Willa's eyes darted between Corey and Haven in surprise. "Hey," Haven said to Corey.

"Are you okay?" Willa blurted out. Haven's eyes were tired and bloodshot from tears. It was then that Willa knew just how badly she'd hurt herself.

Haven smiled at Willa. "Oh, you know me." Haven raised her arm to give Willa a closer look.

"Yeah." Willa gently touched the exposed tips of Haven's wrapped fingers. The touch was so light, but Willa could feel an energy pass between them. "I do."

Chapter Ten

Haven moaned when her alarm broke through her last few moments of sleep. For the first time at camp, she wanted to sleep in. She wanted to pretend that her hand wasn't throbbing to the rhythm of her heartbeat, and she wanted to pretend that rhythm wasn't at double-time every time she thought about Willa. The problem with that was Haven couldn't escape her in sleep any more than she could awake. It had taken a few years, but Willa's dream appearances had become few and far between. When she did come to her, Haven had always woken up exhausted and disappointed. She would spend restless nights chasing, running, and crying with Willa always just out of her reach, beyond the tips of her fingers where she was never able to touch her.

Each one of the last few nights had been filled with those dreams, variations of new and old. The difference was that last night they had finally touched. It wasn't a dream or her imagination when Willa had reached out to her. Haven didn't pull away, and she forgot any pain in that moment as she watched Willa's fingertips touch hers. There had been no crying, no chasing, and no begging her to come back. Unlike in her dreams, Haven had asked for nothing and expected even less, yet Willa had answered.

Haven looked at her bandaged hand and the exposed tips where Willa had brushed her fingers. They were a bit more wrinkled than the day before, which meant they weren't swollen. A good sign. That was until she attempted to make a slow fist. She felt the wounds stretch and rub against the gauze and prayed they weren't stuck to the fabric. She was curious to see the damage she'd done to herself this time around.

She began to unwind the wrapping when Shannon popped her head in. "Eh. I knew you were gonna do that. Get changed and I'll redress it before breakfast."

Haven agreed to wait for Shannon to help her and rolled out of bed to get dressed.

"Um, you're not planning on going out on the river today, are you?" Shannon asked when Haven came out into the kitchen with her gear.

"Um, yeah. Of course I am."

"Sit down," Shannon said. Once Haven sat, Shannon started unwrapping her hand. "Not if you can't move your hand or grip a paddle."

"Once you get this bandage off, I will." With the outer wrap off, Haven grimaced as Shannon peeled the smaller pieces of gauze from her fingers. She took a couple of deep breaths before looking down at her exposed hand. Her stomach didn't flip; it just wobbled a bit at the sight. "Okay. Okay. It's not so bad. It was worse in my imagination." Her knuckles were scraped up pretty good and there was a decent amount of bruising, but overall it wasn't the worst she'd done to herself. "Okay. For these here we could use the waterproof Tegaderm." She pointed to the first row of knuckles. The second knuckles of her middle and ring finger took the worst of it, so she suggested a Tegaderm layer as well. Haven decided to use a beeswax bandage for her other fingers, which would work to keep anything out of those scrapes.

"What about your grip?"

"It's fine. I've done this with a torn rotator cuff. I can manage with a few bruised knuckles." Her defense sounded more convincing than it felt. Honestly, Haven wasn't sure she could grip the paddle all that well, but she had plenty of other skills and maneuvers to make up for it. She hoped. "Damn it!" Haven screamed as Shannon poured the peroxide straight from the bottle over her wounds. "I fucking hate you," she growled.

"If you insist on putting yourself in the river with a literal handful of open wounds, then we need to make sure it's clean first."

"Right. That makes no sense."

"Don't even get me started with shit that doesn't make sense, Ms. I'm-gonna-kayak-anyway." Shannon soaked a cotton ball with rubbing alcohol.

"I don't know what you think you're doing with that, but—"

"It's either this or telling Mama Lu not to let you on the water, for liability purposes."

Haven's mouth dropped open. "You wouldn't!"

"Try me." Shannon dabbed Haven's wounds and the surrounding skin, then blew it dry like she would for a child.

Haven hissed and bit her lip trying to transfer some of the pain and sting elsewhere. Her hand was on fire. She closed her eyes and thought about the way Willa's delicate touch had taken away the pain for those brief moments. Before she knew it, Shannon had finished applying the waterproof dressings. The slow burn of the alcohol was wearing off and so was some of the sharpest pain. A few minutes of ice during breakfast and she would be good to go.

Once Shannon had the scrapes cleaned up, they both headed up the drive to the lodge.

Mama Lu met them at the door. "So? Lemme see." She held out her hand for Haven to show her. "Shannon?"

"It's fine. Just bruised and a little stiff," Haven said before Shannon could answer.

"I didn't ask you."

Shannon looked at Haven and smiled. "She has multiple abrasions and contusions, but no obvious sign of fracture. I recommend rest, ice, and ibuprofen for pain."

"So she's staying at camp today?" Mama Lu asked.

"No!" Haven shouted. "Please?" Haven begged Shannon.

"No. She knows her pain limits. If she feels that she can do it, I don't have a reason she can't."

"I can!" Haven felt like a kid trying to convince her parents to let her have a pony. "I can do it." Haven flexed her bandaged hand to prove her point and instantly regretted it. She stifled a sob of pain and smiled through her clenched jaw.

Mama Lu looked at Haven and agreed. "I trust you, Haven. If you say it's fine, I believe you."

She thought, *Oh, shit. That fucking hurt,* but said, "No worries, Mama." She'd gotten her way. Pain or no pain, she couldn't change her mind now. Haven dismissed herself and headed straight for the drawer of zip baggies and then to the icebox. One upside to being on the river was the ten miles of freezing water to soak her hand in.

She set herself up with her laptop, ice pack, and camera to download the previous day's pictures before they headed out after breakfast. As the images transferred onto her computer, they played through in a slideshow. There were so many amazing shots of the campers immersed in unscripted flashes of joy and excitement that made Haven smile. In these pictures they were so much more than their diagnosis or prognosis. Beyond her love of the water and kayaking, she truly loved this part of her job. As the last few images scrolled across the screen, she knew she'd not taken them. Someone had picked up her camera at the hot springs and captured a handful of images, including the final photo on the roll that took her by complete surprise. There she was wrapped in Willa's arms where for a split second they appeared like they'd been caught in an intimate lovers' embrace. They were half dressed, dripping with water, and pressed against each other in a moment Haven had tried desperately to erase from her mind the day before. "Haven!" someone called, and Haven slammed her laptop closed.

❖

It wasn't like Willa to oversleep, but she had been up and down most of the night wondering how Haven was doing. By the time morning came she was exhausted and slept right through the breakfast bell. Willa hadn't even heard Corey get up or leave, which surprised her. She rushed to get ready and quickstepped it across the lawn to the lodge.

Breakfast was already set out and everyone except a few of

the volunteers had gotten their plates. Several campers, including Corey, had taken their seats around Haven, who looked as tired as Willa felt. It was obvious by her weary expressions that Haven had not slept well either. The pain must've been far worse than whatever medication Shannon had to give her. Yet she laughed and conversed with the group as if nothing had happened.

Corey waved Willa over and scooted along the bench to make space for Willa to sit. She hesitated at first since Corey was sitting and chatting with Haven, but her curiosity and need to check on Haven won out. She set her plate down and slid into her seat without a word.

"Willa, check this out!" Corey motioned toward Haven and the arm resting in her lap.

"Oh, she's eating. I don't think—"

Willa cut her off. "No. It's okay." She wanted to see it. Even if this sort of thing had been something that disturbed her appetite, she would still want to see.

Haven's eyes were wide with surprise. "Oh. Okay." She slowly raised her arm and rested her hand on the table. Although they had already seen it, everyone gasped anyway.

Willa's stomach tightened and her face flushed. "Oh, Haven." She wanted to reach out and caress her battered hand but resisted the urge. "I'm so sorry," was all she could say.

"Don't be sorry. It's not your fault." Haven smiled. "Besides, it looks much worse than it is."

Willa looked into Haven's eyes for any sign of pretense, but there was none. Or at least none she had the ability to recognize. "Well, I'm sorry you won't be on the river with us today, then."

"Yes, she will," Corey interjected.

Willa glanced between Corey and Haven. "What?" Willa asked in disbelief.

"Sure. It's okay. I've gotten worse on the river. See?" Haven stood and raised her pant leg to expose a series of scars that ran up the length of her shin. Everyone, including Willa, craned their necks to see. "Went for a swim on the South Canyon rapid and bounced off a bridge piling. Well, less bouncing, more scraping."

Willa noticed how proud Haven was of her injury. She wondered how many other wounds and scars her body had acquired over the last few years. Haven had always been rather clumsy and managed to injure herself doing the most mundane tasks. Willa recalled the one time she had nearly sliced off her finger while shopping for hurricane lamps, and the day she earned an ER trip after giving herself a concussion with a KitchenAid mixer. She knew she shouldn't ask, but she couldn't help herself. "Are you sure you should?"

"Well, I assure you that whatever doubts you have about my ability to be on the river are misplaced, Willa."

"I only meant—"

"Ha!" Corey interrupted. "We already talked about it before you got here. It's all good." Before the conversation could move forward or take a sharper turn for the worst, breakfast was over and Wingman was shooing everyone to their morning groups. Willa hadn't meant to offend Haven. She just wanted to make sure that she wasn't putting herself in jeopardy to prove a point. Her intention was to express concern, although looking back she could see why Haven had reacted the way she did. Willa had no right to question Haven or her choices. She lost that right years ago.

The bunkhouse seemed to get more disheveled as the days passed. It was no longer just Haven's clothes and equipment piled around the room. It seemed as though it had joined forces and multiplied with all the others. Willa sat with the rest of her group and took several deep breaths. She woke up tired, and now she was hungry because she hadn't eaten any of her breakfast, and she was irritable from her interaction with Haven. And if all that wasn't enough, Spartan felt the need to be the first one heard.

"Was it just me or did I rock the kayaking thing yesterday? Y'all did well, too. Well, maybe not Willa." He paused for laughs, but got nothing. "Someone had a little problem staying on the top side of the water."

"Hey, now. That's not what we're here for, Spartan. It's not a competition," Wingman said.

"Not technically," Spartan said.

"Not at all," Survivor said. "I'm not sure you're understanding the point of this camp if you believe it's about competing against each other."

The entire group was silent when Survivor finished speaking. Willa knew in her heart that she was right. This wasn't a competition, yet here she was being challenged by Mr. Douche in Boots, and boy, did she want to kick his ass in the worst way. Willa sat silently, lost in her own world, as the group discussed the lesson from the day before. When they were dismissed from group, Willa sped from the bunkhouse to find Corey, get on the bus, and then make Spartan eat his own arrogant words. Once they were on the road and headed down the mountain, her stomach growled, reminding her that it was very much empty.

Chapter Eleven

Haven almost wished that today was "ranch day," and not their second day on the river. That way she could get a day to rest her hand while campers were off horseback riding and hiking in the White River National Forest that adjoined the ranch. But that was tomorrow. Today they were going to run the Colorado again. This section was more challenging than the day before and would test their new skills several times along the way. The forecast called for clouds, rain, and temperatures in the sixties, but that was just a part of the adventure. Haven didn't mind the rain in the canyon; it added an ethereal magic and natural music to the experience.

So far that morning the skies were clear and the light began to flood over the walls of the canyon. Haven was careful to use her right hand for any pushing or pulling of the boats and equipment. It was easy enough with help from Diego and his two-armed kayak lifting skills. Haven and Wendy preferred the teamwork method with one of them on each end of the boat. They finished lining up the boats and tossed everyone's gear into their corresponding kayak while MC gave the campers a quick overview of the day's run.

After his safety review, everyone headed off toward their boats. Once everyone was loaded into their boats and launched, Haven would bring up the rear. Everything had gone smoothly until she reached down to grip her paddle with her left hand. It was the first time that morning that she'd tried to grasp anything, let alone pick something up or handle it. She went through a series of stretches and movements with her fingers to try to relieve some of the stiffness.

It seemed to reactivate the throbbing sensation from earlier that morning. As best she could, Haven slipped into the boat and pushed herself into the current, using her core muscles and hips to maneuver the boat to compensate for her weakened left stroke. It would work. Though she already knew she'd would be beyond exhausted at the end of the day. She floated along in her boat not far behind the group and drew her hand along through the cold water. Though not as cold as an ice pack, it did well to relieve the sting of her knuckles, and she was glad for that. Haven was going to have to rely mostly, if not solely, on her helmet camera to capture images for the day. She was thankful that she at least had the option so she wouldn't miss capturing today's moments. They were about to begin as they approached the first rapid of the day, Maintenance Rapid.

She wasn't surprised that everyone made it through without swimming. It was simple Class II with an easy line and no major obstacles, save for the steep pour-over on river left that MC had everyone avoid. A good start to the day all the way around. She noticed that Willa was up front, following closely behind MC and charging into the waves. Haven was pleased to see her getting right back into it after her struggles the day before. If anything, she seemed a bit more gung-ho, and Haven guessed that was her confidence and determination taking over. As Haven approached the rapid, she overcorrected her lineup to compensate for her injury and was sucked into the left line toward the hole. She went over the drop and hit the boil at an angle, causing her to capsize. Instinct kicked in, and she initiated a standard roll technique. She leaned forward against the deck and braced her knees and heels against the inside of the hull to keep herself securely inside the boat during the maneuver.

Haven swept her paddle from bow to stern at an angle to create lift beneath the surface, but her grip on the shaft was compromised by her weakened hand. She flicked her hips and pushed her right knee against the deck to give herself the momentum to right herself, but without the brace from the paddle her attempt was useless. Knowing that a second attempt would be pointless, she raised her arms into the air and waved them. Almost immediately, she felt the bump of another kayak and pulled herself to the surface using Scrat's boat as leverage. Once she had righted herself, the rapid had washed them out into the calmer water where the group had gathered into a huge eddy. *Great.* So much for the perfect start to the day—both she and her ego were sopping wet. Thankfully, that was the only damage she had sustained. Though when she caught a glimpse of Willa's concerned face she took a small hit to her conscience as well. Haven refused to accept that Willa, or anyone else, might have been right about her staying off the river today.

MC gave them a rundown of the next few rapids and what to expect. The busiest portion of the run was within the first four miles of their eleven-mile trip save for a few rough drops and rolls when they reached the infamous South Canyon Rapid at the end of the day. Haven couldn't think about that right now. She had to get through the next few miles in one piece, and then she'd worry about how she would manage that when they got there. Once back in the water, Haven watched Willa zip back toward the front of the pack with MC and Spartan. A part of her hoped that Willa would hang back a little in order to have time to judge the coming features, but she and Spartan now seemed to be jockeying for a lead position, which set of a few alarm bells in Haven's head. She didn't know what they were doing, but she still didn't like it. She hoped MC noticed it, too.

Willa's heart raced. It hadn't stopped pounding since they'd launched the boats that morning. Between anxiety, adrenaline, and watching Haven struggle with a roll that should've been second nature, Willa's system was in overdrive. She had been right about Haven and knew she shouldn't have been on the river with her injury. But Haven had made it abundantly clear that no one was going to tell her what she should or shouldn't do. Willa had little time to worry as they sped toward the next rapid.

She heard the feature before she could see it. MC called out a series of instructions to prepare the first half of the group for the next four consecutive rapids. She struggled to hear him over the increasing roar of the river and the rushing of blood through her ears. Spartan hooted in excitement as the ripples grew larger in preparation of the big water ahead. "Come on, Willa. Don't be scared!"

"Dick," she murmured to herself. Willa watched as MC took the line down center of the left-angled shoot, followed closely by Spartan, who glanced back at her and winked. It seemed easy enough as long as she hit the same line and stayed just to the right of the rollers that threatened her with a swim. "Loose hips," she reminded herself before moving in after Spartan. She splashed through the lateral wave that curled into the flow. The bow of her boat disappeared beneath the surface as the cold water washed up over her and her kayak. Willa paddled through the surf as it bounced her from side to side, threatening to toss her into the water if she would let it.

It was both invigorating and frightening to be at the mercy of Mother Nature. Ahead, Spartan had made it into the green water beyond the action and turned to watch the others come down the drop. The last thing she wanted was him watching and judging not just her, but everyone else, on their technique. Her body tensed, and the river took advantage of the opportunity. Distracted by Spartan and his smug stare, Willa was caught off guard by the last surge as it crashed into her boat, pushing her sideways toward a large boulder near the center of the river.

Her instinct was to paddle against the flow and lean away from the impact with the rock. As soon as she did so, Willa realized her mistake. She corrected herself by jerking her hips and raising the hull of the boat toward the current to hug the rock and push herself around it.

"Whoop, whoop. Careful, now," Spartan hollered at Willa.

As soon as she was free from her hang-ups, she drifted out of the flow and ferried into the eddy with MC and Spartan. In spite of the cold water bath she'd just received, Willa was comfortable. Her rapid heart rate and her flaming temper were keeping her warm. There weren't many things that could send Willa into a mood spiral, but Spartan had become one of them. Cancer or not, he was an arrogant tool, and she would love nothing more than to baptize him in the river with her hand on the back of his head.

Willa found it hard to understand why some people had to ensure they embodied the worst of every masculine stereotype. Assholes could easily be found in every group of people, but some of them, like Spartan, seem to give an extra effort in achieving the designation. Instead of acknowledging him or his instigating comments, Willa focused her attention of the rest of the group coming through the drop. She kept her fingers crossed for each of her friends coming down the chute.

Dunkin's head appeared above the horizon. Willa whooped and cheered as he maneuvered his way through the curling waves. "Yeah!"

"Bet he eats shit," Spartan said.

Willa rolled her eyes and ignored him. "You got this, Dunkin. Paddle through, man. Nice!"

"Nope. He's gonna get washed out," Spartan said. Willa looked at him incredulously but said nothing.

The same rogue wave that caught Willa from the side hit Dunkin too and sent him toward the same rock. "Hug the rock, Dunkin," she called out to him.

"More like eat the rock. Ha!"

Willa's head snapped around. "Shut the fuck up, dude."

"Whoa, woman. Don't get your panties twisted. I'm just having fun."

"At the expense of others, and believe me when I say that you're not funny. You aren't any better at this than any one of us."

"I'm a little better," he countered arrogantly.

"You're a dick, do you know that?" By this time not only had Dunkin made it down successfully, but so had Shark and Diego. "We get it, man. You're amazing, but damn, shut up about it already."

"Whoa, what's going on?" Diego asked as he ferried over and docked against Willa's boat.

"Nothing," she said.

He looked at Spartan for his reply, but he pretended not to be involved in the conversation at all. Diego let it go. "If you say so."

Mateo and Survivor made the descent look effortless even with a boat twice as long as everyone else's. There was a jubilant round of applause and cheers from the group when Survivor lifted her paddle in the air in triumph.

"Why are we cheering? It's not like she made it through on her own."

That was it. Willa had enough of his egotistical and malicious comments. She took a quick stroke and turned her boat toward him. "Who do you think you are? You're just the same as everyone else here and not better in any way. You're just an asshole with a bad attitude, and I don't even know why you're still here if this is all so rudimentary for someone of your caliber."

"Well, someone doesn't recognize friendly banter among friends."

"That is not banter, and you're not my friend. And while I can't speak for others, something you have no problem doing, I'm not sure you can count the rest of them among those 'friends' you talk of." By this time most of the group had now made it down to the eddy and were gathering around and gaping in awe at Willa.

Haven came down the run as MC interrupted the heated conversation and advised the group that they would be stopping here for lunch. Just up the bank from the eddy was a gazebo and picnic area, and for Willa it was a perfect time for a break from sitting in the boat and putting up with Spartan.

Willa beached her kayak and unlatched herself from the boat. She pushed herself out and gave herself a good back stretch from side to side.

"You're not the first person to call me an asshole, Willa," Spartan said when he sidled up to her on the shore.

"That honestly doesn't surprise me at all. Excuse me," she said, scooting around him to avoid any further conversation.

He followed her. "I think people are intimidated by me. Men think I'm too strong, and women—"

"Don't tell me. Can't get enough of you?" Willa rolled her eyes and kept walking.

"Especially the lesbians."

Oh for fuck's sake, he couldn't be serious. Willa spun around to face him. She stood up straight and took a deep breath before speaking. At full stretch, Willa was a good four inches taller and many pounds heavier than he was. "I'm only going to say this once, and for your benefit, I will say it to you alone. I recommend that from this point forward if you feel the need to speak to me or about me, don't." He took a step back and nodded in acceptance in spite of the words she knew hung on his lips.

❖

It was obvious that Haven had missed something between Willa and Spartan. And while he wasn't injured or bleeding, he was sitting off by himself instead of with the rest of the group. It seemed that he was starting to feel the effects of his constant boastfulness, and part of her felt bad for him in a way. She wasn't sure what kind of man he had been before his diagnosis, so she wondered how much of who he was now was a result of the illness.

"Hey. What's got you sitting over here alone?"

"I do better on my own," he said without further explanation.

Haven sat in the seat opposite and decided to dig a little deeper if only to satisfy her own curiosity. She opened a large, waterproof trauma bag filled with a variety of medical supplies and picked out items she needed to tend to her wounds. The organized prep kit seemed to catch his attention. "This should scar up pretty well in a few days, I think."

He scooted over to get a better view of her hand and the items she pulled out of the bag. "That's gauze. You need another Tegaderm bandage. I'd cut it like this to give your fingers more range to bend." Spartan showed her where to cut notches on the film so it would fit more like a glove and less like webbing between her fingers.

"I hadn't even thought about that."

"I'm not surprised."

She looked at him quizzically. "And why not?"

"I'm a trained survivalist, ready and waiting for shit to hit the fan, so to speak. I'll be able to live for weeks out of my backpack when it's time to bug out. People like you aren't smart enough to think about that stuff."

"Wow. Okay then. Good to know on the survival info," Haven said. "How long have you been a prepper?"

"Since Obama was elected. But I got serious after the doctor said I had cancer. I figured I'd pack a bag and hike off into the woods to die."

"Ah. So you figured that personal or collaborative skills weren't a necessity?"

"I've never had those. I think most people are idiots and incapable of doing anything for themselves," Spartan deadpanned.

"Well, that's not exactly true. I'm thinking you'd see that if you stopped being self-righteous now and again."

"Not possible, sweetie." Spartan measured and cut the bandage for Haven's hand and helped her apply it.

"Thanks." He was right; it pulled on her wounds less and gave her better range of motion. He smiled knowingly, although Haven couldn't bring herself to say it aloud. He was a cocky bastard, and it had nothing to do with cancer. Haven was almost positive that he was born a tool.

With lunch over and everyone's bladders empty, MC whistled his rallying cry and signaled to the river. It was time for the last half of the run through downtown Glenwood and into South Canyon. Haven had checked the speed and flow of the water that morning. It was high and fast and guaranteed to be a significant challenge to all of the campers. But before then, they could enjoy a few fun bumps and a hippy dip or two along the way.

They picked up on the river in the same order they had been except for Haven, who now took a place near the center of the pack. Her hand was still pretty much useless for anything except resting in the water or cradling the paddle shaft, although Spartan's bandage technique eased much of the pulling on her wounds, which helped. Haven couldn't figure him out. If she didn't know better, she might have thought he and Willa had been friends. It was probably such similarities between them that contributed to their conflict. But Haven had to give more credit to Willa, as she was nowhere near as self-absorbed as Spartan. Although that opinion quickly changed when she spotted the two of them grappling for position heading into the canyon. Haven could see that they were much too close to each other. The South Canyon rolls and waves were far too unpredictable to have more than one boat tackle it at a time. MC knew this and he whistled for them to hang back, though neither listened. Willa was the first up and probably had no idea that Spartan was so close to her stern. If she took a sharp hit from the right, she and her boat could end up taking them both out. Scrat and Mateo saw the danger as well and called out for Spartan to hold up, but it was too late. The riffle transformed into huge, billowing waves crashing and breaking in no order. Enormous boulders and an ever-changing riverbed combined with 3,000 cubic feet of water per second made South Canyon into an unpredictable series of lateral waves, undulating troughs, and fast water hitting from every direction.

As she feared, Spartan had been hit sideways. It knocked him off balance, exposing his hull to the next surge and pushing him straight into Willa's boat. The impact turned them both over and Haven gasped. The two capsized boats sped downriver and there was no sign of either Spartan or Willa. Haven's heart stopped as she frantically scanned the rapid for any sign of their red PFDs. She heard a shout from downstream river left, on the opposite side of where they had gone over.

Diego and Wendy had headed for the boats, while MC and Scrat each went for a swimmer. Haven tried to push herself through the rapid, but without complete control of her paddle she was left trying to get herself through safely. She watched helplessly as Willa was tossed around and overcome by wave after wave. Spartan was now in the center of the flow headed for the bridge piling much as she had once done. Haven was frozen between saving Willa or Spartan, knowing that she couldn't help either with her mangled hand.

Before she could make her choice, Mateo and Survivor sped past her toward Willa as Scrat and MC raced to Spartan. Willa had managed, either by luck or by maneuvering, to make it toward shore where she could grab hold of the rocks and get leverage to hold herself in position until they reached her. Spartan was in panic mode. He was flailing and struggling against the current, which did nothing but push him closer to danger.

He cried out in pain that could be heard throughout the canyon. Scrat reached him just in time before his body slammed into the piling as Haven had once done. She heaved him up by his PFD and he clung to the side of her kayak as she ferried him toward the pullout just beyond the bridge. Willa was doing the same alongside Mateo and Survivor's boat.

With everyone safe, Haven focused on the remaining campers riding the rapids down to her. One by one, they conquered the South Canyon like champs, something she knew Willa could've done had she just listened and not tried to race Spartan to it. Her impetuous start and his competitive personality caused a chain reaction that could've killed her. Her fear and anxiety morphed into anger and frustration by the time she reached the boat ramp. Haven nearly dropped her paddle from the intense shaking of her hands.

Haven started to jump out of her boat and give Willa a piece of her mind, but her thought was lost when she saw everyone gathered around Spartan. Her stomach sunk; something bad did happen. He was lying on the ground, his face contorted in pain. Wendy was on the phone with Shannon relaying the situation, while Diego was on another line calling for an ambulance. When Haven moved in closer, she saw what they were frantically describing. Though covered by his wet suit, Haven could see that his leg was awkwardly angled in comparison to his other. The sight made Haven feel sick, and her head swirled. Before she made a scene in front of everyone, she ran off into the nearest bush to vomit. She'd never seen something like that, and she didn't think she would ever be able to forget it.

CHAPTER TWELVE

Willa contemplated following Haven into the bushes, but it probably wasn't a good idea for several reasons. Willa was exhausted, and for the first time in hours, her heart was finally beginning to slow down. She just wanted to make sure that Haven was okay, and then she needed to sit down. After a few minutes, Haven stumbled out of the brush and made every effort not to look back over where Spartan and the rest of the group crowded around.

"Hey," Willa said.

Haven's eyes were glassy and filled with tears. She didn't respond when she looked at Willa, almost as if she didn't recognize her. She just jerked her head and hiked up the ramp toward the truck.

"Hav—" Willa was interrupted by Wendy and Diego advising her that it wasn't such a good idea.

"I'd let her go, Willa," Wendy said, coming over to check her for any injuries. "How are you doing?"

"I'm fine, I guess. Tired, but still in one piece, it seems." Willa regretted it as soon as she'd said it. "I didn't mean it like that."

Diego chuckled anyway. "Nice."

"That's not...I didn't...I feel bad, man. If only I'd...I don't know."

"Done what? You didn't do anything. He's the one who didn't leave space between you two. That section tosses everyone," Diego said.

"Sure, but if I'd seen him there. Or if I'd just waited and let him go ahead." She wasn't being honest. She had challenged him, and she would've done it the exact same way even if she had seen him first.

"You can't blame yourself for—" Wendy was cut off by the blaring of the ambulance siren as it pulled into the parking lot. "Sorry, we gotta go."

After they loaded Spartan into the transport, everyone else piled into the bus to head back to the ranch. The silence was deafening and lasted even through dinner. Mama Lu had gone into town as soon as she heard about the accident, and the volunteers were tasked with preparing dinner. Willa assumed that Haven had more than a little to do with the idea of individual pizzas. It always was her favorite way of making dinner without actually making anything. It should have been a fun evening with laughs and mini food fights, yet instead the dough and toppings were set out on the table and everyone quietly created their meals.

When the headlights from Mama Lu's truck shone through the windows, everyone jumped up from the table and flooded outside onto the porch. They watched as the driver's door opened and Mama Lu made her way to the house. Spartan was nowhere in sight. Willa's stomach twisted at the sadness in her face when Mama Lu met them at the steps. "Spartan will be staying at the hospital tonight with a proximal tibia fracture. Once we know when he is being released, we'll arrange for him to return home." Gasps and sighs moved through the group as she herded everyone back into the house. A few minutes later, Wingman reminded them of campfire and sent everyone scattering to get ready.

Willa made her way out to the fire and chose her seat for the evening. It was a cool night, yet she couldn't feel much of anything other than the guilt she had for what she'd said to Spartan before the accident. Even if he had deserved it in the moment, she wished she could take it back or maybe not have been quite as mean about it. It was the way it always turned out, saying things you regret and never getting the chance to apologize for them. This hadn't been the first time, for sure. She stared into the fire and replayed her words when a soft black bundle hit her in the face.

"You're gonna need this." Corey tossed the hoodie at Willa and sat next to her. "And this." She flapped the wool blanket over their laps.

"You always know, don't you?"

"I do. And I know that today wasn't your fault. So stop trying to find a way to blame yourself."

"I hate you." Willa bumped her shoulder into Corey's.

Wingman started the meeting with an update on Spartan, explaining that he received a cast for his injury, but thankfully would not require surgery. "I know we had a pretty intense day on the water, and Spartan's accident was the worst way we could've ended it, so I want to take a few minutes to discuss it."

After several moments of silence, MC spoke up. "Well, I just want to say thank you to my crew for their excellent swift water rescue skills. We train for these situations, hoping that we never have to use them. And to the volunteers, you saw the need and reacted immediately to cover the gaps. I'm grateful for such a great team, and I'm very proud of your work today."

"I wish I could've seen it," Wingman said proudly.

Willa spoke next. "I'm sure it's no secret that Spartan is not my favorite person here. He's arrogant and chauvinistic, to name a few of his obvious qualities. I'm not here to talk shit behind his back, because I've already said it to his face. I think that's why I'm taking some of the blame for what happened today."

"No!"

"What? That's crazy."

"Willa, you know you had nothing to do with what happened to him," MC said. "There were a few errors made on that run, but none of them by you. You didn't smash his knee into that gnarly rock, did you?"

"No, but I encouraged his competitive streak with my own. I wanted to be better than him. I wanted to…I wanted to be as good as he was. Hell, I wanted to be able to do it with a broken hand."

Willa looked up from the ground, meeting Haven's eyes without searching for them. "I wanted to do it with one eye." Haven's expression was confused. Corey reached out and squeezed

Willa's knee and she continued. "I'm going blind in my right eye, a side effect of the radiation. It's important to me that I don't have to rely on anyone, and my pride helps me make very stupid decisions about that. And it seems they're all coming back to bite me in the ass this week. When I was diagnosed with cancer, I'd already known what it was like on the other side. To love someone that you would do anything for, but lose anyway."

Haven's heart squeezed in her chest. Her eyes welled as she listened to Willa speak.

"I couldn't force her to do that. I couldn't trap her in a life that had no future. At least, no future that I could see in that moment. And to—" Willa's voice cracked, and Haven could feel the pain in her voice. "It was my own battle to fight, and I knew that while it would hurt us both for a while, it would save you from worse pain in the end." Willa stared into Haven's eyes.

Haven couldn't hold back the tears. She held her hand over her mouth at first to hide her surprise, and then to stifle the sobs. The fire illuminated Willa's own wet cheeks as she cried. Haven wanted to run to her, to wipe away those tears of pain and guilt from her face, but she didn't. Because in spite of her admission, Willa nearly destroyed Haven the day she walked out on her.

The pain of that moment came flooding back three-fold with the knowledge that Willa had resigned herself to death. She would rather have died alone than let Haven watch her let the disease beat her. The thought of Willa leaving her for someone else had been insufferable, yet she had survived. The idea that Willa could have died with her ever knowing would've killed her. It was too much to bear. Haven couldn't sit in painful silence with a thousand eyes watching her keep closed the gaping wound that had reopened in her chest. "I'm sorry," she said before running into the darkness beyond the ring of the flickering fire.

Haven didn't know where she was going as long as it was far away from there. She walked toward the woodpile, but instead of hunkering behind it she chose to climb onto a large, flat boulder. Stardust twinkled in her hazy vision when she held her head back and stared into the evening sky. Haven lay back on the cool rock and closed her eyes, though it did not stop the tears from flowing down her temples into her hair.

How had she gotten here? Not on this rock so much, but here in Colorado. How was she able to run from her past just to have it reappear before her? The moment she saw Willa step out of the SUV she should have left. Haven knew that nothing good could come from being so close, yet so far away. They were different people now, with new lives, dreams, and futures ahead of them. While some things seemed familiar, the truth was nothing was the same and never would be again. How could it? Even if she had finally been given the chance to say and do everything she had dreamt so many times, it was too late, wasn't it? And would any of it even matter now? Beneath the stars, she cried for all the wishes she had ever made that never came true.

"Hey," Willa whispered from the darkness.

Haven wasn't startled by her voice; somehow she already knew she was there. She sat up and wiped the tears from her face and eyes even though it was too dark for Willa to see her. "Hey."

"I had no idea where you went, but somehow I found you."

"You did."

"Can we talk? Up there preferably, because I'm a little scared a bear followed me out here."

Haven chuckled. "Sure." She moved over to make room for Willa.

"I brought these," Willa said as she pulled out several rumpled tissues from her jacket pocket and handed them to Haven.

"Oh. Thanks." Haven fiddled and folded them in her hands.

"So, about what I said. I didn't mean to upset you. I hadn't even intended on saying any of that, but it just sort of came out."

No kidding. She lay back on the rock again. "I've spent three years wishing on every star in this sky for this moment. And now I'm not even sure what to do with it." When Willa lay down next to her, Haven could feel the warmth of her body next to her in contrast to the coolness of the boulder beneath her. The heat from her closeness spread through her core, and she shifted to increase the space between them.

"Was your wish for me to spill my guts and make a complete fool of myself in front of strangers? Because, wish granted."

Haven laughed. "Well, maybe not that. But I'd be lying if I said that I didn't waste one or two on something almost as petty."

"Hmm. Well, that could explain a few things."

"Why didn't you give me a chance, Willa? You know I would've done anything for you. Didn't you trust me?" Haven couldn't look at Willa or she would lose her nerve to ask these questions.

"I trusted you with my life, Haven. But you couldn't have fixed it, and that would've hurt you more than I did. I couldn't do that to you."

"You didn't give me a choice, Willa. You made the decision without me. How could you possibly know how I would've felt?" Haven began to cry again and sat up to wipe her eyes and nose with the tissues Willa had given her.

Willa sat up as well. "I thought I was doing the best thing for both of us. How could I care for you and keep you safe if I had?"

Haven burst into tears and turned to Willa. "I didn't need you to take care of me. In case you missed it, I'm pretty good at taking care of myself." Haven motioned to the darkness around them. "And I could've taken care of you."

"Yes, you've become quite the independent adventurer. It suits you. Better than being a caretaker would have."

"Dammit, Willa! That's not fair." Haven slid down off the rock away from her. "I spent these last few years doing everything I could to become someone you could love again. Yes, I found a new passion in the process, and I wouldn't change that, but there was no way I could've put those shattered pieces of me back the same way. You gave me no choice but to become this person."

Willa came down from the rock and stood before her. Haven's heart pounded in her chest. The glittering stardust and waxing moon illuminated Willa like a dream she'd had so many times. "Haven, I'm so sorry I hurt you. I was scared and selfish, and I thought I was doing the right thing. Although now I see that I made the biggest mistake of my life. I've regretted it every day of my life since."

Haven couldn't believe that she was hearing those words. She had prayed for the day when Willa would appear before her and say these very things. She felt light-headed, and her knees buckled. Willa's strong arms wrapped around her and held Haven tight against her. "Willa," Haven said as she melted into the embrace. Willa dipped her head, their lips a whisper apart. "Forgive me, Haven. Please?" she asked, looking into Haven's eyes.

Her eyes were dark and soulful, and Haven felt the heat of Willa's breath against her lips. Haven wanted to fall into them the way she had done so many times before. She wanted to stay forever in her arms like she once had. But she couldn't. Haven pressed her palms to Willa's shoulders and gently pushed her away. Against her body's pleading, Haven stepped back out of Willa's arms. "I need some time, but I know that I'll forgive you. I just can't do it this way. I'm not in a position to be caught up in another woman's arms, especially yours. I…I have a girlfriend."

Willa felt like she'd been struck in the chest. She did have a partner. Of course she did. Why wouldn't she? "Oh. I see."

"And I don't think this is a good idea. We never were very good at stopping at kissing."

Willa remembered. Even the first time they had ever kissed had gotten pretty hot. "Do you remember the first time we kissed?" Willa climbed back onto the rock.

"I do. I was sitting on the trunk of my tan Buick and you were leaning against my leg fidgeting with something. A stick?"

"Yeah." Haven climbed up and reclaimed her place next to Willa. Willa noticed it was a little closer this time, and she made no attempt to scoot away again.

"We spent the whole weekend camping, snuggled in the same bag in the same tent. That's when you told me you loved me."

"And you didn't respond, if I recall correctly."

Haven laughed. "I didn't. I knew I loved you, but I was so scared to say it aloud. And then there we were in the woods behind your house, alone and anxious."

"The moon was nearly as bright then as it is now." Willa was surprised by how similar the two nights were.

"I remember. I could see how nervous you were, and I could only imagine that your heart was racing like mine. I'm not even sure what came over me, but I knew I had to kiss you."

Willa's stomach fluttered at the memory just as it had then.

"And that's the last time I had any control over my heart."

"It was so long ago. So much has changed."

Willa knew that was the truth; so much had changed. They weren't innocent kids anymore with their future laid out before them. Somewhere along the way they'd become adults and made their own lives outside of anything they had ever planned together. Sitting on a boulder beneath the infinite sky, Willa knew that they were as distant as they could ever be. "Are you happy here?"

There were several moments of silence before Haven answered. "Mostly." It wasn't the answer Willa had expected. "Don't get me wrong, I love Colorado. My friends are here, Valiant is here, and I guess my work is here."

"You guess? What are you doing?"

"I paint. Professionally, you could say."

"What? Haven, that's amazing! You were always such a talented artist."

"Thanks. It's how I met Bianca. She's also my agent."

And just like that, Willa's excitement died. "Oh, so she inspired you to paint again?"

"Not so much. She just sort of pushed me back into it and encouraged me to make a career of it."

Willa didn't hear a hint of emotion in her voice. "But you don't want to paint?"

"No. I do. But you know that being a professional artist never interested me. I always feared what would happen if I was forced to paint. Seems I was right. I just lose all interest in doing it as soon as someone tells me I have to. There's no freedom in a deadline."

"I see. So why keep doing it?"

Haven sighed. "I don't know. Bianca has put so much into promoting my work, and she believes I have a future. I just...the fire isn't there. Ya know?" Haven pulled her legs up and wrapped her arms around them.

"Why don't you become a professional kayaker? Everyone can see the fire in you when you're on the water."

"Ha! I've thought about it. Wanna hear a secret?"

It had been so long since Haven had confided in her, and she was desperate for it. "I would."

"I've been thinking about starting my own camp."

Again, it was not the response what Willa had expected. "Wow. That's great."

"Yeah. It's just an idea. Just dreaming it all up for now, so it keeps getting bigger. And there's no way I could afford to start it here with everything I'd want to do."

"So you'd move back to Florida?" Willa asked.

"No. I can't go back there."

Willa had no doubt why Haven had left and why she wouldn't return. She had experienced a constant barrage of memories after they had separated. Growing up together in a small town left very few options to avoid each other except to move. Willa had done it herself when she bought the farm with her brother. Although she chose a few counties compared to the several states that Haven put between them. "I'm sorry, Haven."

"I know. It's funny how some things work and others don't. I'd watch all these couples break up and get back together twenty times over and wonder why we never got that chance. Seemed unfair somehow."

Willa had wanted to reach out to Haven so many times, but as time passed it became harder and harder to make that move. She'd thought about her often during her radiation treatment when she was quarantined and alone for days on end. "After what I did to you, I can't believe you would ever have wanted me back."

"We'd been together so long and known each other our whole lives, there had never been anything we couldn't work through if we wanted. I thought it was just a matter of time. But then…you never came back." Haven's voice cracked with emotion.

Willa could no longer hold back the tears as her heart broke hearing the pain in Haven's voice. "I couldn't, Haven. What if I lost my eye? They talked about taking it out. How could you be with someone like that?" Willa was sick to her stomach remembering when the doctor gave her that as an option.

Haven looked at Willa. The moon reflected off her tearstained face. "How could you think that would even matter to me? You didn't even give me a chance to show you that what we had was in here." Haven pressed her hand against Willa's chest.

Willa held Haven's hand in place over her heart. For the first time in years, Willa realized she was right. Across miles and years, Haven still owned each beat of Willa's heart. "And now it's too late."

They sat in a painful silence with the cool night creeping into Willa's skin and into her soul as she held her breath for Haven's response. When she finally spoke, the words sent a frozen spike through her heart. "For some things, it might be."

Chapter Thirteen

Willa stretched and rolled over. Her eyes flung open wide when she saw that Corey was sitting on the edge of her bed. "Morning!" Corey said as Willa all but jumped out of her skin in surprise.

"What the hell, man?"

"Wakey, wakey! Where did you disappear to last night?"

"What time is it?" Willa hadn't slept so soundly since she'd been at camp. It was a welcome change. All except for the last thirty seconds.

"It's eight o'clock. They rang the breakfast bell twenty minutes ago, and when you didn't come they sent me over to check on you."

"Wow."

"Yeah, wow. Have you ever slept this late? Even Haven seemed a bit concerned when you didn't show up."

"Haven? Concerned about me? She said that?"

"Yes. Well, not with words so much. Mama Lu asked me if I'd seen you, and when Haven overheard that you were AWOL she coincidentally began pacing and peering out the windows."

Willa smiled. "Interesting."

"I thought you'd think so. Now come on! It's field day today, with horseback riding and paddleboarding on the lake, and later there's a cornhole tournament. But right now MC is making homemade pancakes as big as your freaking head." Corey jumped up and down on the edge of the bed.

"Ha! Okay. Okay. But stop jumping before I pee myself."
Corey hopped up off the bed and made room for Willa to get to the
bathroom before she made good on her statement.

"And hurry up before Haven wears a rut in the floorboards
waiting for you."

"Shut up. I'll be right there."

"All right. I'll go let *everyone* know you're fine."

Willa couldn't help but feel a little anxious and excited to
see Haven this morning. She jumped in and took a quick shower
before getting dressed and rushing across the yard to the lodge.
It was strange how different this morning felt from all the others.
There was a sense of peacefulness and optimism that filled the air
accentuated by the soft morning light breaking over the mountains.
Just as Corey had said, Haven stood at the window and stared out
toward the cabins. A smile spread across Haven's face when they
saw each other for the first time that day. It was going to be a great
day. Willa knew it.

Haven met her at the front door when she reached the porch. She
offered her a polite good morning and told her about the enormous
pancakes Corey had mentioned. It wasn't anything significant, but
it was more than Willa had gotten from her in five days and it made
her morning.

They hadn't been kidding about the size of MC's noggin-sized
flapjacks. They were monstrous and filled with anything she could've
wanted, from berries and nuts to peanut butter and jelly had it been
requested. Willa placed her special order for her breakfast and made
a plate of bacon and eggs while she waited.

There were three different sign-up sheets hanging on the wall
in the dining room. One was for horseback riding, one for massages,
and the other for those interested in playing in the cornhole
tournament. Willa made a note to herself to sign up for everything
after she was finished eating breakfast. Which she realized could
take all day when MC delivered her pancake order.

"It won't hurt his feelings if you can't eat the whole thing,"
Haven said as she took the seat next to Willa and slid over a cup of
coffee.

Willa smiled. "I can. I just don't think I should."

"Not if you plan on moving at all for the rest of the day. Speaking of, I don't see your name up there yet." Haven motioned toward the sign-up sheets.

"I haven't gotten there."

"Well, it looks like you're not left with many options, sleepyhead. It's not like you to miss a sunrise, if I recall correctly."

"True. Unless I'm out late the night before."

"I see. Well, you should finish eating and get your name up there or you'll miss all the fun." Haven got up from the table and disappeared into the kitchen.

Willa watched her go before getting up to put her name on each of the lists. Since she was late getting up, she had to finish eating, get changed, and be at the barn in less than thirty minutes for the first trip of the day. Part of her had hoped for more time spent with Haven, but she also wanted to try her hand at all of the things she'd never done before, things that Haven enjoyed.

Willa's morning was spent riding through the forest and along creeks of the Rocky Mountains, and then relaxing with an hour-long massage. As she made her way up from the spa she heard the laughter and ruckus coming from the lake. MC, Scrat, and Mateo had pulled out several stand-up paddleboards and were giving lessons to those interested. Corey spotted Willa and hollered for her to join them. She hadn't been interested in putting herself into any physically demanding activities so soon after a massage, but then she spotted Haven. "Is there anything that woman can't do?" she asked herself.

"Not when she puts her mind to it. She's obnoxiously stubborn that way," Wendy said as she trekked up behind Willa.

"Oh, hey. It certainly seems so."

"Get changed and go down. You could learn a thing or two from her."

"I'm realizing that. I'll see you down there," Willa said before she rushed off to change.

It didn't take her long to get into her suit and then down to the lake where everyone was trying out their SUPing skills, or lack of them. By now Corey and Haven were involved in some sort of paddleboard handstand competition that she wanted nothing to do with. Diego was whipping around making figure-eight movements that resembled a surfer in the ocean. Considering that she lived in Florida, it always surprised people when she told them that she'd never been on a paddleboard.

"Willa! Stop being a chicken and get your feathers out here," Corey yelled from where she had joined up with the girls now doing yoga poses in the middle of the lake.

"Ha! I get it now," Haven called. "Willa. Free range. Chickens. Ha!" The revelation had broken her concentration and sent Haven toppling over into the lake.

Willa held her breath until Haven popped out of the water with an enormous grin. "Oh, good grief."

❖

Once back onto her SUP, Haven saw that Willa was getting a quick lesson in the art of paddleboarding and getting into her PFD. Everyone had opted for little more than suits and trunks. Haven knew Willa was going to be rather startled by the temp of the mountain lake. The lake was a cool sixty degrees. Her assumption was confirmed by Willa's shout when she stepped into the water and then onto the board. "And here I thought it was gators I had to worry about! Damn!"

Haven laughed because she completely understood Willa's wariness of water. It reminded Haven of all the times they had caught and wrestled any gator under five feet just for funsies. She knew there was a world of difference between you sneaking up on them and the other way around. Even so, it probably wasn't one of their wisest adventures. Even though she knew better, the thought of alligators made Haven pull up her feet.

Corey called out for Willa to meet them in the center of the lake. But by the looks of it, it was going to take her more than a few minutes to make it that far. Willa resembled a newborn fawn on fresh legs as she danced awkwardly on top of the board. Scrat stepped into the water and showed Willa an easier way to start out. She held the SUP steady as Willa lowered herself onto her knees and sat back on her feet. Haven knew Willa's best chance of staying on the board was to lower her center of gravity until she could get the hang of balancing herself upright. Haven smiled.

"That girl is bound and determined to impress you. Or at least die trying," Corey said as she floated up alongside Haven.

"Impress me? What?"

"You're kidding, right? She hasn't stopped pushing herself since she got here."

"Shut up." Haven laughed nervously. "Why?" The Willa she knew was only worried about not looking like a fool.

"Come on. You're practically Superman. Kayaking the wild whitewater of Colorado, risking your life when someone needs you, forging through the pain to fulfill your passion. I'm not even gay, and you've got me hot and bothered." Corey laughed.

"Oh geez. I'm not Superman. You know that I did this by smashing it between two pieces of wood, right?" Haven held up her healing, but still damaged, hand.

Corey scrunched up her face. "Well, it goes way beyond that. I mean, look at how hard she's trying." She pointed over to where Willa was finally making her way out into the water toward them.

"Oh my. It might be faster if we meet halfway."

"No. Let's make her work for it," Corey said.

Haven liked the way Corey thought. She was flattered by the idea that Willa was working for it and doing what she could to impress her. Willa had always had Haven's heart and never had to do much to win her over. She certainly never had to go out of her way to try to impress her. It was kind of nice. And dammit, she looked so great trying even if her technique was a whole lot of mess.

"There you go. Stay centered," Haven said as Willa floated toward them.

"Oh, for heaven's sake, Willa. Put your back into it!" Corey said.

"Hey! I'll get there when I get there. And when I do…"

"What? You'll tip over."

"No!" Willa yelled, and as she did, her balance faltered. She danced back and forth.

Corey burst out laughing, and Haven tried to keep a straight face. "It's all right. You'll get it. Just takes practice." Haven turned to Corey. "I'd be careful. She'll get you when you least expect it."

"So it seems." Corey winked at Haven.

"Wha—Hey, you made it!" Haven welcomed Willa to the middle of the lake.

"I did."

"Great. Are you ready to learn how to perform the standing part of stand-up paddleboarding?"

Willa's expression was uncertain. "I guess so."

"Can I just sit back and watch?" Corey asked.

Willa smirked at her. "Yes. Do that. Lean all the way back. Like right into the water."

Haven laughed. The relationship these two had built in the last few days surprised her. They bantered like siblings and giggled like childhood friends. It brought out a side of Willa that was so rare and authentic, and one that she had once been lucky enough to experience. It made her happy to see Willa share that with someone else, and also a little jealous. "Okay, kids. Play nice."

"Yeah, Willa."

"Shut it. Now go away so I can concentrate."

"Not a chance."

Haven took the brief pause in their sisterly badgering to interrupt and start teaching Willa how to SUP. "Okay, both of you. Let's do this."

Haven positioned herself onto her knees and instructed Willa to first watch her. She placed her paddle across the board several inches in front of her knees. Slowly, she replaced each knee with her foot and moved into a squatting position. With her feet planted and her body balanced over the center of the board, she lifted her paddle and stood upright. "And there we go. You try."

Willa looked at Haven like she had just performed a miracle and walked on water. "Uh. Yeah. Easy for you to say."

Haven knelt back down. "Take your time. Just keep your feet

shoulder width apart and get your balance before you stand up. You can do it. Ready?" Haven looked into Willa's eyes and locked onto them. She relayed each step to her without breaking the contact. It was an intense connection, and Haven could almost feel the energy sparking between them. They moved in unison through each step until they were almost upright. "Now, stand."

"Or poop. You look like you've gotta poop."

"Corey!" Haven whipped her head in her direction. She laughed with Corey until they heard the "oh shit" and then the splash.

Corey broke out in maniacal laughter, and Haven tried not to when a soaking wet Willa popped up from the water and threw herself onto the board. "Dammit, it's fucking freezing."

"Oh my gosh. Are you okay?" Haven asked through stifled snorts of laughter.

"I am. But she isn't going to be." Willa snarled and lunged at Corey, making her spook and jerk backward. The sudden movement threw Corey's own balance off, and she toppled back into the water with her own curse and a splash.

It was now Haven's turn to lose her composure and break down into hysterics. "You guys are ridiculous. So childish." Sure she thought it was childish, but in an "adulting sucks" kind of way.

"Childish?" Willa looked incredulous. "Corey, did you hear that?"

Corey feigned shock and surprise. "Why, Willa, I do believe she has just sullied our honor."

Even Haven knew what was coming next, but she had no way of escaping them. Willa grabbed onto the stern of Haven's board, while Corey latched onto the back. She dropped down onto her butt to keep from falling in. Haven gripped the side rails of her SUP as Willa and Corey rocked it back and forth, trying to dump her into the water with them. She refused to give in. The board was far too long and wide to simply turn over, so as long as she could keep her grip Haven could hold out.

"Come on in, baby. The water's fine."

The sultry sound of Willa calling her baby undid more than her grip on the board. A wave of butterflies fluttered through her.

Her body was weak and her resistance was down, allowing Willa to reach up, take her by the waist, and pull her into the water. The shock of the icy water was nothing to fight the heat that built within her as Willa held her close.

❖

Willa could've spent all day floating in the water with Haven in her arms. However, in spite of the desire boiling in her core, she was beginning to lose feeling in her feet. There was nothing quite like reality to bring her out of the moment. Before Willa could release her, Haven put both hands on Willa's head and dunked her under the surface. The sudden face-freezing rush cause her to relinquish her hold and let Haven go. "Jeeezus! That's enough."

All three of them shimmied themselves back onto their boards, and Willa willed the sun's energy to reverse her hypothermia. After several minutes, she was warm enough to have full use of her extremities. In spite of her desire to master the art of standing on a paddleboard, she was more than okay with trying it again some other time. Like when the water wasn't two degrees above freezing and Haven wasn't there to distract her.

The lunch bell rang from the lodge and everyone raced toward the shore. The smell of barbecued meat made Willa's stomach growl loudly. In spite of her desire to run like a starving wolf toward the scent, she stayed to help Haven out of the water and pull up her board.

"You don't have to do that," Haven said.

"I know."

"I think there's a brisket up there with your name on it."

Willa's eyes grew to the size of dinner plates. "You didn't."

"I did." Haven smiled, and Willa's entire body quivered.

She didn't know what she was more excited over, the fact that Haven made a brisket, or that she remembered and made one for her. There was nothing in the world that could compare with Haven's hardwood smoked beef brisket. Willa was surprised she didn't have gluttonous dreams about the delicious slab of meat. Her mouth was already watering with anticipation. Willa didn't know which of them she wanted more at that moment. "You're killing me. Corey, you will not believe how good this thing is. It's heaven in your mouth."

"I must say I'm a little uncomfortable with your excitement over a piece of meat," Corey said.

"You say that now."

"It's actually pretty good," Haven confirmed.

"And you made it just for her. How sweet." Corey winked, and Willa saw Haven blush.

Willa was the first in line for lunch, and she had no shame for it. She spooned a small selection of salads onto her plate but saved two-thirds of the plate for meat. She skipped the chicken, burgers, and dogs entirely. "Here," she said as she served several slices to Corey as well.

"Whoa. That's enough." She stopped Willa before she put the last piece onto her plate. Willa shrugged and gladly put it on hers instead.

She and Corey sat at the table, and Willa wasted no time before she dug into her food. It tasted just as she had remembered, "full of love and a dry rub," as Haven had always joked. As she stuffed her face with lunch, she noticed the new sheet that Wingman hung in place of the tournament sign-up. The names had been rearranged into teams, and Willa's stood out boldly next to Haven's. "What?" she asked with a mouthful of brisket.

"Ohhh, yeah. They put that up while you were getting your massage. Such fun, right. I guess since we can't be on a team together, that's the next best thing. Ha!"

"Why do I think you had something to do with this?" Willa raised her eyebrow at Corey.

"Meee? Nooo."

"That's fine. You don't realize what you've done. Back home, we're standing champs of Nancy's Memorial Day BBQ and Cornhole Tournament."

Corey laughed. "That's fine. Shannon's my teammate, and I heard that besides Wingman, she's the best there is."

Willa stuffed a piece of meat in her mouth and said, "Until now."

Once everyone had their fill of barbecue, Wingman announced the teams and arranged the tournament bracket. Willa realized they didn't kid about cornhole in Colorado either. She was sitting on the picnic table when Haven came up and handed her a wad of junk. Willa picked apart the tangle of stuff and pulled out a rainbow bandana, a sequined clown tie, Mickey Mouse ears, a pink tutu, and an inflatable alligator pool toy. "What is this?"

Haven giggled. "So, it's tradition during the game that we wear a fun and unique outfit to express our personality, and I picked a few things I thought we could use."

"Was this what was left at the bottom of the pile or what?"

"Ha! Nope. I picked it all special. These are my lucky goggles, though," she said as she lowered a pair of frog-shaped children's swim goggles down over her eyes.

Willa couldn't help but laugh at the way they mushed her eyes and pinched her cheeks because they were way too small for her head. "How can you see anything in those?" she asked, covering her mouth to keep from cackling at how ridiculous she looked.

"I can't. It's what makes me so good." Haven pulled the goggles off with a loud sucking sound.

"You're a nut."

"I know. Now let's get you geared up." Willa stood and Haven held up an item in each hand for her to choose. Given the options she had no chance of selecting anything inconspicuous, so she decided to go all in. She chose the mouse ears, clown tie, and the alligator, leaving Haven the ballerina tutu that she probably picked more for herself than for Willa anyway. Haven tied up her wild blond hair into the bandana, which looked less silly and more badass than it would have on her. Willa slipped on her mouse ears and tie while Haven stepped into her skirt and pulled it up. The tulle had seen better days, but she put a punk rock spin on the whole ensemble that worked in her favor. She looked more stunning in this awkward costume than anyone else could have. Her smile, her energy, and her confidence made her glow with a bewitching beauty. "You're captivating, Haven." Willa reached out and brushed her fingers against Haven's soft, blushing cheek. Willa watched as Haven's eyes fluttered closed at the touch of her hand. Time slowed around them for that moment. Willa wanted to pull her into her arms and kiss her with a desire she hadn't felt in years. She stepped in close and raised Haven's chin with her fingers. Her soft pink lips parted so slightly, begging to be kissed.

Corey's voice broke through the spell and brought them crashing back into reality. "Let the games begin!"

Willa could've strangled her for interrupting the moment, until she realized that she actually saved them from embarrassing themselves in front of everyone. Corey motioned to all of the people who now gathered around them, and she thanked her. Haven cleared her throat nervously and fidgeted with her tutu, pretending to ignore the entire situation.

"Are you ready to kick some ass?" Willa asked Haven.

Looking at Corey, she grinned. "Yes, I am."

Chapter Fourteen

Haven second-guessed her decision to jump into Willa's arms, but only after she was already there. It felt great to knock Shannon off her winner's perch after almost an entire season as the tourney champion. It felt even greater to have done it with Willa. They still made a great team. Willa released Haven slowly enough so that her body slid down the front of hers in the most provocative way. The friction sparked a fire in Haven's belly. As soon as her feet touched the ground she stepped back away from Willa. "Good game." Haven cleared her throat and tucked an imaginary strand of hair behind her ear.

"It was." Willa blushed as pink as Haven felt.

They were saved by the interruption when Wendy and Diego charged up and reminded Haven about the traditional hot tub challenge scheduled after dinner and the campfire. "Oh right. I'll be there," Haven said.

"The what?" Willa asked.

"Every camp we try to see how many campers and volunteers we can fit into the hot tub at the same time," Wendy answered.

"It's steamy, and sexy," Diego added.

"And crazy crowded," Haven said.

"That sounds like a literal hot mess, but in the best way." Willa looked right at Haven and smiled.

"It is." Diego winked at her.

As soon as they were dismissed from the evening campfire,

everyone scattered toward their bunks to get changed into their suits and trunks. Haven, Wendy, and Diego had already changed earlier, giving them a few extra minutes in the tub before the others arrived. There was nothing like a good soak after a day on the cold river or lake. It rounded out the experience.

"So, things seem to have taken a turn from earlier this week," Diego said.

"I know. Seems this tub isn't the only thing getting steamy," Wendy added.

"There's nothing going on. We had a pretty long talk the other day and got a few things out on the table. We're just friends. Or at least we're trying to be."

"I think that's great and all, but you can't be friends with an ex. Not like real friends," Diego said.

"Why not?" Wendy and Haven asked in unison.

"You're joking, right?" Diego asked, looking at Wendy.

"No. I know that's true, I just knew that's what she was gonna say."

Diego laughed. "So did I."

"Whatever. Give me a reason why we can't be friends."

"Just one? That's easy enough. Answer me this: do you still love her?"

"What? Like...*love* love her?"

"Yes. Do you?"

Haven knew the answer. It was one she had asked herself a thousand times over. Every stage of their lives together she asked herself that question. Did she love Willa? The answer had been yes in junior high band class. It had been yes the night they shared the same sleeping bag when they camped. It was yes every day of the three years they were apart, and it was yes now. "I'm not going to answer that. It's irrelevant."

"Unfortunately, it's the only question that matters, Haven. You cannot be *just friends* with someone you're in love with, especially if they don't feel the same. One of you will always be wishing things were different, and they never will be. It's not fair to you."

"But that's my choice. I'd rather have her in my life as a friend than nothing at all. I've done that."

"So let me ask this. Could you be friends with her if she started dating someone else?"

The mere thought of Willa with someone else sent a wave of sickness through her. Why would that bother her? She was dating someone else herself, and it didn't bother Willa. Did it? She hadn't said it had when Haven told her about Bianca the night they almost kissed. And obviously it hadn't affected any of their encounters since then. So Willa didn't feel the same way as she did. She could live with that, couldn't she? The truth was, she had no idea if Willa already had a girlfriend at home. They hadn't even talked about Willa, or her life in Florida. "Um."

"Hey, Willa. Corey. It's about time y'all got here," Wendy announced and spooked Haven out of her spiraling confusion.

Haven saw Willa, and her entire body lit up. She had no control over how Willa made her feel, even if moments before she had been lost in her own perplexed thoughts. Willa set her towel on the bench and slipped into the tub directly across from Haven. The move surprised Haven a little since she assumed that Willa would've sat next to her. A part of her might've even hoped, although it was probably for the best that she hadn't. Even more so now that Diego and Wendy had gotten her mind racing with their questions.

Soon everyone else arrived, squeezing themselves into the open spots around the tub. Willa moved across the tub and squeezed in next to Haven, and her pulse quickened. The ten-person tub now held sixteen people, with four of them squatting down in the center of the spa. Water splashed and poured over the sides onto the deck with each addition to the human soup bowl. Haven had no idea when or how it happened, but suddenly she was sitting on Willa's lap as the count reached eighteen. Screams and squeals of laughter echoed through the darkness as everyone piled into the water.

Once again, Haven and Willa found themselves pressed against each other, with their mouths just a heartbeat away. Whether it was the frenzy of the moment or the preoccupation of those around them, Haven closed the space between them and pressed her lips to Willa's. Willa pulled back in disbelief, but quickly reclaimed Haven's lips with her own. Their kiss was hard and fevered, with Willa's arms wrapped tightly around Haven's body.

Haven attempted to relay three years of emotion in mere seconds of time. They were, after all, in the presence of sixteen other people, albeit in a distracted whirlwind of bodies and hot water. She didn't know that she'd ever get another chance to feel Willa's lips on hers, and Haven couldn't let that moment pass by. The truth was, she would never see Willa again after they parted ways on Saturday. As much as she wished it weren't true, she knew they wouldn't be able to be friends. She wouldn't be able watch Willa move on with her life, especially with someone else.

Haven pushed herself back from Willa and got out of the tub. The cold air shocked her skin, but she needed it. Without saying a word to anyone, Haven wandered off into the night toward the safety of her bunkhouse.

❖

Haven was embarrassed to show her face the next morning at breakfast. She didn't regret that she had kissed Willa, just the way she'd run away afterward. Her dreams had been filled to the brim with images of Willa and various arrangements of their bodies entwined together. If the kiss did anything it stoked the fire in Haven's belly.

Haven was stirring her coffee when she overheard Willa talking to the others at the table about a beautiful woman named Carmelita. She craned her neck to listen and heard that she was describing the various features of one of her prized chickens. Willa ran through a list of her favorite birds and their quirkiest traits. No doubt the weirder the bird, the more Willa adored it. She always had a penchant for the smallest, runtiest, and underdoggiest of every species.

Haven sat and joined those who listened to Willa tell them about her farm back home. Goats, chickens, and a couple of sheep made their home with her in Florida, along with her brother. Haven listened intently for any mention of a girlfriend or partner waiting for her to return, yet she heard nothing of the sort. It seemed that besides her farm babies and her brother, the one true love in Willa's life was an Australian shepherd named Annie Oakley. Haven couldn't help but feel relieved by the information, not that it mattered in the end.

Willa had been raised on a farm and longed to one day start her own. It was something that she and Haven had talked of frequently when making plans for their future together, though they never had a chance to make it happen before everything went belly up. A part of Haven was jealous that Willa had gone ahead with their plans on her own. In spite of that, she was glad that she hadn't let cancer keep her from her dreams.

Wingman came into the dining room and gave them all a rundown of their final day on the river. Today they'd be starting on the Roaring Fork, which fed into the Colorado near Glenwood Springs. It was a challenging run, perfect for their last day.

After he filled them in, he scooted in next to Willa at the table. "Do you want to stick with the hard boat, or do you want to take a ducky today?"

It wasn't meant as an insult. Haven knew that Wingman was just looking out for everyone's best interests. He wanted to make sure that Willa would have fun and also be safe if she was feeling uncertain after the accident the other day. Everyone looked at her, waiting patiently for her answer. "I don't know."

"It's up to you," he said.

"You've made it this far, Willa. You don't need a ducky," Corey said, but Willa wasn't certain.

Haven went up behind Willa and set her hands on her shoulders. She leaned down and spoke into her ear. "It's up to you, but I think you're going to kick this river's ass today."

"I'll stick with my boat," Willa said.

"That's our girl." Wingman gave her a light punch to the shoulder.

Within a few minutes, everyone had loaded up onto the bus for their last ride to the river. On the way Scrat held up a bag of permanent markers and explained that they were used to make a mark on the bus like all of the other campers had before them. Haven was always sad to see her new friends leave, but this was going to be the hardest good-bye of them all, and Haven was dreading it. Unfortunately, she couldn't think about that now. There was still more than thirty-six hours left of camp and the next eight were going to be on the water.

The Roaring Fork River was created by snowmelt and was therefore almost fifteen degrees colder than the Colorado. While the difference was most noticeable where the two rivers met, it was obvious upon setting the first foot into the water, too. If Willa was going to miss anything, Haven knew it was not going be spending day after day in freezing water. Whether or not she would miss her was another matter entirely. They were each going to return to their lives and pick up where they had left off. It was a task that Haven prayed that she would make it through easily.

For now, Haven just wanted to enjoy the last day on the river. It was hers as well as the campers'. The summer season was over and winter camps would start within the next few months. Haven was not a winter camp volunteer. She had done it once, and the only thing she hadn't blocked from her memory was the two hours she spent dog sledding. Everything else was a jumble of ice and tears because she had been so cold and miserable.

The ride down to the put-in was wild and loud. The music Scrat chose for their last day was fun and funky and had everyone singing and seat dancing, including Willa. The difference was that she *sang* along to the background vocals or add-ins rather than the main lyrics. It always cracked Haven up when Willa would mimic the "ows," "yeahs," and "uh-huhs" instead of singing the actual words. When "Build Me Up, Buttercup" came on the radio, both Haven and Willa began singing. For those three and a half minutes, they laughed, sang, and belted out the lyrics to the song without thought or concern that everyone might think that were completely nuts.

The entire bus was pumped up for the day when they pulled into the parking lot and unloaded. As had become the routine, they grabbed their gear, suited up, and pulled their boat to the water's edge to wait for the all clear to launch. Willa seemed apprehensive as she hung back behind the group instead of being the first in like the days before. Haven assumed that she was having second thoughts about choosing the hard shell instead of the ducky, and no doubt the memories of Spartan's accident echoed in her mind.

Haven went and stood next to her. "We have a ducky ready to go if you've changed your mind. You could just lay back and enjoy the ride today."

"I thought about it. But I'm good. I'm just not in any rush today."

"Me neither," Haven said as they stood in companionable silence, watching the rest of the group push their boats into the water for their last run on the river.

❖

Willa waited on the porch of her cabin. The sun had yet to even suggest its eventual rise as it was just now 5:30 in the morning. Last night they had agreed to meet early that morning and hike up to the ridge and watch the sunrise on their last day on the ranch.

The morning air was cool as she paced along the gravel drive looking for Haven in the direction of the bunkhouse. The ethereal blue of early morning light and fog floated around them. A warmth spread through Willa when Haven broke through the dense haze and appeared before her like an apparition. She was a stunning, celestial dream.

"Good morning," Willa said when Haven stopped before her.

"Morning."

"You made it."

"Of course I did. I set my alarm, premade the coffee, and had Wendy push me out of bed so I could get here on time." Haven held out a steaming cup to Willa.

"You are an angel."

"Are you ready? It will take about thirty minutes to get to the ridge, so we should get going."

"Lead the way."

The hike was a steep one and there was little conversation as Willa needed to save every breath of air to feed her lungs. For the first time, she was feeling the altitude and limited oxygen. When Haven grabbed her arm and pulled her to a stop, Willa was thankful, yet confused. "What's wrong?"

"Listen," Haven whispered.

Listen for what? Willa could barely hear anything over the sound of her huffing and puffing, but there it was. A strange, unfamiliar sound like an untrained trumpeter. It was a difficult sound to describe. "What the hell is that?"

Haven laughed. "That's an elk bugle. There must be a herd moving through. Come on!"

Haven grabbed Willa's hand and pulled her up the hill. "Oh, Lord."

Haven trudged up the hill, along the fence line, her head darting back and forth as she looked for the origin of the elk call. "There!" she said as she jumped up onto her tiptoes and pointed across the clearing to the edge of the aspens. "There he is."

"Holy shit." Haven was right. Just two hundred feet away stood an enormous elk bull with antlers that stretched at least three feet on either side of his head. "Look!" Willa said, pointing at several females making their way into the clearing.

Haven was determined to get closer. She clasped Willa's hand tighter and continued upward. They seemed to be on an intersecting route with the herd. Willa pulled back on Haven's hand. "It's okay. Just a little closer. You'll never see something like this again," Haven said.

Willa knew that was true. It was a once-in-a-lifetime experience and was already putting the entire rest of the week in second place. The excitement in Haven's voice and on her face was also priceless. The haze of the early morning had been washed away, and she glowed with passion. She was beautiful. Willa didn't protest. At that point, Haven could've led her over the side of a cliff to her ultimate death and she would've gone.

The herd moved across the field toward them, oblivious of their presence until they froze in their tracks. The bull bugled loudly and snorted. "Stop. They smell us," Haven said.

"What's that mean?" Willa had no idea if they should run or hide or both. "What do we do?"

"Don't move." Haven backed into Willa and stood with their bodies pressed together. "Watch."

Willa did just that as the herd of females lunged forward and took off at a gallop toward the fence. The bull brought up the rear of the group as they jumped the fence twenty feet from where Willa and Haven stood. One after the other, they cleared the barbed wire and disappeared into the tree line. Willa felt Haven shiver so she wrapped her arms around her shoulders and pulled her against her chest. "I've never seen anything like it."

"Amazing, isn't it?"

"Yes. But I think we're going to miss the sunrise."

"Oh shit," Haven said.

They hadn't even realized in the midst of watching the elk that the sun had begun to rise. Willa didn't even care that they hadn't made it to the ridgeline. She had seen many suns rise and set, but she had never seen anything like this before. "It's okay. I think this is right where I want to be right now." Willa held on to Haven, who made no attempt to move away. They stood together in the peaceful quiet as the sky transformed into a brilliant display of color and light. The low clouds reflected the yellow of the sun and mixed it into flames of pink and orange that streaked into the sky, pushing away the last of the darkness. Willa could feel her body heat from the light of the day and the warmth of Haven's body against hers.

"I'll miss you, Willa. It's a strange feeling, ya know. I know I missed you before, but now…now it's different."

"How so?"

"Because it's a more permanent thing. Before, I always held on to that small glimmer of hope. This time it's much more final, it seems."

Willa's heart ached at the thought. She loosened her grip on Haven and turned her around. "It doesn't have to be," Willa said as she looked into Haven's glistening eyes. "We could—"

"We can't, Willa. How can we be friends, knowing how I still feel about you? Not to mention the miles between us now, and... and..."

"Bianca."

"It's not fair to either of you, or me. I moved away so that I'd never have to do this, to feel this way, to—"

Willa didn't want to hear it. She couldn't hear that Haven was choosing someone else, even if Willa had no right to be hurt after what she'd done to her. "Shh, my love. It's okay. Another time and another place, it seems."

"I'm sorry," Haven said as the tears streamed down her face.

"No. Don't you ever be sorry for being happy." Willa could no longer hold back the tears that blinded her. "You've changed my life, Haven. This place has changed my life." Willa brought her hands to Haven's face and brushed her thumbs across her wet cheeks. Haven closed her eyes, and Willa was overcome by the need to kiss her one last time. She held Haven's face in the palm of her hands, and Willa gently pressed her lips to hers. It was a soft, languid kiss filled with pain and sorrow. She kissed her for the years they had lost, for the pain she had caused, and the lives they would live without each other.

Chapter Fifteen

The ride back into the city was long and quiet. Haven had little to say about the week, and Wendy respected her desire not to discuss it. She and Willa had exchanged phone numbers and made the awkward obligatory promises to text and keep in touch. Haven had wanted to text Willa every moment since watching the black SUV pull away from the lodge that afternoon. She wanted to know if Willa missed her, if she had made it to the airport all right, if she had eaten lunch, anything to start a conversation. But she didn't. Haven ignored every urge she had to start something she knew she wouldn't be able to finish.

She dropped Wendy off at her place and declined the invitation to come in for a drink. She just wanted to get home and maybe take a long, hot bath. A drink sounded like a perfect addition to a soak, so she swung by the store for a bottle of wine.

Haven felt extra drained from the week. It was always both physically and emotionally exhausting, yet this time it was doubly so. She hefted her duffel onto her shoulder and decided to leave the rest of her gear in the car until the morning. She was going to have to make room for it in the closet anyway since she was finished with camp for the season. She stumbled into the house, dropped the bag in the foyer, and headed straight to the bathroom. Haven grabbed a wineglass and bottle opener from the kitchen on her way through.

She started the tub, stripped down, and poured herself a full glass of wine. She dangled her feet over the edge into the water as it filled. The steam that rose from the bath reminded her of the night she had kissed in the hot tub. "What were you thinking? Ugh." Haven could still feel Willa's lips on hers as they stood on the hillside waiting for the breaking of the sun over the ridge. "That one wasn't your fault. That was all her." Albeit Haven had done nothing to stop it from happening. She even allowed herself to be wrapped up in Willa's embrace well before it had happened. "Okay, maybe it was partly me." Haven groaned and slunk down into the half-filled tub.

Haven lost track of time. The water was cooling off and her bottle of wine was nearly gone. She decided it was best that she got out before she became another tub-drinking statistic. She patted dry but chose to forgo wrapping herself in a towel. Haven poured the last of her wine into the glass and sauntered down the hall to her studio.

Several finished paintings lined the walls, two abandoned pieces were stacked on her desk, and one in-progress piece was propped on the easel in the center of the room. It was her third attempt to capture the same image, and it wasn't faring any better than its predecessors. Haven stood before the painting stark naked, tilting her head back and forth, sipping from her glass. It had potential; she just couldn't find the inspiration. She grabbed the corner of the piece and tossed it on top of the other two on her desk and set down her glass.

Haven chose a larger canvas, already primed and ready for her brush strokes. She normally worked on smaller scale, but this one called to her. She laid out a variety of blues and greens, with several shades of red and orange onto her palette. Using a wide brush, she wiped and mixed the colors together, creating new blends and variations of those colors. When Haven achieved what she desired she began wildly placing strokes and sweeps across the white surface.

A background began to appear around an empty space in the center of the canvas. Streaks of orange and red carved out an image reminiscent of the red rock walls of Glenwood Canyon towering over the rushing movement of the rapids below. In the center was the shape of a woman that Haven began to fill in with the smooth caresses of her brush. A bare back emerged from the canvas as

Haven shaped the figure slowly. A wild mane of hair formed with the drips of paint that ran down onto the skin, mixing with the wet background. She stepped back from the piece and picked up her wineglass. Haven sipped as she gazed at the piece she had just created. It was Willa. There was no doubt. It was a fast, wild, and passionate depiction of the woman she had loved all her life, in a place she adored. Haven caught a glimpse of herself in the mirror and laughed at the sight. She was shit-faced, naked, and covered in paint. Any other time she would've thought that a particularly good evening. Haven dropped her brushes into the water bucket and tossed her palette onto the stool. She was done, and she needed to shower again.

Once in the hallway, Haven heard her phone ring. Her stomach flipped with excitement. Had Willa been the first one to give in and make that phone call? She ran down the hallway still completely nude and rummaged through her bag for her phone. "Dammit. Hello? Hello?" she said after swiping the screen blindly.

"There's my beautiful baby, back from the wilderness."

A wave of disappointment washed through Haven. "Hey, hon," she said, less than enthusiastically.

"Ouch. Everything all right?"

"Yeah. Sorry. Just a little tipsy. I added a bit too much wine in the bathtub."

"Added? You put wine in—"

"Had. Had wine. While in the tub."

"Oh. Do you want me to come over?"

"No."

"Ouch, again."

"Sorry, Bianca. I need to go. Dammit, I need to shower again and sleep. Maybe tomorrow or something."

"Um, okay then. I'll call you?"

"Okay. Night night," she said before hanging up the phone. Haven scrolled through her contact list and stopped on Willa's number. She contemplated for a few moments before clicking to start a new text. Haven began and deleted three different messages before giving up, dropping her phone onto the couch, and stumbling off toward the bathroom. She paused just for a moment in the doorway of her studio to take one more look at the painting on her easel.

❖

The air was thick, hot, and heavy, a drastic change from the Colorado mountain air. Willa could almost breathe in her daily intake of water. The day before had been her longest one on record, and her internal clock was bonkers with the time change. Between a five-hour flight, two hours lost to time zones, and four for the drive time both here and there, Willa had lost an entire day to math. By the time Kyle had picked her up from the airport she was running on fumes without even the energy to run on about her week in Colorado. She most definitely didn't have the energy for the inevitable barrage of questions she would get as soon as she mentioned Haven's name. Part of her wanted to live with that secret a little while longer, anyhow.

She sat on her front porch swing, just as she did every morning after feeding the flock and letting them out of their coop. She heard Kyle on the ATV coming up the path toward her house. Willa propped her feet up on a feed bucket and leaned back into the seat. She was going to need a few days to get back into the grind of farm life after her week at the ranch.

"Mornin'," Kyle hollered as he pulled up and hopped down off the four-wheeler. "On a break already?"

"Eh. Can you call it a break if you haven't technically started?" Annie came running over from where she'd been herding the sheep for entertainment.

"Even Annie's working harder than you are this morning," Kyle said.

"Yeah, yeah. It's a facade. Besides, I had a very busy week that I need to recoup from."

He sat on the swing next to Willa and gave Annie a rub on her head. "Let's see if I ever suggest sending her away again," Kyle said to Annie. "So, how was it?"

A thousand words flashed through Willa's mind, one for each

ever-changing minute that she'd spent in Colorado, but she said, "Interesting."

"Interesting? Not shitty or amazing or a damn nightmare? Just interesting."

Willa laughed. "Well, the trip was amazing. Life changing, actually. The Haven part, that was interesting. Not at fir—"

"Wait, what? Haven? Like your ex, Haven?"

"The one and only." Willa couldn't help but smile.

"You're shitting me. Where? How did you even run into her out there? Weren't you on some ranch in the middle of nowhere?"

"Believe it or not, she was a volunteer at the camp. It was her sixth one in a row or something."

"Wow. That's shitty, man. I had no idea."

"Actually, it wasn't bad. It was awkward more than anything. But after everything that happened, it turned out better than I'd have thought." She touched her lips, recalling the sweet taste of Haven's.

"Does she know? That's a stupid question; it's a cancer camp."

"She knows everything."

"And you're still in one piece, I see."

"It's strange, Kyle. She's a different person now. A pretty wild one, actually." Willa's mind flashed with the recent memories of her hair and clothes and how happy she'd been the moment they'd won the cornhole tournament, tutu and all.

"Haven?"

"Yes. She's a whitewater kayaker with short, bleach-blond hair, tattoos, and she's tough as shit."

"Well, I'll be damned."

"Yeah."

"So, are y'all gonna start talking again?"

Willa recalled the minutes she and Haven shared on the hillside as the sun rose on their last hours together. "Probably not. Even if she didn't live out there now, she has a girlfriend. Not that I wouldn't expect her to have one, I just don't want to hear about it, or know all that much about it, actually."

"Makes sense. Man, I can't believe she was there. I mean, what are the odds? Crazy shit."

When Willa's phone buzzed on the bench beside them, she jumped. She looked at Kyle like a deer caught in headlights. There was no way. Haven wouldn't possibly be calling her. Her heart thumped in her chest as she turned it over and looked at the screen. A small pang of disappointment struck her, yet she breathed a small sigh of relief when she saw that it was a video call from Corey. "Corey!" she hollered when the call connected.

"Willa! I miss you, and it's only been a day," Corey said.

"I know. I've been talking to my brother for thirty minutes trying to avoid returning to reality. Say hi." Willa turned the camera toward Kyle, who now looked as stunned as she had moments earlier.

"Hey," he said.

Willa laughed and panned back to her. "Man of many words, my bro."

"He's cute. You didn't tell me he also had that going for him."

"What? No. I mean, yeah. He's all right, I suppose."

"Damn. Thanks, Will. I think," he said as he fidgeted with the brim of his ball cap.

"Oh, geez. Both of you, stop. This is getting weird," Willa said.

Corey laughed and Willa smiled. It was a great laugh. She did miss her. "How's it going up there in North Carolina? Glad to be back?"

"It's good. Folks didn't waste any time giving me listings to show now that I'm home. Good thing I like my job."

"You work for your parents? Why don't I remember that part?" Willa asked.

"Because, I probably didn't mention it. I usually leave that part out so I don't get the whole nepotism bullshit from people."

"Makes sense. What are you doing?" The angle of the camera had tilted, and Willa couldn't make out what was going on.

"Oh. Sorry. I'm getting ready for work and painting my eyebrows on. It's a girl thing."

"Uh, I'm a girl," Willa retorted.

"Yeah, and you also have eyebrows."

Willa hadn't even noticed before Corey had drawn them in darker, that they were thin and light without makeup. She preferred them in a more natural way, but now understood what Corey meant by it being a "girl thing." "Looks like a whole lotta work to me." Kyle popped his head into the video frame. "You know what else is a lot of work?"

"Being that handsome?" Corey quickly replied.

"Um, no. Not exactly." He blushed and rubbed at his chin.

"Oh, good grief. What is happening?" Willa asked.

Kyle cleared his throat and said, "I was gonna say running a farm by yourself."

"Well, that too, I suppose. Hey, Kyle. Willa, hand me to your brother."

"What? Why?"

"Just do it."

Willa did as she was told, but with extreme hesitation. Kyle was equally hesitant to take the phone, but did. "Hey. What's up?"

"I love this woman. She is a diamond and means a lot to me. She's been through a very stressful week in a hundred different ways. So go easy on her, or you will have to deal with me."

"Promise?" Kyle replied with the unexpected comeback. Willa and Corey both gasped in surprise.

"Oh! You better believe it."

"Okay, okay, children. That's enough of that. Say good-bye." Willa took her phone back from Kyle. "What was that?"

"Just looking out for you. One more thing, have you heard from you know—"

"No," Willa said without elaborating.

"Well, I expect that you will soon enough."

"Unlikely. But anyway, I should get to work before Kyle's head explodes or the goats start a revolt."

"Hopefully, not both. Okay. Miss you, bye."

Willa ended the call and slipped her phone into her shirt pocket. "That was Corey, my bunkmate at camp. She lives in North Carolina, and she's six years younger than you. So don't even think about it."

Kyle shrugged and smiled. "I ain't gotta clue what you're talkin' about." Willa knew better.

❖

Haven's phone rang again. It was the fifth time that day, and she promised that if it was Bianca again she was going lose her shit. She waited until it finally went to voice mail and focused her attention back on the blank canvas. Haven had been sitting in her studio for four days waiting and praying for inspiration. She hadn't created a thing since her drunken session days before. Every image that came to her mind was of Willa. She wasn't going to finish her required pieces for the exhibition if she couldn't get her out of her mind. As stunning as it was, she couldn't use that piece in the show even if she wanted to. It was so far from her signature style that it would stand out like a sore thumb at the gallery. Not to mention that Bianca would probably hate it.

Haven wasn't sure she wanted to share that painting with anyone else, let alone sell it. She would keep it turned around, leaning against the wall in her studio right where it was. When Haven's phone rang again, her sanity snapped. She threw her brush onto the floor and took the palette full of paint and slammed it against the canvas. It slid down the white surface in a streak of color and crashed to the floor. Haven stormed out into the kitchen and answered the phone. "What the fuck?"

"Uh, hey," Bianca said on the other end.

"What, Bianca? No, they aren't done. No, I don't want company. No, I don't even want to have this fucking exhibition!"

"Damn, Haven."

"Sorry. But every time I try to start painting, my damn phone rings. You know I hate deadlines. I never wanted this, and it's stressing me out." Haven couldn't believe she'd said it aloud.

"Just think about how great it will be when it all pays off."

She cared about Bianca, and her head was in the right place for Haven's art career, but her heart wasn't. Haven didn't want to be a professional artist, and the more Bianca pushed, the more she resented her for it. "Bianca, I don't want this. It's too much."

"Just take a break today and get back to it tomorrow. Let's go out."

"Bianca, I don't—" Another call beeped in and Haven paused to see who it was. "Hey, it's my sister. I gotta go." Haven didn't wait for Bianca to say good-bye before she took the other call. "Hey, Gianna. What's wrong?" Members of her family usually didn't call unless it was something that couldn't be said over text.

Gianna didn't waste time on pleasantries, knowing that Haven was on a deadline. "Hey, sis. Nothing. Mom went to the doctor yesterday, and I was just calling with the results."

"Oh, God." Haven's stomach twisted.

"Relax. There's nothing to worry about, right now. He's wanting to run some more tests and a CT to check for blockages in her carotid arteries. Depending on what they say, she may need surgery."

"Surgery? What kind of surgery?"

"An endarterectomy, or something like that." Gianna described the procedure in detail, and Haven's knees buckled.

"Stop. I have to sit down." Even the thought of blood and fluids made Haven queasy.

"The vascular guy seems pretty confident, and he says he does at least three or four a day. So it's pretty routine."

Haven was dizzy and a little sick to her stomach. "So, what? Like, I don't understand. When?" Her anxiety over health issues extended beyond her own.

"Calm down, Haven. If something is wrong they'll take care of it as soon as possible. There's no sense in getting upset until we know something. Even then—"

"I'm coming home," Haven said.

"What? No. That's silly."

"I am." Haven opened her laptop and searched for the cheapest last-minute ticket home.

"Haven. Listen to me. Even if there is a blockage or whatnot, they aren't just gonna cut her open. Surgery could be a week or more out if that's what she needs."

Haven didn't care. Between Bianca, the paintings, Willa, and now her mom, Haven wanted to run away, and that was just what she was going to do. The earliest she could get a flight was for 5:00 a.m. the next day for almost nine hundred dollars. She booked it on her credit card without hesitation. "I land in Orlando at one thirty tomorrow. I'll rent a car so you don't have to come get me."

"For heaven's sake, Haven. You're ridiculous, but I can't say I'm not a little excited to see you now."

"Me too, actually." Haven didn't know how long she was going to be in Florida, but she knew that Bianca was going to blow a gasket when she found out. Maybe it was time. "I'll see you tomorrow. I need to make some calls and get my bags together."

Haven pulled her bags out of the back of the closet before sitting down on the bed. She was preparing to call Bianca and tell her she was going to Florida. She was also psyching herself up to let Bianca know that she would also be going there alone. And single.

It wasn't a spontaneous decision that Haven was making. It had been a long time coming, even before her week on the ranch with Willa. Bianca had asked her a hundred times to move forward in their relationship and buy a house or start a family. Haven always said no. While Willa wasn't the exact reason for this decision, the kiss she shared with her was filled with more passion than all the times she and Bianca had sex combined. That had to mean something.

Bianca deserved to have someone who was able to give her everything, 100 percent. She needed a woman who shared her life goals and dreams of success, and most importantly, who wasn't in love with someone else. Even if Haven and Willa would never be together, she knew that she could never love Bianca the same way. She might never love anyone again, and Bianca deserved so much more than that.

Haven had almost packed her entire closet before she decided that she needed to stop procrastinating and call Bianca. She took several deep breaths and dialed the number.

"Hello?"

"Hey, we need to talk," Haven said, her voice cracking.

CHAPTER SIXTEEN

It had been almost a week since Willa had returned from camp, and she was surprised that the emotional and physical highs had yet to wear off. Even though digging postholes for the new chicken coop wasn't comparable to tackling a whitewater rapid, there was a sense of accomplishment in both. She had caught the kayaking bug in Colorado and had done extensive online research just about every night on where and when she could try it again. Florida was eighty percent water, but its lack of elevation gave it a zero percent chance of whitewater, and a one hundred percent chance of alligators.

Willa set the last post in the ground and packed the dirt around it with her boot. A few cross beams for support and it would be ready for the wire. Her frosty beer bottle called her name from where it sat on an inviting log. "I think I *will* sit, thank you." She plopped down onto the tree trunk and reached for her beer. The darkness in her right eye caused her to misjudge the distance and knock the bottle over. As she lunged for it her knuckles brushed the rough pine bark. "Shit," she said, looking down at her lightly scraped knuckles.

It reminded her of Haven. Not just the injury itself, but the determination that Haven had to push through with it. It was more than just a stubbornness or a need to impress others with her skills. It was a sense of commitment and dedication, a responsibility to finish what she had started. The Haven she remembered from a few years ago would've kicked it over in frustration and run away from it. Not that anyone would've blamed her this time, if she had. Haven had always struggled with having to do it versus wanting to do it. Willa reckoned that was the difference.

"Hey, Will," Kyle said. She didn't know where he came from or how long he'd been there.

"Yo. What's up?"

"Do we have everything we need if we get a storm this year?"

"I reckon. Why?"

"They're talking about a low pressure system in the tropics and it had me wondering if we had supplies."

"Yeah. I mean we have wood and tarps and whatnot."

"Cool. I'm not worried about it, but you never know about these damn things."

Willa had lived in Florida her entire life. Most of it had been on the east coast where tropical storms and hurricanes were just another thing about living in the state. Where kids in the north had snow days, she had hurricane days. It wasn't until she was in her early twenties that she experienced her first serious storm. Willa had been living with a friend before she and Haven had officially moved in together.

Haven's and Willa's families had all taken shelter at their homes except for Haven's sister, Gianna. When her roommate took off for her parents' house, it left the three of them to hunker down at the house with three dogs and a cat. It hadn't started out all that bad, until it made its landfall as a strong Category 3. By the time things really picked up, Haven's sister had medicated herself with anxiety drugs, and somehow Haven couldn't keep herself awake even with the sound of the patio awning slamming against the house. The days afterward proved worst of all with extensive flooding, power outages, and dreadful humidity. By the time they could bathe and get out of the house, Willa was surprised that they hadn't killed each other.

Kyle rolled out the chicken wire next to the coop. "Hey, daydreamer. You call her yet?"

Willa hated being so obvious with her inner musings. "Of

course not," she said, getting up from the stump and walking over toward him. "I told you, I wasn't—"

"Just call her. What can it hurt to say, 'Hey, just checking in. How are things?' Ya know?"

"Yeah, but—"

"Just call her." He looked at his watch and clapped the dust off his hands. "I need to run up to the house for a few minutes anyway."

After he left, Willa contemplated his statement. Why didn't she call her? What could it hurt just to see how things are going for her first week back? Willa knew that unless she made the first call there wasn't going to be an opening of communication between them. "Fine!" she hollered after Kyle who was at least a hundred yards away by now.

Willa returned to the stump she'd been sitting on and took her phone from her pocket. She sat down but then stood up again. The anxiety bubbled in her chest. "What are you so afraid of? Just call her." For a brief moment, she thought of sending a text instead. That way Haven could reply in her time. Or she could pretend she never got it in the first place, and that would leave Willa in limbo. She decided that was worse than calling.

She paused for a few more seconds with her thumb hovering over the call button. When she had hesitated long enough, she pressed the button. It rang almost four full times before Haven picked up.

"Hello? Willa? Sure, that's fine. Is everything all right? No, no GPS, thanks. Hello?"

"Haven?" Willa had no idea what was going on or who she was talking to.

"Yeah, sorry. Hold on one sec," Haven said. Willa heard Haven's muffled voice and then the shuffling of papers and keys. "Willa. Hi. Sorry about that."

"No worries. Is everything okay?"

"Yeah. Uh, yeah. Just renting a car."

"A car? What happened to yours?"

"Nothing. I…I needed a car while I'm here…in Florida."

Willa's stomach dropped like a balloon filled with lead. "What?

Why are you here?" There was no way she'd come to Florida to see Willa, and any other reason had her concerned. "What happened?"

"Nothing. Mom is having some tests done today, and I thought I should be here. And the timing seemed right, I guess."

"Is she all right? Timing?"

"It could be nothing. Gianna just called during…well, it just worked out this way." Haven seemed short with her words. Maybe it hadn't been a good idea for her to call after all.

"Oh, okay then. Wow."

"Yeah. I just got to the car. Can I call you back later when I get to the house?"

"Of course. Let me know about your mom. And if you need to talk, you can come out here and hang out for a bit." *What the hell, Willa? She is here to see her mother, not have a visit,*

"Thanks, Willa. That could be nice. I'll let you know."

Willa hung up and slipped her phone into her pocket. *Shit.* There was no certainty she'd come, but if she did, Willa needed to get her ass in gear.

❖

"When did it get so damn hot here?" Haven asked when she walked in the door of her mother's house.

"Haven?"

"It's me, Ma!"

"Haven Louise, what are you doing here?" her mother, Camille, said, getting out of her chair and rushing over to where Haven stood in the foyer.

"Gianna called and said you were having some tests."

"Gianna called? Gianna!" she called down the hall.

"What? Oh yeah! You're here," Gianna said when she came into the living room.

"Why did you call your sister?" her mother asked Gianna.

"I called to tell her about the doctor's appointments. She's the one who decided to come out here."

While her mother and sister argued about her presence, Haven herded everyone into the living room and out of the foyer. The three of them took a seat and continued the conversation. Haven had come all this way because of these tests, and she wanted to hear about them before getting into anything else. Gianna explained that doctors had discovered blockage in her carotid arteries, but nothing that had them overly concerned or put her in any immediate danger. Nothing that they weren't going to try medications on first.

"You should've waited before wasting your money coming out here, sweetie," her mother said.

"Well, regardless, I'm here. I'd rather be here than out there right now, anyhow."

"Oh no, what's wrong?" her mother asked.

Haven knew she was eventually going to have to explain her trip home, but she hadn't wanted to do so straight out of the gate. She knew that neither of them were going to be particularly grieved over her breakup with Bianca. While she didn't know for certain, the end of their relationship was likely to impact her career, and that would send her mother into a panic. Especially when Haven told her that she'd just walked away from it on impulse. Gianna raised an eyebrow at Haven when she hesitated to answer the question.

"Can't she just be concerned about her mother?" Gianna said.

"Of course she can. I'm happy you're here. How long are you staying?"

Haven had no idea. She hadn't even purchased a return ticket to Colorado. Nothing about this trip had been planned beyond how she was getting to the Denver airport that morning. And the call she had received from Willa not more than twenty minutes after landing was another uncalculated turn of events. "For a bit."

"And you want me to think nothing's wrong. Gimme a break." Her mother got up from her chair and headed off to the kitchen. "I'll be in here pretending not to know that Gianna is breaking you down to get the real reason you're here."

Haven wished that her mom was kidding. But after the look

she'd gotten from her sister a few minutes earlier, there was no way she wasn't getting the third degree. Just as expected, Gianna sat forward in her seat. She crossed her legs, propped an elbow on her knee, and rested her chin on her fist.

"Really?" Haven said.

"Oh yeah. Because I have a feeling this is gonna be gooood!"

Haven could just spew out the highlights, but she knew that would never satisfy her inquisitive and annoying little sister. "Okay, so I guess it all started about two weeks ago."

"Okay. First of all, I'm going to ignore the fact that it's been two weeks building up to whatever this is," Gianna motioned her hand sarcastically all around Haven and her luggage, "and let you continue."

Haven could already tell that this was going to be the longest conversation ever. "Okay, shut up. No more talking until I'm done." It was an impossible request, because as soon as Haven mentioned Willa, Gianna was going to lose it. "Promise?"

"Of course not. But if it makes you get on with it already, then yes. I promise." They both knew it was a lie, but Haven continued anyway.

She began the story from two weeks earlier and built it up to the moment the SUV arrived with the guests. "It had been just another camp welcome until Willa threw her bag on my boots and climbed out of the truck."

"What?" Gianna said at the same time their mother's head stuck out from the kitchen and repeated the question. That was all it took, and her mother was sitting on the couch next to Gianna with matching expressions of surprise.

"Yeah." Haven continued her story. She told them about the first few days, and then the incident with Spartan and how it had caused a complete shift in each of them. Haven also broke the news that Willa had been diagnosed with cancer and had lost most of the vision in her eye. Both Gianna and her mother began to straighten when Haven explained Willa's reasoning behind their unexpected separation. Gianna scoffed, and her mother rolled her eyes.

"Stop," Haven said. "I know what you're both thinking, and it's nothing I haven't thought myself."

"So, did you cheat on Bianca?" her mother asked.

"Are you here to see her? Be honest," Gianna said.

"No. Not really. Maybe? I mean...we didn't...it was just a kiss. But Bianca and I broke up." Haven buried her face in her hands and took several deep breaths.

"So *you are* here to see her," Gianna said.

Haven looked up. "I wasn't. I'm not. I hadn't even talked to her until two hours ago when I landed in Orlando."

"And you broke up with Bianca?"

"Yes. I've been struggling with finishing my pieces for the gallery, and she kept calling and calling. Then Gianna called about you, and that's when I decided that I needed to come home. So I called Bianca and told her I couldn't do it. Any of it." Haven still felt little sadness at her decision to end things with Bianca. There was the guilt of having kissed Willa at the ranch, but there wasn't that sense of loss that she knew she should feel. The hurt from missing Willa every day, even after three years, hung heavier on her heart. And the last week without her had eclipsed all of that. While it hadn't been the reason Haven had returned to Florida, it had been the thought of Willa that made her ultimate decision.

"I see. So seeing Willa after all this time wasn't the closure you wanted," her mother said.

"Not at all, Mom."

"So, let's ask it this way, when are you going to see her?" her mother asked.

"What? I'm not. I can't. I'm here to make sure that everything is all right with you and give Gianna a break. Not to go see her."

Once again, Gianna and her mother explained that everything was fine, and there really was no need for her to have come all that way for nothing. As it turned out, her mother didn't even have another appointment for a month.

"That's great, but I can't."

"Listen, Haven. It's been like three years or something since y'all broke up and you still haven't gotten over her. Sure, it's probably a little unhealthy from a psychological standpoint. I guess the difference between you and someone else would be that y'all have been together in one way or another for more than twenty years."

That much was true. There was hardly a memory from all those years that didn't have Willa in it. "Yeah."

"Great. So we've established that you're going to see her. Now we need to spend the next thirty minutes squeezing the when out of you," Gianna said.

"Maybe…or maybe I could just call her back and see what she says?" Haven said.

"Well, I'll be damned. That was easier than I thought it would be."

"Speak for yourself."

❖

"What are you doing?" Kyle asked Willa as she paced around, and he tightened the last piece of wire around the gatepost. They had finally finished the barbed fencing along the front half of the property and up to the gate. *They* was a relative term as Willa had been too distracted that morning waiting for Haven to arrive.

"Nothing. Why?"

"That much has been obvious all morning. Why are you pacing around like a nervous sow?"

"I'm waiting for…" Willa paused in mid-sentence when she saw a vehicle coming up the road.

"For who?" Kyle asked, following her line of sight to the vehicle. "Who is that?"

"I dunno yet. Could be Haven."

"Haven? How? Uh, you said she lived in Colorado."

"She does. But she just happens to be here visiting her mom. I found out yesterday when I called. She'd just landed. Curious coincidence, don't ya think?"

"To say the least." Kyle and Willa watched the car as it came

BETWEEN SAND AND STARDUST

and went past them. "I have so many questions I don't even know where to start."

"Maybe save them for later. I think this one's her." Willa spotted another vehicle going a bit slower than the first.

"But—"

"It is! Oh, shit. She actually came."

"Oh, shit is right," Kyle said, crossing his arms over his chest. Willa smiled and waved as Haven pulled into the gravel drive and up to the gate. "Hey! You made it," Willa said. Her heartbeat was quick and her stomach fluttered when Haven smiled back at her. "I did. No way, is that Kyle?" Haven squealed. "It is," Willa said. Haven put the car in park and killed the engine as Willa opened her door.

"Oh shit!" Haven jumped out of the vehicle and rushed to him. He picked her up in his arms and spun her around. "What happened to you?" she said when he set her down. "What is all this? So manly." She ran her fingers through his full beard.

"Me. What happened to you?" he asked.

He was no doubt talking about Haven's dramatic physical changes, most noticeably her hair. It was in two wild pigtails with hair sticking out in every direction. Willa noticed that the ends were pink now, a new addition since camp. So was her makeup. A week on the river made no time or need for hair and makeup, so this was the first time Willa had seen Haven in "real life." She wore a denim skirt, combat boots, a vintage camera tank, and some flowy kimono thing over it all. Willa was both intrigued and aroused by Haven's curious ensemble and attitude, but it was her incredible smile that pulled her all the way in. Willa couldn't believe that after all the time that had passed, Haven was here.

"Look at you. All cowboyed up and sexy as hell. Both of you," Haven added as she looked Willa up and down.

Willa stood frozen under Haven's gaze until she looked away. "Hey, Kyle, get the gate and I'll pull her car in." Willa pulled the car up to the house, while Kyle and Haven followed her on foot.

"So, Kyle says y'all were working hard running fence all morning. It looks great."

"Yep. With that done we can open it up as another pasture for the sheep and goats."

"Nooo. You've got goats? I love goats."

"Well, we have to move them over anyway. We can just do it now, if you don't mind?"

"No way. Don't let me interrupt what you're doing," Haven said.

They headed off toward the barn as Kyle began giving Haven the brief overview of the property. "This is my place. Haven built hers over that way like some sort of secluded hermit."

"I'm not a hermit. It's more wooded and closer to the lake is all."

"There's a lake?" Haven's eyes grew wide.

"Yeah. Over that way. You can kinda see my place through the trees. See?" Willa stood behind Haven and pointed over her shoulder toward a small speck of red in the distance.

"Wow. What is this, like a thousand acres?"

"Nope, about sixty. Kyle has the large animals over here, and I keep my chickens and the llamas over by my place." Just then, Annie came hightailing it across the yard toward them. Willa whistled and called her over to introduce Haven. "This is my girl. Officially, the best dog I've ever had. I don't know what I'd do without her."

"Hi, sweetie," Haven said as she bent down to give Annie a few chin scratches.

"No getting rid of her now," Kyle said.

"Awww. That's okay." Annie planted a wet nose kiss right on Haven's lips.

When they reached the barn, Haven's smile was already stretching from ear to ear. She looked like a wound-up top waiting to be let loose, and that was before she saw the kids that came running up behind their mothers. "This is Fanny, Clara, and Eunice and their babies, Bert, Reba, Jenny, and Benny. They're twins."

"Ooh! Can I pet them?" Haven was visibly shaking with excitement.

"Ha ha, yes." Kyle opened the gate, picked up one of the babies, and set Bert into Haven's arms.

The mothers circled around, waiting their turn for attention while the other kids jumped and pronked over each other. "I'm in heaven," Haven said.

The mothers began to wander off to explore their new pasture, calling for their little ones as they left. Bert began to call after his mom, so Haven reluctantly set him down to rejoin his family.

"We can track them down again later, if you want," Willa said.

"Hey, I need to ride up to the north side and bring down Harold. I'll be back," Kyle said.

"Harold?"

"He's a bison. We rescued him from an animal entertainment company. You know, like ones that lease animals for commercials and stuff. We got him, two llamas—Fred and Ginger—and Leland."

Haven laughed. "You're killing me with these names. Who, or should I say what, is Leland?"

"Leland is an ass, literally. He's a donkey. Those are the only four residents here without a real job."

"You mean, food?" Haven raised her eyebrows and her smiled sunk into a frown.

"Well, yes and no. We're a farm, after all. Here, let me show you." Willa took Haven by the arm and led her off toward the rest of the property. "We have meat chickens and egg chickens. We breed sheep for their wool, and goats for meat and sale, although so far we've only used them for milk, cheese, and soap."

Haven's frown eased. "Well, we have to get it from somewhere."

"Right." Willa stopped them in front of a large hut flanked on each side by large wire pens. "These are my babies." The chickens knew when she was coming and they poured out of the coop and came running from every direction.

Haven squealed in surprise. "Oh, shit!" she said as they circled around them like a hungry mob. Haven grabbed onto Willa's shirtsleeve.

She laughed. "They won't hurt you. Well, Rudolpho might; he's a dick. You just poke him like this." Willa grabbed a broom handle and demonstrated her practiced stick poke.

"They just run loose like this? Won't something hurt them?"

"They're in the coops at night, but during the day when we're out working they have free range." Willa winked, and Haven moaned. They both laughed. "Come here," Willa said as she opened the door to the coop and led Haven inside. "Reach in there."

Willa pointed to a hay-filled box, and Haven hesitated. "What?"

"It's okay. Here." Willa grabbed Haven's hand and together they reached into the nest, and Haven pulled out two eggs.

"Oh, wow! They're blue."

"Look here," Willa said, pulling two deep red colored eggs from the next nest.

"What?" Haven said.

Willa laughed. "Those are from an Ameracuana, and these are from a Copper Maran. Or as I call them, Carmelita and Barbara."

"Do you eat them?"

"Every morning for breakfast. I'll make them for you. Um, sometime. Whenever." Willa could've smacked herself. She hadn't meant to imply anything, and it probably could've been ignored if she didn't trip all over her own tongue.

"I'd like that," Haven said.

CHAPTER SEVENTEEN

Haven stood inside the doorway of Willa's home in stunned silence. She had been so overwhelmed from the moment she arrived at the farm, she didn't think that it was possible to be more so. Every inch of her house was built and decorated to match Willa's style and personality. Quirky knickknacks and antique farmhouse collectibles filled the large open room made up of the kitchen, dining, and living spaces. The tall ceiling exposed the trusses and open loft over the rear of the house that Haven guessed was the bedroom area. When Willa led her down the short hallway, her assumption was confirmed. There was also a large laundry room on one side and a bathroom on the other. Both were decorated with a similar rustic farm style as the rest of the house. "I cannot believe you built this all by hand."

"Well, Kyle made most of it happen. He did the hard work. I just did a lot of holding and pointing."

"I doubt that very much. This is incredible, Willa."

"Thanks. It's small, but it's home. Great thing is that it's portable and almost completely off-grid."

Haven listened as Willa described the different features of her composting toilet and solar power. She was blown away by all of the hard work and engineering that went into constructing the house. "These would be amazing ideas to use if I ever find myself starting a camp like Valiant." Willa had everything that they'd always talked about, even down to rescuing abused animals. As amazing as it all was, it hurt, and she was more than a little bit jealous.

"Do you think you'll start your own camp one day?" Willa asked.

Haven could hope so, but in reality there was no way she could do it alone. "Not in Colorado, that's for sure."

"You could start it someplace else, like Florida?"

"As much as I like Florida, I don't think I could make it work here either. I'd need someplace with mountains and rivers, trails for horses, lakes and creeks, and maybe a few less deadly predators."

"I see." Willa had set out a plate of cheese and snacks, and they both devoured it within minutes. "Stay for dinner? I'll put some chicken on the grill and whip up a potato salad if you're interested."

"One of *those* chickens?" Haven asked, almost afraid of the answer.

Willa laughed. "No. Not this time."

"Whew. Okay. I might need a warning for that. Or maybe not." Haven couldn't decide if she would want to know the chicken before she ate it.

"I'll keep that in mind for next time. Beer?"

"Yes. Thanks." Next time? That was the second time Willa had made reference to visits beyond this one. Haven had let this one slide. "Would you like help?"

"Actually, I sort of made it all up last night after I talked to you on the phone so it would be ready if you said yes."

Haven laughed. "Seriously?" Haven was flattered that Willa prepared everything based solely on the hope that Haven would accept.

"Yeah."

"You're so cute." Haven stood up to her tiptoes and kissed Willa on the cheek.

Haven followed Willa outside to the grill and sat on the porch swing. She rocked and sipped her beer while she watched Willa master the grill like she had done so many times before. "It's weird."

"What's weird?" Willa asked.

"Sitting here, with you there. It's a little surreal." So much so that Haven expected at any moment to be jolted awake and find herself passed out on the couch in her studio.

"I can understand that."

Haven wondered how she had ended up here in this moment. She had dreamt so many times, in so many ways, the different fantasies of how she and Willa could find their way back to each other. There wasn't a single one that any realist would've ever thought possible. Even Haven's wild, escapist imagination never could've come up with the story she was living now. Haven pulled her legs up against her chest and rested her cheek on her knees. She looked up at Willa, who had moved closer to her. "I can't believe it's you."

Willa sat down next to Haven. "It's me."

"I broke up with Bianca." Haven had no idea why she'd said that. Willa hadn't asked or even made mention of Bianca at all that day.

Willa sat back in the swing and sipped her beer. "Wow. Okay. I'm sorry?"

"Don't be. It was inevitable. I probably should've done it months ago, like the first time she asked me to marry her."

"The first time?"

"Yeah. She is persistent and doesn't take no for an answer to anything. Thankfully, her attention span is short, and she's easily distracted."

"So she didn't see it coming?"

"I don't know. If she didn't, she was the only one. She's a great person and a talented agent, but…but she isn't you."

"Well, I am pretty unique. If I do say so myself."

"Oh, and humble, too." Haven laughed.

"She's so humble," Willa said in reference to an inside joke they had once shared about Janet Jackson.

"You remembered!"

"I remember a lot of things, Haven."

Haven stared off into the distance, afraid to make eye contact with Willa. "Me too."

"I remember holding you as you cried yourself to sleep after getting disqualified from the high school drill competition. I remember stealing those trading cards from the flea market because you didn't have money to buy them," Willa said.

"I remember the night I showed up at the bar to surprise you and the look on your face when you saw me from across the room." Haven turned her head and looked at Willa.

"You were wearing a strapless black dress and knee-high leather boots. Who could forget that?"

"I tried." Haven swallowed around the knot that tightened in her throat. "And when I couldn't erase you, I did everything I could to cover you up with new people and places."

"I don't blame you. You had to do what was best for you."

"And now I'm sitting on a porch swing, on a farm in Florida, with you. What the hell?" Haven blinked away the tears that had threatened and laughed instead.

"Maybe we should stop wondering how or why and just sit here and enjoy the mystery."

"And beer." Haven threw back the last swig in her bottle.

"And beer."

❖

Willa had lost track of both time and beverages. After dinner, Kyle, Haven, and Willa sat around a large fire drinking and reminiscing about their childhood. They had been at it for hours when Kyle looked at his phone. "Holy shit. It's two in the morning."

"What?" Haven and Willa said at the same time.

"You heard me. And by the looks of the beer situation, it's time for me to stumble home and pass out."

Judging by the wasteland of empty cans around his chair, it was for the best. Willa had gone easier on the beverages, but she still had a decent buzz. Haven had switched over to water hours earlier in preparation for her drive home. "As long as you make it home and don't pass out on the trail between here and there."

"Oh, no. My car is over that way. I could just walk you home and then head out."

Before Willa could protest, Kyle did. "Na, no…nope. I can do it myself. Me. I can walk home."

"Don't worry. We have a lot of practice. It's usually much worse, for both of us."

"Okay. If you're sure."

"Sure as eggs is eggs, as my daddy always says," he said as he stumbled off into the dark.

"I ain't never heard Daddy say any such thing," Willa called after him, and Haven laughed.

"Although I do recall your dad offering up some equally interesting things," Haven said.

Just as Willa was about to agree, they heard a loud hoot and a thump from the trail. "Oh, good grief. Kyle?"

"Yup. I'm good. Tripped over this log while I was having a piss. It's all good."

"Good Lord. Should we get him a flashlight before he walks off into a swamp or something?" Haven stood and squinted into the night where he had stumbled away.

"Lucky for him there ain't no swamps between here and there, but I reckon I can go find him a flashlight." Haven followed Willa into the house. "I'll be right back. He better not lose this." Willa waved the large red Maglite.

"Okay. I'll be here." Haven dropped herself into the couch.

"Good."

Willa hadn't been gone for longer than five minutes, but when she got back Haven had slipped off her boots and curled her feet up onto the couch. Her back was against the arm, and her head rested against the back cushion. Haven's eyes were closed and she appeared to be sound asleep. Willa stood motionless for several minutes, content to watch her sleep. In that moment, she fit perfectly right there in Willa's home and in her life.

"I feel you staring at me over there," Haven said without opening her eyes.

"What? No, I'm not."

Haven opened her eyes and raised a skeptical eyebrow. "Sure. Did you get him the flashlight?" Haven sat up on the couch.

"No. He was already up the road near his place when I got out

there. If he passes out up that way the goats will keep him company."
Willa sat down on the couch next to Haven.

"Wha—"

"Kidding. He's fine. See." Willa held up her cell phone with a text from Kyle on the screen saying, "Hme."

"Oh, okay. Good."

Willa adored how even after all these years Haven still cared a great deal for Willa's family, and she wasn't afraid to express it. It also surprised her how much in this short time Haven had forgiven. Willa didn't think she could ever be so merciful to someone who had done what she had to Haven. She just stared at Haven sitting mere inches from her willing herself to believe that miracles do happen.

"You're staring at me again."

"I am. I'm just trying to convince myself that I deserve this."

"Deserve what, Willa?"

"Your forgiveness and your friendship. You."

"Well, you have my forgiveness whether or not you think you deserve it. As far as friendship, that one is harder for me to give you."

Willa went from feather to lead in a split second. "I understand."

Haven moved closer and put her hand on Willa's thigh. A fire ignited where their bodies connected. "It's not because I don't want to be your friend, but because I don't think I could ever settle for just that."

Willa set her hand on Haven's and wrapped her fingers around her slender wrist. "Me neither." She slid her hand up Haven's forearm to her elbow and gripped it firmly.

"I realized that it's not enough for me. It never was," Haven said.

Willa could no longer resist the urge she had to pull Haven into her arms. Their bodies melted into each other as Willa claimed Haven's soft lips with her own. Her passion flared when Haven opened her mouth and welcomed Willa's tongue. Their kiss was desperate with need. She twisted her fingers into the back of Haven's hair, and Haven purred. Inspired by the sound, Willa clenched her fist tighter. Haven pulled back from their kiss and gasped for air.

Willa could see the desire burning in Haven's deep and darkening eyes. "Are you sure?"

Haven moved swiftly and straddled Willa's thighs. She could feel the searing heat of Haven's core press into her leg. "As sure as eggs is eggs." Haven grinned before resuming their hot, wet kisses.

Willa slipped her hands up the back of Haven's skirt and squeezed her ass. The move fueled Haven's need as she pressed herself down onto the seam of Willa's jeans. The pressure pierced her as Haven rocked herself against the ridge. A rush of heat spread between her legs and her clit pulsed against the friction Haven was creating. Willa gasped for air and cried out, "Shit." Her breath caught in her lungs as Haven released the button and zipper of her jeans and slipped her hand down between them. She slid her fingers into Willa's wetness and teased her clit with well-placed strokes. Willa's fingertips dug into Haven's flesh and made her cry out with pleasure. The rhythm and the heat built up inside Willa until she was ready to explode, and Haven stroked her closer and closer to the edge of ecstasy. Her power and control over Willa in this moment was unlike anything she'd ever experienced before.

Haven knew what she wanted, and she was taking every bit that Willa was giving her. Willa needed to feel Haven in her hand. She wanted to feel just how aroused she was by her dominance over Willa. She slid her hand down her ass and slipped it under her thigh, pushing her panties out of the way at the same time. Haven was on fire and so wet. The smooth liquid on her fingertips sent Willa over the edge. Her body tightened and shook as Haven stroked hard and steady, pulling every ounce of pleasure from her body.

❖

Haven cupped her hand over Willa's mound as she continued to pulse with aftershocks beneath her fingers. She could feel Willa's own fingers lingering between her legs and fueling her ravenous desire. She wanted Willa in her and on her. Haven wanted to feel the passionate touch of hands long forgotten. "I need you, Willa."

Willa shifted beneath her and lifted Haven from her lap.

Disappointment flashed for a moment before Willa stood and pulled Haven up from the couch. She wrapped her arms around her and kissed her hard. Haven's body melted and her knees buckled when Willa pressed a firm thigh between her legs, but Willa held her tightly. Lost in a haze of emotion and hunger, she led Haven to the bedroom. Without releasing her from her grasp, Willa laid Haven on the bed.

Her kisses moved from her lips to her neck and down to the dip of her neckline. Haven shrugged out of her cover-up as Willa slipped her shirt up and exposed her bare breasts. Willa wasted no time taking a firm, rosy nipple into her warm mouth. She flicked the tip with her tongue and scraped her teeth over the sensitive skin. The light pain fed the fire that was roaring within her. She needed to be free of the clothes that separated their skin. She tugged and stripped Willa of her shirt, accidentally popping off two of the buttons she was too impatient to manage. Willa kicked out of her jeans as Haven did the same with her skirt and panties. Willa's eyes ran up and down the length of Haven's nakedness and she could feel her flesh burn under her gaze as she hovered over her. Unable to tolerate it any longer, Haven pulled Willa down and their bodies pressed into each other.

Haven wrapped her legs around Willa's waist and pressed herself into her. Their smooth, slick centers met and Haven bucked against Willa as she thrust against her swollen clit. Their connection eclipsed time and distance with each pulse that passed between them. Haven had never missed anyone or anything so much. Once she let Willa back into her life and heart she was afraid that losing her again might just kill her. But love and passion took over and Haven gave herself into this moment. "Touch me," Haven begged her. "Please." On her command, Willa slid her fingers into Haven, and she cried out.

"I've missed you so much, Haven."

When she heard her name on Willa's lips, her heart soared. She never thought she'd once again hear her name spoken with such intensity. Haven opened herself up as Willa filled her with her fingers and circled her thumb in rhythm with each thrust of her hand. Haven could feel herself tighten around Willa's fingers. She was so close, but when Willa raked her teeth against her neck and bit down with a sharp sting, Haven climaxed. She gasped and hissed in pleasure as pain and ecstasy surged through her entire body. Haven dug her nails into Willa's bare shoulders as she rode out each wave of her orgasm.

Willa collapsed, panting and breathless, beside her, their wet bodies weak and sated. Tears escaped Haven's eyes as she struggled to maintain her emotions in the swirling aftermath of intimacy.

"Are you okay?" Willa asked as she propped herself up on her elbow and brushed away the hair that stuck to Haven's forehead.

"I am. Just a little overwhelmed, I think." She downplayed it significantly because she was more than a little overwhelmed. Just two days earlier, she had been in Colorado working on her art for her girlfriend. And now she was in Florida on her ex-girlfriend's farm making love to her. She was beginning to think a set of Class V rapids would be less of a risk to her life than this was to her heart.

When Willa wrapped her arm around Haven and pulled her close, some of the uncertainties faded away. She still had no idea what had lead her here, but in Willa's arms she was content with the mystery of the moment. "Close your eyes, sweetheart." Willa pulled the covers up from the side and threw them over.

"I can't," Haven said.

"Why not?" Willa looked down into Haven's eyes. Her own filled with concern.

"I'm afraid if I do, then tomorrow it will be but a dream." She'd had so many dreams of such an idea, but they disappeared each morning after she opened her eyes. Sometimes they'd made love, and sometimes they'd just been in love, but each night Haven felt at peace and whole just to wake in the morning and feel the gaping wound of Willa's absence.

Willa lay back down beside Haven. "I'm not going anywhere. I promise I'll be here tomorrow when you wake up. It's my house, after all."

"Yes, it is. And a beautiful one at that. I'm a little jealous, ya know."

"Jealous? Of what?"

"Of the life you've made for yourself here. Everything you always wanted. You did it."

"It may seem that way, I suppose. I do love it here, but look at everything you've done, who you've become. That's more impressive than anything I've done here."

"There's nothing impressive about running just so you can distract yourself from everything you don't want to deal with in life."

"Well—"

Haven shifted onto her elbow to look at Willa. "I didn't mean it like that." Haven could've kicked herself.

"I know." Willa brushed her fingers across Haven's cheek. Her eyes flickered closed and she lay back down in Willa's arms.

"I can't say that everything to come out of our separation was bad. I found great friends, a worthy cause, an exciting hobby, and a new path for the future. But all I ever wanted to do was share each of those things with you. No matter how far away I ran, you were always here." Haven took Willa's hand and pressed it against her heart. "I'd have given them all up to be with you again."

"And that's why I had to leave. You never would've done any of these things had I stayed. You would have given up your life to save mine, and that…I couldn't let you do that."

"But that was my choice to make, Willa. We could've fought the cancer together and then done it all together."

"And what if I had died?"

Haven's stomach lurched, and she felt sick. "Don't ever—"

"But what if, Haven? You would've stayed by my side wishing for a miracle and missed out on your own life. This wonderful life."

"You were my life." Haven didn't even try to hold back the tears any longer. "And you're alive, and look at all the time we missed together."

"Believe me, my love, there is nothing about those years to be missed. Now go to sleep."

"Hold me," Haven said as she closed her eyes.

"Forever," Willa said as Haven drifted off to sleep.

CHAPTER EIGHTEEN

Willa woke up with the sun just as she always did. Haven was sound asleep wrapped in her arms where she had been all night. She was afraid to move for fear that she would wake her so Willa took a few minutes to stare at Haven's peaceful, sleeping face. When the roosters began their morning wakeup call, Willa was helpless to stop them.

Haven stirred and stretched until she opened one eye and growled. "What the hell is that?"

"That, beautiful, is a farm clock. Wakey, wakey." Willa leaned down and kissed Haven.

"Meh. Where's the snooze button?" Haven moaned.

"No snooze. It's breakfast time."

"For us or them?"

"Both. I'll go take care of them first and then come back for you. That will give you a few more minutes to sleep."

"No, no. I can help."

"Okay," Willa said. "Would you like a cup of coffee first?"

"Oh God, yes." Haven sat up and Willa couldn't help but chuckle. Her funky and fun hair was even more so this morning.

"I like it," Willa said, nodding and eyeballing Haven's bedhead.

"I can only imagine. It'll straighten itself out after some caffeine."

"Coming right up." Willa jumped out of bed and grabbed a pair of jeans and a shirt off the clean clothes chair in the corner as she headed to the kitchen.

She had expected Haven to go back to sleep as soon as she left the room. But she came shuffling out of the bedroom right behind her wearing one of the flannels from her chair. "I've never seen a more beautiful sight."

"You're full of crap. But thank you."

While the water heated, Willa ground some fresh coffee beans for the press. She apologized to Haven for the barrage of noise but promised her it would be worth it. After a few minutes, she plunged the strainer and poured out two dark and delicious cups of coffee. "Ready?" Willa asked as she grabbed the kitchen scrap bin from the counter.

"Let's do it."

Willa slipped her feet into a pair of bright red rubber boots and offered her spare pair to Haven. They were much too big for her, but it added to the oversized theme Haven had going with the shirt. "Do you need shorts?" It had dawned on her to ask when she noticed that Haven appeared not to have anything else on beneath the flannel.

"Nope," Haven said when she lifted up the hem to show that she was wearing her skirt from last night. "Not that it matters any since I couldn't find my panties."

Willa laughed. "I'll help you find them when we're done out here."

"Okay." Haven followed Willa out toward the coop. "What's that?" she asked, pointing to the container Willa had.

"Kitchen scraps." She opened the lid and showed Haven the vegetable peels, eggshells, and other food waste that she fed the chickens each morning.

"Um. They eat their own shells? Isn't that chicken cannibalism or something?"

"They eat the rest of the egg too, sometimes. Chickens eat almost everything. Bugs, mice, lizards."

"Oh yuck. Stop. Mice?"

"Oh yeah. You'll never need a barn cat with a flock of chickens around. Hold this for a sec." Willa handed Haven the scrap bucket as she unlocked the shed and scooped out a couple of buckets of feed.

The ladies were ready and waiting for breakfast when they got to the coop. Willa filled the pans and feeders and then unwound the hose from the side of the building. Haven stood back with the bucket held to her chest and watched the chickens scramble for their food and freedom. It wasn't long before they recognized the black bucket she held and began to gather around her feet.

"Uh, Willa," Haven said with a nervous tone.

"It's okay. Just toss the scraps out onto the ground right over there." Willa pointed at a clearing about five or so feet from where Haven stood.

"Okay."

Haven removed the lid and then slung both the bucket and its contents all over the flock of chickens standing between her and the space Willa had pointed out. "Uh. That's not what I meant." Willa laughed hysterically as the startled birds flapped and scattered at the unexpected assault of food scraps.

Haven looked equally startled by her epic failure. "It slipped." She blushed.

"It's okay," Willa said as she leaned down to pick up the bucket and dump out what was left in it. "Good thing you're cute." Willa moved in and kissed Haven on the lips.

"Whoa, hey now. Not in front of the chickens," Kyle said as he sauntered up.

"Morning," Willa said.

"Morning, ladies."

Except for his comment about their brief kiss, Kyle gave no other awkward glances and mentions to the fact that Haven was still there that morning. Willa assumed he would save all that for after she left. "What brings you over this way so early?"

"I assume you haven't had the television on yet this morning, but the storm track was updated last night and it's making a turn."

"Storm?" Haven asked.

"They also upgraded it to a Cat Two. The new report should be out at eight o'clock. I think we need to get ready for this one, Will."

"Eh. I'm sure it's fine. We're inland now, remember?"

"Right, but if it turns and comes in at an angle, like they think it might, we'll be on its bad side. And that's if it doesn't get stronger once it's over the Gulf."

"Willa, it couldn't hurt to be prepared," Haven said.

Willa refused to let some storm put a damper on this moment. Haven had spent the evening in her arms, and now they were doing chores as naturally as if it had always been. Everything in her world was going better than she could've ever thought it would again, and she would fight reality as long as she could to keep it that way. "Let me finish this first, and then I'll check out the Weather Channel."

"All right. I'll be over in the barn seeing what we've got. I've got some, but we'll need to make shutters for your place." Kyle headed back off toward his house.

"How'd I not know there was a hurricane coming?" Haven asked.

"Because up until Kyle came running over here like a nutcase it wasn't a big deal."

"Well, you know how Gianna is. I imagine if it was something to worry about she'd be all over it."

Willa laughed. "Good to know that hasn't changed."

"Are you kidding? I think her spider senses have evolved. It can be good or bad, depending on how much caffeine she's had."

"If you want it known, get Gia on the phone." Willa recited their long-held motto for Haven's sister, and they both laughed.

"So now what?" Haven looked around at the chickens that now milled about minding their own business.

"Now, *we* can eat," Willa said.

"And shower?" Haven added with a sexy spark in her eye.

It reignited the memories from hours earlier. Willa stepped close to Haven, slid an arm around her waist, and pulled her in. "Or just shower," she offered.

❖

Willa had barely waited until they had closed the door before her hands started searching for the buttons on Haven's shirt. They pulled and tugged at each other's clothing on their way toward the bathroom leaving a trail of garments behind them. When Willa bent over to start the water, Haven couldn't resist the urge to run her fingers along the round curve of Willa's smooth bottom. Her body was soft but sturdy, and she dipped and swelled in all the right places. Years of working on the farm had added onto the strength of her best assets. Haven wanted to lick and taste her way around every inch of her skin.

The sound of the shower hissed to life and the room began to fill with a thick steam. The heat and condensation built up salty beads of sweat on their flesh. Haven pressed her body into Willa's and ran her hands up slick arms and shoulders and gripping her neck to pull her down into a fevered kiss. When Willa picked Haven up into her arms and stepped into the hot spray of the shower, Haven felt a rush of excitement flood between her legs. Haven wanted her, but she wanted more than just her hand and fingers. She leaned in close to Willa's ear. "Do you have a cock we can use?" she whispered.

The request caught Willa off guard, and she looked at Haven with surprise. "Really?"

"Yes, really."

Willa hesitated for a split second before she jumped out of the shower dripping wet and vanished. She reappeared just as quickly grasping a pearly white dong in her hand. Haven's body shuddered with anticipation of having Willa fuck her with the sinfully sexy dildo, but first she wanted to please her with a few well-placed licks. Haven took the cock from Willa and sat her down on the far end of the tub. She spread her legs open and slid down between them onto all fours using a washcloth to cushion her knees.

Haven kissed up the inside of Willa's wet thighs as the searing water stung her back and dripped down the cheeks of her ass. She teased her tongue lightly over the lips between Willa's legs with a few quick flicks of her clit. Willa hissed and bit her lip, and Haven felt herself throb with need. Looking up into her eyes, Haven took Willa fully into her mouth and her head fell back against the wall. Willa's fingers threaded through Haven's hair and twisted with a painful pleasure.

When Haven slid the cock into Willa, she cried out. She pulsed and thrust it inside her as she licked and sucked on her swollen lips. Willa begged for release. "Please, Haven."

Haven's name on Willa's lips was a sound she had only dreamt of hearing again. The breathless desperation and need in her voice drove Haven into a frenzy. She wanted her to come. She wanted to taste her pleasure in her mouth. Willa gripped the edge of the tub with white knuckles. She was close, and Haven could feel it.

"I'm coming, Haven. Shit," Willa cried out as her body shook with wave upon wave of ecstasy. Haven stood, a sense of victory rushing through her. She was smug and pleased with herself as she watched Willa struggle to catch her breath. Haven rinsed her hair and body under the spray, allowing Willa as much time as she needed.

❖

Willa's entire body was useless. It took every ounce of energy she had left to hold her head up. She watched Haven close her eyes and stand back into the water. Rivulets flowed down over her body, following along every sinewy ridge and supple curve of its length. Beads dripped from her firm nipples, onto her belly, and down between her legs. Willa wanted to be the water, exploring in and out of every delicious dip of Haven's flesh.

Unbridled desire was all Willa needed to find the strength she lost giving herself to Haven. She was running on primal need when she stood and took Haven into her arms. Willa pulled one leg up over her hip and thrust her thigh between Haven's legs. She pinned her against the wall with the weight of her own body as she kissed Haven with ravenous desire. Haven began to run her hands down Willa's arms, but she gripped them both with one hand and held them firmly above her head. Willa's free hand gripped the cock, and she slowly slipped it in, out, and along Haven's wet folds, teasing her with it.

Willa released Haven's hands and hooked her arm under Haven's raised leg, pushing her open and thrusting inside her. Haven screamed with pleasure and grasped onto Willa's shoulders. Willa repositioned her arm, looping around the small of Haven's back and supporting her as she dipped her to take a hard nipple into her mouth. When Willa twisted it gently between her teeth, Haven gasped. She bucked against each of Willa's thrusts, each one growing faster and harder as Haven neared climax. Willa kissed her, the sweet taste of her lips mixed with her own scent was intoxicating.

"You're so beautiful, Haven. Come for me. Just for me."

As if she had just been waiting for permission, Haven cried out Willa's name as she came. Her body tightened as Willa pushed the cock deep inside her with one last, slow thrust. Willa held her close as small shudders pulsed through her. "I've missed you so much."

Willa had no idea how they had ended up in bed, as everything after Haven's staggering orgasm was a bit of a blur. She rested her head on Haven's bare chest and listened to the rhythmic beat of her heart, and slow, soothing breaths. Willa brushed her fingers lightly over the bare skin of Haven's back. Its effects were both relaxing and arousing. She was surprised by the latter after their intense and exhausting shower. When she ran her hand down Haven's belly and she didn't protest her arousal surpassed relaxed. It wasn't long before Willa had Haven straddling her hips ready for another round.

❖

"So we never went into it, but if you can't start a camp here or in Colorado, where would you go?" Willa asked as she went about making breakfast hours after they had planned.

Haven sat on the stool on the opposite side of the island and sipped her coffee. "Well, it would have to be someplace between the two, I suppose."

"What is between the Florida sand and the Colorado stardust?" Willa waved her spatula dramatically.

"Oklahoma tumbleweeds?" Haven laughed.

"Well, yes. But I was thinking more along the lines of, I don't know, the Tennessee Smokies." Just then the reality that Haven lived in Colorado struck her. She hadn't given it much thought up until that point. Even if she did decide to move again, it wouldn't be back to Florida, and that's where Willa was. "It is closer than Colorado. So I reckon that's a plus."

"I have looked at property costs in North Carolina, believe it or not. I ran the Nantahala River with Scrat last year. There's definitely a lot of potential for a great camp there." Haven swirled the coffee in her mug.

Willa was reluctant to offer advice that would ultimately take Haven away, but the truth was she would be leaving soon, anyway. The thought tore at her. "Well, Corey's family owns a real estate agency in Asheville. I'm sure she'd be more than happy to put some feelers out for you."

"Hmm, interesting."

Willa set down the plate of fried ham, eggs, and hash browns she made for breakfast, and Haven eyed it quizzically. "What?"

"Are these the eggs?"

"Uh. What?"

"Are they…the yard eggs?"

Willa laughed. "They are fresh eggs from the coop, not the yard. They're normal, regular, edible eggs."

"Okay." Haven poked at the yolk as if it were going to hatch into a baby chick.

"You realize that's not how eggs work, right?" She laughed again.

"I don't know. I've never had a—"

"Yard egg," Willa finished. "Just eat it." Willa dug into her own plate without hesitation, and Haven seemed less skeptical about her own.

Haven took a forkful of egg and potato. Just as she was about to put it into her mouth her phone rang. "Hello? Hey, Gianna. Yeah. No, we…we were busy. Okay. Okay, bye."

"What's up?"

"Gianna's noon o'clock news. We need to turn on the TV." Haven finished the bite she had started. "Mmm. Yard eggs are delicious."

❖

Haven and Willa stared at the screen of brightly colored graphs and maps of the state. Just as Kyle had said, the morning update shifted the storm named Jennifer toward the east and increased its strength to a Category 3 storm. At its current speed, they anticipated landfall within two to three days. The worst news of it all was its expected upgrade to a devastating Category 4 or 5 hurricane.

Satellite images did little to ease Haven's anxiety, as its sheer size was set to eclipse the entire state. The prediction cone had the eye aiming for the city of Cape Coral with the swath of danger extending out a hundred miles on either side. Haven's anxiety was increasing as quickly as the storm.

"What are you going to do?" Haven asked, looking over at Willa. "What am *I* going to do? I don't even know if my mom has shutters." Her heart was beginning to race.

"We'll put up boards and shutters. I'll run some ratchet straps over the coop and the sheds. It'll be fine, sweetie." Willa scooted up next to Haven on the couch and squeezed her knee. "I'll come over and help y'all get ready."

Haven couldn't believe she would even offer at the risk of her own livelihood. "No. No way. You have too much to do here. I mean, how are the two of you going to manage on your own? And I'm just going to leave?" She couldn't leave, but she had to leave.

"Babe, relax," Willa said, cupping Haven face in her hands. "Breathe." Willa kissed her softly.

Haven took a deep breath. "But—"

"We have a couple friends that I'm sure will come give us a hand. Besides boarding up the houses and the coop, there isn't anything we can do. All we can do is hope the barns and sheds hold up. We'll do what we can."

"What about the animals?" The thought of Willa losing any of her flock or the rest of her livestock was heartbreaking.

"We will put the large animals out to pasture. Their instincts will keep them safer than a barn would. The back thirty acres has a lot of tree coverage. The goats and chickens we'll put in Kyle's garage, with the extra feed and supplies."

"Out in the storm?" Haven couldn't imagine just opening the gates and letting them fend for themselves in the wind and rain.

"I'm scared, too. But it's part of the job. We do everything we can to prepare, but there's always risk. You know this. You think you know how it's all gonna go, and then whoosh, a rogue wave tosses you into the river. It's about the prep and the recovery."

Haven adored Willa for trying to use river analogies to ease her fears.

She needed to go. The longer she delayed going home, the longer she kept Willa from taking care of the farm. She couldn't believe that their beautiful reunion was being destroyed by a raging hurricane headed their way. "I should go."

"It'll be okay." Willa kissed her long and hard.

Haven wouldn't let Willa walk her up to her car. She didn't want her to see how much it hurt her to leave, and she especially didn't need to see the ugly crying Haven did all the way there. Something didn't feel right about leaving. She was so afraid that once she did everything was going to change. She waved good-bye to Kyle, who stood in the doorway of the barn and waved back.

Once Haven was on the road, she called Gianna to let her know she was on the way. She was relieved to know that her mother did have shutters for her house. It was one less thing she was going to have to worry about during the storm. When she hung up with her sister, she immediately dialed Wendy's number.

"Hello?" Wendy said.

Haven didn't waste time with a hello. "Girl, you're never going to believe this."

CHAPTER NINETEEN

I told you, Will. I told you the storm was coming and we should've started this shit days ago." The storm was at least two days out from landfall, but the wind had already reached them.

"We couldn't have known it was coming this way, Kyle," Willa said as she tossed a strap over the shed.

"Are you fucking kidding me? I told you, but you were too busy daydreaming and playing house with Haven." He hooked the ratchet strap to the anchor and tightened it down.

"What the hell, man?" She understood that he was on edge about the storm, but there was clearly something else bothering him.

"What?" He stood up and set his hands on his hips, breathing in heaves.

"What was that shit about Haven? She has nothing to do with this."

"Willa, what are you doing? She doesn't even live here. Hell, she doesn't even live in this state or on this side of the damn country. Everything we have worked for is right here, and you're gonna let it go to shit in some storm because of her?" He threw the next strap and set off to secure it.

"What are you talking about, Kyle?" Willa grabbed for his arm, missing it the first time. Her second reach caught his elbow before he could get past her. "Stop for a second!"

"Listen, don't think I don't know that you still care for her, but she isn't coming back here. So what else could that mean?"

Willa couldn't remember the last time her brother had been so upset. "Kyle, I'm not going anywhere." Sure, she'd had the occasional thought of how to make things work with Haven. But she was forced to admit that unless she gave up her farm, there was no way they could be together. As much as she had tried to avoid it all weekend, it seemed that she was going to have to accept it. "I can't. We've put too much into this place."

"I'm sorry, Will."

"For what?"

"That things aren't gonna work out the way you want."

"Hey, I made a decision years ago that lost me every chance there could've been for us. This is just another result of that decision."

Willa had been fooling herself into thinking that somehow everything would work out, mostly by ignoring the reality of the situation. She'd just allowed her heart to lead her wherever it took her without giving any thought to what the meaning was behind it. But the truth was, she and Haven couldn't be together. Too much had changed, and the space between them was just too great. Willa knew it, but she just didn't want to believe it. "I'm the one who should be sorry." And she truly was. "Toss me another tie down."

Kyle picked out one from the back of the Gator and tossed it to her. "Will!" he yelled as the end unraveled and the metal hook caught her in the face.

She literally hadn't seen it coming. The hook was covered with plastic, but the way it had whipped around hit her like a brick. "Shit!" she hollered, covering her eye with her hand.

Kyle ran to her. "Lemme see, Will." He tried to pull her hand away.

"I didn't see it. Son of a bitch." Willa could feel the warm trickle of blood start through her fingers.

"Fuck. You're bleeding, dammit. Let me see."

Her fight or flight instinct fought against him as he continued to try and pull her hand away. "It could be your eye."

"Why would that fucking matter, Kyle? I'm blind."

"What?"

She could tell it wasn't her eye, but just below it, right on the bone. "I'm blind in this eye. From the radiation. It's been gradually getting worse, but now it's just dark." She took her hand down, and Kyle's face flushed pale.

"Um, okay. Sit. Sit down here." He cleared the seat on the Gator and helped her into it. "Why didn't you...never mind." He paced nervously looking for something, and pulled a handkerchief from his pocket. "Here, put this on it."

Willa took the cloth and pressed it to her face as Kyle jumped into the driver's seat and sped off toward the house even though it was less than a hundred feet away. "I could've walked, ya know."

"Dammit, Will, this is no time for jokes. Come on." He rushed her into the house and into the bathroom.

"The kit's under the sink in the kitchen."

When he left to fetch it, Willa removed the cloth and inspected the damage in the mirror. Blood covered the side of her face and her hands as well as her neck and shirt. Willa thought of Haven and how they'd probably still be outside trying to get her off the ground after passing out. She wet a clean washcloth and wiped away most of the blood. Once that was done, she could see the large gash that ran just under her eye along her cheekbone. "Shit," she said, realizing that she was going to need stitches. She grabbed a clean cloth and met her brother in the hall.

"What? Is it bad? I mean, face wounds bleed a lot anyway, don't they?"

"I need stitches. You stay here. I'll go up the road to the walk-in clinic and be back in a few."

"No. I'm driving."

"No. I'm quite capable of doing this on my own. I don't need your help, Kyle." The pain was growing worse and Willa was getting agitated. The injury felt like a culmination of everything that was going on. "If we hadn't been rushing at the last minute because I was distracted by Haven, I wouldn't have been smashed in the face. And I got smashed in the face because I've been blinded by the cancer that caused all of this bullshit in the first place." She was on the edge of a breakdown for the first time in her memory, and the more she struggled the more she slipped.

"Okay, Will. One thing at a time, and right now that thing is your face." He hooked his arm in hers and walked her to the truck.

Kyle didn't leave her side the entire time they were at the clinic. He sat with her in the waiting room and followed her back for her exam. He even sat and talked to her about nonsense while they stitched up the wound.

When they were back in the truck and headed home Willa apologized. "I'm sorry, Kyle."

"You're sorry? For what? You didn't hit me with a ratchet strap."

"No, I didn't. And we'll deal with that later. I'm sorry I didn't tell you about the whole eye thing."

"Yeah. That one caught me off guard a bit. I can understand that you didn't want people to treat you different or whatever. But I'm your brother, Will."

"I didn't want you to think I needed help or that I couldn't do shit on my own."

"What I won't understand is why you think that needing help or having support is such a bad thing."

"I'm working on it."

❖

"You're breaking up. Are you there? Willa?" Haven disconnected and redialed, but this time it went straight to voice mail. The storm had made official landfall an hour earlier, and so far the west coast was being hammered unlike anything they'd seen since 1960. Major news networks had set up camp in St. Cloud about twenty miles northwest of Willa and Kyle's farm, including the famous Jim Cantore from the Weather Channel. There was already word of several tornadoes forming along the eyewall causing significant damage along the eastern side of the storm.

"Channel Nine says the cell towers are down southwest of

Orlando, and they've lost power almost everywhere south of Lakeland."

"She's closer toward the east than west, but if it keeps on track it won't matter."

There was nothing about this storm that trackers or prediction models were getting right. It came in as a strong Category 4, but it was lower and slower than they planned, and on a path that would send it straight between Haven and Willa.

"It should weaken a bit as it moves across, Haven. That's what they said."

She knew what they'd said. That's what they always said, and she had been through enough of these to know all the jargon. But it didn't make her feel any better. Especially when they showed image after image of the damage being sustained. And she didn't understand how every major storm to come through always had to hit in the dead of night. "Why are these damn things always at night?" she asked, looking out one of the gaps they had left in the shutters.

"Channel Six just said that they lost the roof on the city hall in Lake Wales."

"You're not making this any better, Gianna."

"Sorry. I'll turn it off for a bit."

"No!" Haven said. As nerve-wracking as it was, the news was her one connection to Willa.

"Okay, I'll just turn it down then."

Haven sat at the kitchen table and turned her phone over and over in her hand willing it to ring. She just wanted to hear her voice and know she was all right. It was bad enough that Willa had gotten hurt getting things ready. Thankfully, she'd said it wasn't anything major. "I can't say I miss this nonsense. We don't have freaking hurricanes in Colorado."

"No, but you have snow, and that's worse."

"Normally, I'd agree with you, but right now it's a toss-up. Besides my family, there's only one thing about Florida that's missing out in Colorado," Haven said.

"And the chance of getting us, or her, out there is less than that of getting a hurricane."

"I know." As much as she could dream about Willa moving out to Colorado, she knew it would never happen.

"And you are not giving up your new art career to move your ass back here and be a pig farmer."

Haven was blindsided by Gianna's statement. This was coming from the same woman who had practically pushed her out the door to go see Willa. "First of all, she isn't a pig farmer. They don't even have pigs. And secondly, what the hell?"

"Whatever. I'm just saying that you've made such a great life for yourself out there and it would be stupid to give it up and move back here."

Haven wasn't going to deny that she had a pretty good thing going on in Denver. But moving back to Florida would never be an option for her, no matter what she planned on doing with her future. "Gianna, I'm not moving back here."

"Good. You can't become a world famous artist if you're busy plucking chickens all day, or whatever."

"What the hell kind of farm do you think she has? And besides, I don't even want to be a famous artist. Sometimes I don't even want to be a regular one."

"Wait, what?"

"There's more to being an artist than just painting. It's about deadlines and contracts and kissing people's asses. None of which I enjoy. I don't even like most people, let alone want to kiss their ass. It's political and cliquey."

Haven was surprised to be saying it aloud. Sure, she'd mentioned it here or there, but never let it all out. She'd never been the popular girl in school. And the art scene in Denver, and probably everywhere else, was full of snobs and egotists, and that was before getting involved with clients and dealers. Someone was always better or at least knew more people, so their talent was irrelevant. Even Bianca's first priority was always about making people like her.

"Please don't tell me you want to give it all up to be a farmer."

Why should it even matter? It was her life, not Gianna's. "So what if I did?"

"Then I'd say you're full of shit," Gianna said, pushing herself away from the table.

Before Haven could respond, she had turned up the volume on the television. Power outages were now affecting more than 600,000 people throughout Central Florida, and they were reporting major flooding in counties across the state. Haven's heart dropped like lead when they mentioned the Kissimmee Chain of Lakes area, near where Willa lived. Witnesses stated that massive oaks were toppling over onto homes and vehicles and uprooting entire foundations. Willa and Kyle had at least twenty hundred-year-old oaks around the property and near their homes. As if her anxiety couldn't get worse, an emergency broadcast sounded declaring a tornado warning for Haven's immediate area. Her senses heightened as she struggled to listen for the telltale sounds of a freight train headed toward their house.

"Help me get the mattress into the bathroom," Haven said. Her face was hot with anxiety.

"Okay," Gianna said.

"Ma, bring the radio and the flashlights from the kitchen."

"Already in there, sweetie."

While Haven and Gianna were sitting at the table, her mother had moved the supplies and water into the master bathroom and set them in the shower. The tub was filled with water, but there was plenty of space for the mattress and sleeping bags. The electricity flickered, but stayed on, and Haven was glad. The three of them got comfortable on the floor and settled in to wait for the all clear.

"So, you wanna be a farmer," her mother said.

"Ugh. That's not what I said. I...I want to start my own camp. There. Happy?" She glared at Gianna. "And yes, I want animals, too. So?"

"I think that sounds like fun, sweetheart."

"Seriously, Mom?" Gianna said.

"Sure, why not? If that's what she wants to do, then why not. What's it matter to you?"

Haven smiled. She hadn't expected her mother to come so easily to her defense. "Exactly. What's it matter what I do?" A booming clap of thunder rattled the walls and Haven jumped. "Dammit."

"It doesn't matter to me. I just think that she shouldn't mess up a good thing, that's all."

"I guess that depends on what your definition of good is," her mother said.

And with that, they sat in silence and listened to the sounds of the storm outside.

❖

When Willa attempted once more to leave the house, Kyle didn't stop her. She had tried several times to stick her head outside and get some sense of damage, but each time, Kyle had pulled her back into the house. It was for her own safety, but they nearly had a knock-down drag-out after the fifth time he'd done it. It was early morning, and while the storm had passed, there was a steady wind and the sky was still eerily dark.

Willa stepped out into the yard and her heart sank. Four of the giant oaks that lined the driveway had toppled over, their entire root systems pulled from the ground, taking with them the surrounding soil and road gravel. The large holes left behind were flooded with water, while branches, palm fronds, and other debris covered the ground. Willa turned to face the house. It remained intact except for having lost most of the roofing shingles. Her stomach jolted the instant she realized that the barn was no longer towering in the background. "No." Willa hurdled broken limbs as she ran around to the back of the house. She stopped when she saw Kyle standing frozen before an enormous pile of debris where the old barn had stood. Tangled metal and wood was collapsed onto itself or twisted with what was left of the surrounding pine trees. The steel pole barn still stood, but entire sheets of roofing had been peeled back like the lid of a sardine can.

The sound of steady wind and scraping metal filled the air. Without it, the deafening silence would've been unbearable. Just then, Annie went barreling past them toward the barn. "Annie, no! Come." Willa and Kyle chased after, calling her name. It wasn't like Annie not to listen. In the clearing behind where the barn had stood was a sight that squeezed Willa's heart.

"I can't believe it," Kyle said. Annie barked and circled the herd of animals that stood in the middle of the field. They were wet and matted, covered in mud and rubble, and all huddled together into a safe, protective circle.

Willa's relief was short-lived when she realized there was no red peeking through the tree line at her from where her house should be. Her stomach turned as she made her way along the mangled fence toward her home. She scrambled over the fallen trees and broken limbs that blocked the path. Her feet sucked into the ground that was soft and saturated with rain and overflow from the lake. When she got to the end of the path, her breath caught in her lungs.

She hadn't realized Kyle had followed her until she heard him gasp. The thick canopy of a massive tree blanketed Willa's small house. She was crippled in disbelief, petrified to the spot. Her ears buzzed, and tears stung her eyes. It was as if there had been no house there at all, just a tree and its enormous spidery branches.

"Willa? Kyle? Hello?" a voice called out from amidst the destruction, muffled by the rush of blood through Willa's ears.

"Shit. It's Haven," Kyle said, turning toward the sound of her voice, but Willa didn't move.

"Oh, Willa!" Haven said, wrapping her arms around Willa's shoulders.

Willa still didn't move or hug Haven back. "What are you doing here, Haven?" she said without tone or inflection.

"I've been going crazy. I had to come see that you were all right." Haven rubbed Willa's arms, looked up at her, and touched the stitches on her face. "What—"

Willa stepped back from Haven's touch. "You shouldn't be here. It's too dangerous, and you shouldn't even be out on the roads right now."

"I don't care. I had to see you." Haven reached out and stroked Willa's arm.

She had to see her, or she had to see her lose everything? "You need to go. There's no reason for you to be here," she said, pulling her arm away.

"What are you talking about, Willa?"

"This isn't your problem. You need to go home."

"I'm not going anywhere. I can help. Kyle, help me get in here," Haven said, squeezing herself between the branches to get to the front door.

"Stop, Haven. You're going to get yourself killed," Willa said as she grabbed Haven by the elbow. Because that's all she needed was for Haven to get hurt trying to save her stuff.

"You don't always have to rescue people, Haven. Some of us can do it on our own."

"Will, don't," Kyle said.

"But you don't have to. I'm here. Kyle's here. We can—"

"Go home, Haven." It was all gone. She had nothing left, and she refused to let Haven stick around to salvage the pieces.

"Why?"

"Because you don't belong here, Haven. This is my farm, my life. You have your own, and it's not here. You're not going to give that up for this…this mess. Just go."

Haven grabbed Willa's hand and squeezed it. She refused to let go when Willa tried to pull away. "Don't do this. Not again. Don't push me away."

"Please, let go," Willa said, tugging her hand away.

"Willa?" Tears ran down Haven's cheeks; Willa's heart shattered. "You can't just push me away because you're too prideful to need help! You're not that person anymore, remember?"

"Kyle, get Haven back to her car."

"Will, but—"

"Now," Willa said, turning to walk away.

Haven came around and stood in front of Willa, pulling her shoulders back and wiping the tears from her face. "I can't do this again. It will kill me. I know it will."

"It won't. It's best for both of us, you'll see. You deserve better than this, better than me."

"I love you, Willa, and you love me, too. Please, don't do this," Haven cried.

"Good-bye, Haven," Willa said. Her heart was breaking into a thousand pieces, but she had to do it. It was for their own good, and she was saving them in the long run, she told herself, over and over again.

"Kyle, don't let her do this," Haven begged him.

"You know she won't listen to me. Wait a few days. Maybe she'll come around."

"Not this time. If I leave, I'm going back to Colorado. I've waited so long already." Haven looked once more at Willa. She could feel their connection crumbling as they stared into each other's eyes with tears falling.

"I'm sorry," she said, her voice cracking. It was all Willa could manage to say before she turned and walked away. *So very sorry.*

Chapter Twenty

Two weeks had passed since Haven had returned from Florida. Her mother's home had sustained minor damage with a few downed limbs, some missing siding, and a handful of shingles. The day after the storm, her mother had already called her handyman to get on his list for repairs. There wasn't a single reason for Haven to stay.

For days on end, Haven locked herself away in her studio to finish the last paintings she needed for the gallery opening. Despite not wanting to go through with it, Haven would fulfill her obligation to Bianca. However, save for a few pieces she'd already completed months earlier, Haven explored a new style for the rest of them. A style that was born from a whirlwind of love and loss, and had begun with the drunken painting of Willa she'd created weeks earlier.

Each time Haven closed her eyes, Willa was there, standing before her exposed, waiting for Haven to reach out and touch her. But once again, she was just beyond her grasp. The heart and soul she had once held in her hand was as distant as the stars in the sky. Haven's brush moved quickly against the canvas. The black emptiness framed the painting, moving inward and fusing with deep blue and midnight purple into the shape of two women, the curves of their breasts and bellies close to touching but separated by a vast darkness. Their flesh was made of astral swirls and a million specks of stardust that created a sense of eternal movement forever suspended in time. It was the last piece she needed to complete her set for the opening. It might have even been the last painting she'd ever finish at all.

She closed the door to the studio and went out to the living room. She stood in front of the television deciding whether or not to turn it on and get lost in some mundane home and garden show. Haven decided instead to plop down onto the couch with her phone. She had downloaded a real estate app and saved a few searches with her ideal, albeit farfetched, property features. As expected, Colorado was far too expensive for what she wanted, and remembering her conversation with Willa, she had added Tennessee and the Carolinas to her list. Something always drew her back to North Carolina with its mountains, lakes, and rivers. Haven was surprised and a bit overwhelmed by the selection and varied price ranges. She'd love to buy a working ranch with house and outbuildings on forty acres, but a million dollars was more than out of her price range. Yet, two listings down was another with home on a hundred and twenty acres for a quarter of the price. While the latter was certainly more reasonable, what was the catch? Although none of it mattered, because she couldn't afford the down payment on either. She decided it'd be less depressing to check her email.

Haven had gotten Bianca to print a few dozen extra invitations that she could send out to her friends from camp. To her surprise, nearly everyone she'd invited had RSVP'd to the positive, including several people who didn't even live in the state. It didn't hurt that the annual fundraising gala for Valiant Adventures was being held that same weekend and most would be in town for that. She was determined to fill the room with people she liked with hopes of minimizing the number of pretentious art critics she'd have to talk to. It broke her heart that one of those people would not be Willa. Not because she hadn't yet RSVP'd, but because Haven didn't even bother to invite her.

There had been a time when Haven would daydream about Willa walking into the room during some such event just to surprise her. They would see each other from across the room, and the world would fade away around them. But Haven knew that was crap, and real life didn't work out that way. Real life drops a duffel on your foot, tries to drown you, sends a hurricane to kill you, and then punches you in the face. "Good grief, Haven," she said to herself. She needed to get out of the house. She had no more tears to cry, and she needed to move on once and for all.

Haven sent out a text to Wendy, Diego, Scrat, and a few other locals to see if anyone would bite on the idea of heading over to the wave park at Clear Creek. Within minutes, all of them had replied with a resounding, "Yes."

"Hell yeah," Haven said, jumping up from the couch to gather her gear.

Since they were scattered around Denver and the suburbs, they agreed to meet there within the hour. Haven loaded her boat onto the rack of her car and tossed her dry suit, helmet, PFD, and dry bag into the back. The idea of being on the water thrilled her. She arrived in Golden within twenty minutes of getting on the road. Scrat had beat her there, having just gotten finished with a rolling lesson at the pool. By the time Haven had unloaded her kayak, Diego and Wendy had pulled in. Haven was so excited she could barely contain herself, even if they were just going to spend a few hours playing in the waves and not running the river. "Hey, y'all!"

"Hey, stranger. Welcome back," Diego said.

"How's it feel to be out in the sunlight? You've been locked up in that studio of yours since you got back. Is that paint in your hair?" Wendy asked, reaching up and pulling on a clump of Haven's hair.

"Ouch. Must be." Haven picked at the dried mat of blue paint. "It feels good. I was gonna sit on my ass and watch TV and cry after I finished my last piece, but then I started talking to myself. I figured I should get out."

"As long as it wasn't a two-way conversation," Diego said as he tossed down his SUP and rummaged for his gear in the bed of the truck.

Wendy leaned in close to Haven. "Are you doing okay, otherwise? Ya know, with...Florida?"

"I don't want to talk about it right now," she said, a lump forming in her throat.

"I can understand that. But have you heard from her at all?"

"No, and I doubt I ever will again. She made it very clear that whatever we had…whatever that was, it was a mistake."

"It just doesn't make sense, ya know?"

"Believe me, I know. She's afraid of ruining my life or forcing me to take care of her. I have no idea, but it's bullshit. And right now I don't want to think about it, or her, or what happened in Florida. I just want to be on the water." The river always had a way of carrying away the stress and pain of a day or a lifetime. If she had to, Haven would spend every day trying to do just that.

"Woo-hoo," Diego hollered as he picked up his board and ran off toward the water.

"Uh, where are his pants?" Scrat asked, pointing at Diego, who was sans bathing suit.

"What the hell, Diego!" Haven slapped her hand over her eyes and screamed.

"You're going to get arrested," Scrat called after him.

"You're going to get hypothermia," Wendy added.

"You can probably get a smaller boat!" Haven said before they all broke out in hysterical laughter.

Kyle walked the adjuster to the door and returned to the table where Willa sat. Stacks of forms, papers, pictures, and files covered every inch of the surface. She spun the piece of paper around with her finger several times, stopping every few rotations to look at the dollar figure highlighted at the bottom. It was more than they had expected, but not enough to rebuild everything they'd lost, especially the hundred-year-old barn. Sure, they could replace it with a modern structure much like the steel pole barn, but so much more than a structure had been lost with the building. Not to mention the sheds, lean-to shelters, pens, and the coop, and then there was Willa's house.

Kyle sat back down at the table beside Willa. "So, what are you thinking?"

"I don't know anymore, Kyle. My brain is toast." They'd been looking at numbers, values, and replacement costs for nearly four weeks. They had pages and pages of inventory, supplies, buildings, each one with a dollar amount next to it. The only amounts missing were ones that represented the value of the time and labor that went into making it what it was.

"If we take the replacement value we can rebuild everything and then some. We can sell the timber from the barn, or salvage what we can and raise something smaller."

"If we take the cash, we can sell the whole lot," Willa said.

"Right, and we can still sell the barn timber for a nice bit of cash."

"We'd have to start over from scratch." The thought of it pulled at her wounded heart.

"We'd have to do that here, too."

He was right. No matter what they decided to do, they'd have to start from the bottom. Unless they got lucky and found a run-down start-up like they had there. "What about my place?"

"It's not too bad. We'd have to repair the roof and the loft, but considering that a fifty-foot oak tree fell onto it, I'd say it could be a lot worse."

"True." She wouldn't have believed it had she not seen it. The biggest of the limbs managed to miss the house altogether and acted as braces to keep the bulk of the tree from crushing everything beneath it. It had come out with some damage, but considering that it was built by hand, it withstood a great deal.

"Maybe it's time we got out of here, Willa."

"What are you talking about? We have to make a decision." Willa waved the piece of paper at him.

"No. I meant Florida. We've lived here our entire lives. What if we made a change? People do it all the time."

"I can't even believe I'm hearing this from you. And where would we go? Huh?"

"I don't know, how about North Carolina? They have decent farm land, it's not terribly cold, and best of all, no hurricanes."

He was out of his mind. She thought she was losing her grip on reality, but he had slipped right off the deep end. "You're nuts, man."

"Why? Come on. Think about it. We can expand the farm and start a u-pick. We can't grow shit in this sandy soil here, and it's so damn hot to boot."

"What about the animals? Harold and Leland. The girls. My chickens? I'm not leaving my chickens, Kyle."

"They'll come with us. Hell, it'd probably be better for them, too."

Willa rubbed her hands over her face. What was happening? "I…I don't know. I need air," Willa said, pushing herself away from the table.

Annie followed her outside and went off in search of her charges. Ever since the storm, the animals were all enclosed in the same pasture, and while they had several acres, they insisted on moving and migrating together. Annie had become their self-appointed babysitter and became restless if not allowed to check on them several times a day. It was an interesting sight to see. Willa knew Haven would've been amused by it.

The thought of selling the farm wasn't inconceivable. It was in their best interest in terms of future growth and financial opportunity. But Willa couldn't help but fear that if they left, Haven wouldn't be able to find her. It was an idiotic notion, and she knew it. Why would Haven ever come looking for her after the way Willa had treated her? She'd done exactly what she had promised never to do again. Willa had begged for her forgiveness, and at her first test of faith, she failed.

She walked the property, surveying the mounds of debris they had spent weeks gathering into piles to be burned. The roof of the house was tarped and waiting for repairs, as was her house. Bare patches of dirt were all that remained where different outbuildings had stood. They determined that their damage was caused by a tornado and not the high winds of the hurricane itself. It was evident by the path of destruction it left across the property. It was no longer the farm it had been days or even hours before the storm came through.

Willa stopped by the makeshift coop they had made from what remained of the one she had just finished before the hurricane. It wasn't as pretty, but it served its purpose for now. She let the flock out for a few minutes of free-range yard time while she sat in the grass and teased the ones who came close enough. "How would y'all like to move to North Carolina?" she asked. Thankfully, they didn't answer.

After a while, Willa gave them fresh water and threw down some scratch to get them back inside for the night. She saw Kyle pacing in the side yard when she got back to the house. She hadn't realized he was on the phone until he turned to face her. When he spotted her his eyes widened in surprise. "Hey, she's back. I'll call you later," he said quickly and quietly before pushing the phone into his back pocket. "Hey."

"Uh, hi. Who was that?" It was obvious he had either been talking about her or didn't want to talk in front of her.

"Oh. Who? Jason. I was just telling him that we got our settlement amount."

"Ah," she said, although she knew he was lying. "So are you serious about selling this place?"

"Yeah, Will. I am."

She took a deep breath. "Okay, we'll do it. But we're taking my house."

❖

The car pulled up in front of the gallery and Haven hesitated. Despite having everyone, including Bianca, ask if she wanted them to accompany her, Haven chose to go alone. After seeing how many people were already inside, she was regretting her decision. Before she could ask the driver to whisk her away from the crowd, Wendy approached the car and opened the door.

"Get out of the car," she said.

"There are sooo many people here. What the hell?"

"That's a good thing. Now, get out."

As soon as she was out of the vehicle, she was swarmed by guests welcoming and congratulating her, most of whom she didn't even recognize. Wendy did her best getting her inside and putting a drink in her hand, which Haven downed in a few large swallows. When Bianca approached from across the room, Haven relaxed. While things had been awkward between them over the last few weeks, Bianca was the consummate professional, always able to put business before anything else.

"We have several interested buyers, three potential commissions, and everyone's hand to shake," Bianca said.

"Commissions?" Haven asked as Wendy slipped another cocktail into her hand. "I don't take commissions, Bianca. You know that." She downed this beverage as quickly as the first.

"You will if they pay you, Haven. That's part of the job," she whispered as a finely dressed man approached them.

"Good evening, Ms. Thorne. Exceptional compositions. I enjoy the…"

Haven tuned him out, nodding at his pretentious accolades, but not listening. When he was finished, she thanked him and excused herself. Both Bianca and Wendy chased after her.

"What was that, Haven? Besides rude," Bianca asked, her face red with anger.

"I'm sorry. I just don't want to listen to all that bullshit all night from every Joe Blow who thinks he understands the meaning of my decision to use cobalt to represent the trials of woman or some shit."

"These are art critics and collectors, Haven. Let them say whatever they want as long as they give good reviews and spend a lot of money."

Another glass appeared in her hand. "Thank you," she said before drinking it down.

"Slow down on those, please," Bianca said.

"Oh look! My friends," Haven said, leaving a frustrated Bianca standing alone.

Haven couldn't believe how many of her friends had showed up for her. Campers, fellow volunteers, and even a few river guides she'd met through Scrat and MC.

"These are amazing," Wingman said.

"I wish I could afford one. That's for sure," Corey said.

"Don't do it. They're overpriced." Haven was not the one who put the dollar amounts on the pieces. She had even argued with Bianca about the outrageous numbers she was putting out there.

"But I like this one, a lot." Corey said, pointing to *Midnight Stardust*.

"Yeah. Don't tell anyone, but it didn't take me more than an hour to paint that," Haven said.

"Has she seen it?"

"Who?" Haven knew who, but she was caught off guard by Corey's question.

"Willa. It's her and you, isn't it? Has she seen it?"

"Um, no. It's not. No, she hasn't, and she probably never will."

"Well, that sucks. She should. It's quite amazing. Maybe someday she will."

"You're a strange little bird, Corey," Wendy said, changing the subject. "So I hear you're in the real estate game out in North Carolina."

"Yeah. I'm a showing assistant for my parents' agency."

"Well, Haven here might be in the market for some adventure property out that way."

"No way. That's great! What are you looking for?"

"Oh, uh, nothing right now. Anything over a dollar is out of my price range at the moment. I'd have to sell all this stuff at these insane prices to even have a down payment," Haven said.

"Yeah, I understand that. Well, keep me in mind, though. I bet I could find you some great places."

"See, Haven. You just gotta know the right people," Wendy said as Bianca walked up.

"Hey, all. I'm going to have to steal her away for a while. There's a few big players that we need to make friends with," Bianca said, hooking her arm with Haven's and leading her away.

Haven swiped a glass from the passing tray. When Bianca gave her the look, she sipped at it instead of just tossing it back.

"I know you don't want to be here. But please, Haven, this is my career," Bianca said.

"Fine. Whose ass do you want me to kiss?"

They moved through the crowd talking and schmoozing with the diamonds and tuxedos that filled the room. Haven let them each tell her what they thought about her work and what they felt it meant. She nodded and smiled while she sipped on her drink. Looking around the room, Haven noticed that several of her new style pieces already had red dots, as did at least two of her others. She was stunned to see that people were not only buying her works but spending insane amounts of money on them.

When two women approached arm in arm, Bianca went into action. She was damn good at her job. "Good evening, ladies. Isn't this a wonderful showing?"

"It most certainly is. It's such a pleasure to meet such a talented artist." She introduced herself and her wife before continuing with her compliments. "Stunning work. Especially your latest pieces. They're very passionate."

"Thank you very much," Haven said.

"We're interested in a number of pieces for our collection, but we wanted to inquire about commissions."

"Haven, this is the couple I spoke about earlier."

"Yes. But I'm sorry, I don't—"

"We've never discussed them in detail, as Ms. Thorne has been working primarily on her own ideas."

"And they are exquisite, and a steal at these figures."

A steal? At least two of the paintings already marked sold had price tags of over $12,000 each. It was highway robbery in her mind. "Thank you. I'm so glad you like them," Haven said. She opted for polite instead of what she had wanted to say.

"So how much for a commission, Ms. Thorne?"

"Oh, I don't—"

"One moment please, ladies," Bianca interrupted, pressing her hand on Haven's back and stepping back out of earshot. "What are you doing?"

"I told you, I don't want to take commissions. I don't like the pressure."

"Haven, do this and you can have the entire price. I won't even take my agent fee. This is what every artist dreams of, and I can't let you miss this opportunity."

Haven knew Bianca was right. For a time, this had been her dream. But like all dreams, they end. She loved painting, and she always would. But it wasn't what she wanted to do. She knew what she wanted, and she knew just how she was going to do it. Haven turned back to the women and smiled. "I'd love to take your commission."

Chapter Twenty-One

It took six months after going on the market for the farm to sell. Willa had begun to get discouraged as time dragged on without an offer, and she found herself second-guessing their decision to move. One of the last potential buyers to come look at the property had stopped Willa in her tracks and sent her pulse racing. Yet the young woman with wild blond hair was not the one her heart hoped it had been.

Willa could find Haven in anyone and anywhere. There was always a trait or quirk that would remind her of something that Haven would do or say. She had thought to call her many times over the last six months. But as life complicated things and time continued to pass, Willa's opportunities to reach out diminished. Any attempt to contact her now would only hurt one or both of them, and Willa didn't want to hurt Haven ever again. If that meant disappearing from her life forever, she would do so.

Kyle pulled around the house in his truck, hauling a thirty-foot, bright red stock trailer. "I saw the hauler coming down the road for your house," he said, jumping out of the vehicle.

Willa was probably paying more to move her place than it had cost in materials to build, but it was full of her blood, sweat, and tears. It was going wherever she did. They had already packed up all the roosters and chickens into their cages and stacked them in the bed of Willa's truck. That just left her house and their blended herd of misfits.

The household movers had come the day before to pack up their personal items. Willa thought she'd be uncomfortable having someone else pack and move her stuff, but she had been wrong. It left her plenty of time and energy to stress about how they were going to get her house onto a trailer without wrecking it. Although she had built and designed it for such an occasion, when she saw the trailer they arrived with, she had her doubts that it was going to work.

To her surprise, the whole process took no more than thirty minutes. Willa stood back and held her breath as she watched a hydraulic remote-controlled trailer back up to her house. It tilted and shifted until the rails and beams lined up. Willa watched as her house began to tip backward until she thought it would be almost perpendicular to the ground.

To her relief, it never got that far before the motors whirred and it began to lower back down. Two men tightened the straps that held the house to the rails. Once it was level to the ground it was securely atop the bed of the trailer. It took a few more minutes as the hauler adjusted and locked into position for the transport. "That's that," Willa said, breathing a sigh of relief. It was really happening. All that was left was to load the animals, and they would be on their way. Willa and Kyle walked along behind her house as they hauled it off the property and out onto the road. It was a surreal vision to see her home driving off on a flatbed.

"Let's get these buggers loaded and we will be on our way. Ready?"

Willa took a last look around at the property. Grass had already covered in most of the spaces where buildings and oak trees had once stood. There was a feeling of closure that washed over her, and she was content with the decision she was making. "As I'll ever be." She had fear, but she also had hope that everything would work out the way it was meant to.

Kyle patted her on the back and set off for the gate where the entire herd waited as if they knew they too were starting a new adventure. "They're not gonna be so excited when they realize they're going on that trailer."

"They know."

"Well, let's hope they load themselves calmly and politely."

"Well, Harold and the goats will, but I already know Leland is gonna be an ass about it." Willa snorted as she laughed at her own joke.

Kyle gave her a look and rolled his eyes. "That was so stupid," he said, but chuckled anyway.

Willa put the lead on Harold and walked him up into the trailer, latching the gate behind him. They repeated the process with each of them, putting Harold and Leland in their own stall, the two llamas in theirs, and the sheep and goats filled up the back. The kids had a different idea, it seemed. Every time Kyle managed to get them blocked in on one side, someone escaped out the other side by jumping on and over the bigger adults. At one point, Willa had to step back because she was laughing too hard to be of any use. With the use of all their arms and legs, Kyle and Willa managed to block them in long enough to close the gate with everyone inside.

"That went pretty well, I think," Willa said, still fighting the giggles.

"Well, it could've been worse," he said. "That's it, Will. Let's blow this Popsicle stand."

Willa checked the cover on the chickens one more time, and then each of them loaded up into their trucks. Willa waited for him to pull out onto the road before following along behind him.

In less than ten hours, they'd be pulling in to their new farm, and for the first time in her life, Willa would no longer live in Florida. She wondered if this was what Haven had felt like when she decided to move from the only home she'd ever known. It was a mix of excitement and trepidation. Her eyes filled with tears as she passed familiar landmarks and old haunts on her way out of town. She didn't know if she'd ever be back, but without a reason to return she imagined not. Haven would've been the only reason.

❖

Haven stood on the curb with her luggage looking for anything that resembled a silver Ford Explorer. She determined that far too many people drove silver vehicles. Haven checked her phone again to make sure the volume was up and that she hadn't missed any calls or messages. That's when she heard her name.

"Haven!" Corey shouted as she came around the front of the truck with her arms wide open.

"Corey!" Haven welcomed the offer of a giant hug.

Haven couldn't believe that it had already been almost eight months since she'd last seen Corey at her gallery opening in Denver. She would never forget it. She had made close to $80,000 in sales and commissions that night. Bianca had promised her a hundred percent of the profit. It was enough money for a strong down payment on the property she had dreamed about. It was all going to happen, and Corey was there to help make it so.

"I'm so excited!" Corey said, putting Haven's bag into the back of the truck. "Are you tired? If you are I can take you to the house to relax, or if you're not we can get started." Corey chattered at a thousand miles per hour.

"I'm all right. It's a two-hour time difference. I probably won't fall asleep until tomorrow if I'm lucky," Haven said.

"Still not sleeping, huh?" Corey asked, pulling away from the curb.

"Nah. I haven't slept an entire night going on four years now. Except for…eh, it's been a while." Haven was going to say since Florida, but thought otherwise. She knew that Corey and Willa had remained good friends since camp, and she didn't want to make things awkward.

"Okay. Well, I have three properties I have to show you. Maybe four, but I'm not sure if we'll have time today for all of them."

"That's fine. I'm here all weekend."

"I know! This is going to be so much fun!"

Haven was very much looking forward to the adventure. She had gone over and over the listings that she and Corey had narrowed down over the last few weeks. They all had so many great features that she was looking for that it was nearly impossible to decide without seeing them in person. Haven hoped that once she got there and saw the property that she would feel a connection or something of the sort, and she would know.

The first property on Corey's list was over a hundred acres with a lake, two springs, and plenty of pasture land. The old barn would need to be taken down, but Haven could use the timber to build other things. The price was well within her budget, and that would leave enough to construct several of the buildings herself. "It has such amazing views, I wish I didn't have to start from the ground up, though."

The next property had fewer acres than she wanted, and no streams or springs, but it did have a three-acre lake. The other plus was a main cabin and a middle-aisle barn in great condition. She would still have to bring in the containers for the cabins, and her own place, but she felt a very positive vibe with this property.

"I like this one a lot. But the next one is my favorite. It was part of a multi-listing. The previous owners broke it out into separate parcels to make it easier to sell," Corey said.

Haven shuffled through the listings pages that she had printed out. "Is this 608 Winding Ridge?" She agreed with Corey. This was a gorgeous property. It was the one she kept going back to every time she looked through the papers.

"Um, no. That one…it's been sold," Corey said. "I'm sorry."

"Oh," Haven said. She couldn't have been more disappointed by the news. Her heart sank as she looked down at the beautiful pictures on the page.

"I'm sorry. But this next one is just over on the next ridge. The views are just as spectacular, I promise."

"Okay. Just one more though." Haven felt the jet lag kick in, spurred on by the devastating blow that she was too late in making a move on that property. It would've been perfect. A quaint cottage built in 1895, a well kept, six-stall barn with a loft, and an actual river as its eastern border.

"Okay. This is the last one."

Haven was beginning to have second thoughts about the whole thing as they drove to their next destination. She was hoping that the next time she got out of the car that she would've found a place to call home. Her future. Her happiness. But as the sun began to set, Haven hadn't yet found what she was looking for. It was a feeling that always seemed to be just beyond her reach, and she didn't know why. It was as if every time she got close to finding her forever it was taken away from her. The only difference this time was that it hadn't been Willa who took it away.

They pulled onto the property, and Haven sat up in her seat. They crossed a bridge over a swift running river. The drive opened into a gorgeous green pastures lined with old timber fencing on either side of the road. When the road forked, Corey turned in the direction of a beautiful red barn and several matching outbuildings. Beyond the buildings stood a small ranch house with wraparound porch across from acres of tilled fields ready for planting.

"Corey, this is incredible, but there is no way I can afford this."

"Oh. This isn't the property. This is the half that was bought a couple months ago. They own the right-of-way to the parcel back that way." Corey pointed back to where the road had forked. "I just need to let them know we're here."

"Oh." Haven was once again disappointed. She had no doubt this place was well beyond her budget, but it was certainly beautiful. It was also a bit more farm and less camp than she was looking for, so that helped ease the sting.

"I'll be right back," Corey said, getting out of the car and walking up to the house.

Haven watched as a man answered the door and Corey pointed back toward the car where Haven was waiting. As he stepped down from the porch, Haven's stomach jumped into her throat. She squinted and blinked several times over, but her eyes saw just fine. It was Kyle Bennett. "What the fuck?" Haven said as she got out of the car and walked toward them.

Corey and Kyle met her halfway between the house and the vehicle. "This is—"

"I know who this is, Corey. What is going on?" Haven said, choking on the knot in her throat.

"Hey, Haven," Kyle said.

"Kyle, what the hell is going on?" She glanced between him and Corey.

"Don't be mad," Corey said.

"I'm not mad. I'm confused, but that's going to change in a second if someone doesn't please tell me what is happening here."

"I'll explain it."

Haven felt her knees buckle beneath her at the sound of Willa's voice from behind her. She was afraid to turn around for fear of falling over. Tears filled her eyes and Corey smiled before covering her mouth with her hand. Haven felt fingers intertwine with her own and pull her around. She came face-to-face with the last person on earth she would ever want to see again, and her emotion turned to anger. "What are you doing here, Willa?"

"I live here."

"We," Kyle added.

"*We* live here. We bought it with the insurance settlement and profit from the Florida property when we sold it."

"What?" When Kyle spoke up, Haven turned around toward him.

"We settled the damages and packed it all up to come here. It was my idea, Haven."

She turned back to Willa. "So why am I here? You wanted to gloat or something?" Haven felt like she was in a trap and snapped back around. "Corey?"

"It wasn't my idea. Although I did help, obviously."

"What about the property? The right-of-way? All a lie? Was that other land even really sold?" Haven wanted to scream. She wanted to cry.

"Yes. It was sold. But the right-of-way story is true. There is an adjoining hundred and thirty acres for sale, and they do own the right-of-way. Willa thought that—"

"It's what you've been looking for, Haven."

"What I've been looking for? How could you possibly know what I've been looking for, Willa? Every time we get anywhere close to what I'm looking for you run away, and break my... No, I can't do this," Haven said, waving her arms in defeat and starting back toward the car. The small pieces of her heart she had left were being crushed into dust. Nothing was safe from Willa, not her heart, her soul, or even her future.

"Haven, please." Willa chased after her.

❖

What had Willa expected? In spite of how she had hoped the situation would turn out, it was going as she should have guessed—badly. "Haven, please. Hear me out."

"Hear you out?" Haven spun around to face Willa. "You want me to hear you out? You've got to be shitting me!"

Willa could see the anger that rose in Haven's face as the tears filled her eyes. "I know. I don't deserve it, but—"

"That is the understatement of the century. You destroyed me, Willa. Not once, but twice. You broke my heart so badly I thought I'd die. I blamed myself for years. Years!"

At some point, Corey and Kyle had snuck off back to the porch away from them. "I'm so sorry." Willa reached out for Haven's hand, but she jerked it away.

"Don't touch me," Haven said, crossing her arms close to her chest. "How can I believe anything you say, Willa? You promised me that you'd never hurt me again, but you did. Your sorry means nothing."

"I know."

"And you tricked me. All of you. You plotted this horrible plan to get me up here and then ripped the rug out from under me. That's not all right."

"It's yours, Haven."

"What?"

"The land Corey brought you to see. It's yours, if you want it."

"What the fuck are you talking about?"

"The land that Corey brought you here to see. It's ours. It was a split parcel, but they gave us a deal if we bought both. It's mostly wooded, with a stream running to the Green River. It has a lake and a great clearing, perfect for the cabins, and—"

"Stop, Willa. You bought me property?"

"Yes. Well, no. It came with this property. We were going to let it go until I saw it, and I knew it was for you." Willa could see everything Haven had ever dreamed laid out on those 130 acres.

As Willa and Kyle made the move to North Carolina, Willa found herself fantasizing about the possibility of Haven moving and starting her camp there. Willa even imagined how she could help achieve her goals. When Corey informed her that Haven was coming out to look at property to start her camp, Willa finally believed in fate again. This was going to be her last chance to get back together with Haven, and this time she would do whatever she had to make it last a lifetime.

"There's no way I can accept that."

"You can. I'll sell it to you. At a very reasonable price, too." Willa could see Haven's demeanor begin to change. She saw the possibility in her eyes, and Willa's heart lifted. But as quick as it came it was gone.

"No, Willa. This is insane. I ran across the country to get you out of my life, twice."

"And I moved six hundred miles hoping to make this work. I'm all in, Haven. I want to be with you. Forever. I don't want to run or hide or push you away ever again. I may have lived through cancer, but it's not a life without you in it. I love you, Haven."

Haven's tears ran down her face and Willa ached to brush them away. She hesitated at first, but when she reached out to touch her face, Haven didn't pull away. Her eyes fluttered closed and Willa stepped toward her. When they opened, Haven was staring into hers.

"How do I know I can trust you, Willa? How do I know this is real?"

Willa folded Haven's hand into hers and dropped to her knee. "Because I love you, Haven Thorne, and I want to spend the rest of my life with you. No one knows how much time we have left, but no matter how long that may be, I don't want to do it without you." Willa's heart raced and pounded in her chest. She didn't know if it was her hands or Haven's that were shaking. When she reached into her pocket and pulled out the ring, Haven gasped. "Will you marry me?" Willa held her breath waiting for Haven's answer. Seconds seemed like hours, and she began to lose hope with each passing moment.

Haven covered her mouth with her hand and stared down at Willa. "Willa…I…" Haven's words caught in her throat.

"Please, Haven, I need you." Willa grabbed Haven's hand and held it to her chest where her aching heart pounded. "I've done so much running from everything in my life, because I didn't want to fail. I didn't want to fail you, and I didn't want to disappoint you if I couldn't fight the cancer and win."

"Oh, Willa," Haven said, dropping to her knees before her. "You could never have disappointed me. You are a fighter. You are the strongest, and most obstinate, woman I've ever known. It kills me to this day knowing that I couldn't be there for you when you needed me the most."

"I didn't want to need you, Haven. I didn't want to need anyone. But I do need you." Willa's stomach turned and tumbled. She had finally realized there was no one else on earth that she wanted by her side through sickness and health than Haven. "I need you, and I want you by my side every day for the rest of our lives. No matter how long that may be. I'm so sorry for hurting you, and I will do whatever it takes to make it up to you. I will show you every day how much you mean to me. Please." She let the tears stream down her face, and Haven's soft hands cupped her cheeks and brushed them away.

"Promise me, Willa. Promise me that no matter what happens from this point forward, you and I are in this together, win or lose."

"Haven, I can't promise that I won't do everything in my power to protect you. But I know that by pushing you away I wasn't saving anyone, least of all you. I can't imagine living even one more day with you by my side. I promise, my love, with every breath I have, we are in this together."

"Then yes. I'll marry you," Haven said, her own tears flowing freely.

Willa slipped the ring onto her finger and they jumped to their feet. She took Haven into her arms. "And I promise I'll never let you go again. I love you."

"I've loved you my whole life, Willa Bennett, and I always will."

CHAPTER TWENTY-TWO

Haven stood on the front porch of the main lodge as she had many times before, watching as the SUVs pulled up the drive. Her excitement was palpable, and she squeezed Wendy's hand. "I love this part."

"I know. Are you ready?"

"Of course," Haven said as the vehicles came to a stop in front of the house. The doors swung open and campers began to pile out with their bags and packs.

Haven and Wendy went around to the back to start unloading the luggage when Willa stuck her head around the back end. "How exciting is this? It's finally here, your first camp."

"I know, babe." Haven jumped into Willa's arms. "How was the drive?"

"It was great. It's a really fun group."

"Oh, I can't wait." Haven's entire body hummed with excitement.

She couldn't believe that they'd made it happen. For more than a year, they worked their asses off building cabins, raising money, and getting the mountains of paperwork in order for what seemed like every agency in existence. Scrat had agreed to come out and work out all of the river running and permits. Wendy came to keep Haven's head above water and to be her right-hand lady, while Corey handled all of the volunteers. Willa and Kyle had the farm to run as usual, but they would be handling the farm-related activities like horseback and trail riding.

Haven and Willa were happier than she could ever remember being. In the middle of all the chaos of starting the camp, they had made the time for a small, intimate wedding ceremony. Surrounded by their closest family and friends, they vowed to always depend on each other and never be afraid to lean on one another to get through the tough times in life.

For the first time in her life Haven felt like she was where she was meant to be. "Thank you."

"For what, my love?" Willa said, wrapping Haven into her arms.

"For finding me and choosing me out of all the other stars in the sky." They had lost and found each other so many times on their journey through life, but Haven knew in her heart they'd never be lost again.

"In every life I ever live, I'll always choose you. Thank you for giving me the chance."

"Forever and for always, Willa."

About the Author

Tina Michele is a Florida girl living on the banks of the Indian River Lagoon in the biggest small town on the Space Coast. She enjoys all the benefits of living in the Sunshine State. During the day, she pretends to do what they pay her for but really spends most of that time daydreaming and plotting some wild adventure. She graduated from the University of Central Florida with her BA in interdisciplinary studies—the most liberal of the liberal arts degrees—majoring in fine art and writing with a minor in women's studies. To say she is motivated by her Right brain is a major understatement. Afflicted with self-diagnosed Sagittarian Attention Deficit Disorder, she spends a lot of time starting projects that she might, possibly, one day, probably finish. When she isn't writing, playing, drawing, painting, or creating something of some sort, she feeds and waters the three dogs that are permanently tethered to her hindquarters.

Books Available From Bold Strokes Books

Between Sand and Stardust by Tina Michele. Are the lifelong bonds of love strong enough to conquer time, distance, and heartache when Haven Thorne and Willa Bennette are given another chance at forever? (978-1-62639-940-2)

Charming the Vicar by Jenny Frame. When magician and atheist Finn Kane seeks refuge in an English village after a spiritual crisis, can local vicar Bridget Claremont restore her faith in life and love? (978-1-63555-029-0)

Data Capture by Jesse J. Thoma. Lola Walker is undercover on the hunt for cybercriminals while trying not to notice the woman who might be perfectly wrong for her for all the right reasons. (978-1-62639-985-3)

Epicurean Delights by Renee Roman. Ariana Marks had no idea a leisure swim would lead to being rescued, in more ways than one, by the charismatic Hudson Frost. (978-1-63555-100-6)

Heart of the Devil by Ali Vali. We know most of Cain and Emma Casey's story, but Heart of the Devil will take you back to where it began one fateful night with a tray loaded with beer. (978-1-63555-045-0)

Known Threat by Kara A. McLeod. When Special Agent Ryan O'Connor reluctantly questions who protects the Secret Service, she learns courage truly is found in unlikely places. Agent O'Connor Series #3 (978-1-63555-132-7)

Seer and the Shield by D. Jackson Leigh. Time is running out for the Dragon Horse Army while two unlikely heroines struggle to put aside their attraction and find a way to stop a deadly cult. Dragon Horse War, Book 3 (978-1-63555-170-9)

The Universe Between Us by Jane C. Esther. Ana Mitchell must make the hardest choice of her life: the promise of new love Jolie Dann on Earth, or a humanity-saving mission to colonize Mars. (978-1-63555-106-8)

Touch by Kris Bryant. Can one touch heal a heart? (978-1-63555-084-9)

A More Perfect Union by Carsen Taite. Major Zoey Granger and DC fixer Rook Daniels risk their reputations for a chance at true love while dealing with a scandal that threatens to rock the military. (978-1-62639-754-5)

Arrival by Gun Brooke. The spaceship *Pathfinder* reaches its passengers' new homeworld where danger lurks in the shadows while Pamas Seclan disembarks and finds unexpected love in young science genius Darmiya Do Voy. (978-1-62639-859-7)

Captain's Choice by VK Powell. Architect Kerstin Anthony's life is going to plan until Bennett Carlyle, the first girl she ever kissed, is assigned to her latest and most important project, a police district substation. (978-1-62639-997-6)

Falling Into Her by Erin Zak. Pam Phillips, widow at the age of forty, meets Kathryn Hawthorne, local Chicago celebrity, and it changes her life forever—in ways she hadn't even considered possible. (978-1-63555-092-4)

Hookin' Up by MJ Williamz. Will Leah get what she needs from casual hookups or will she see the love she desires right in front of her? (978-1-63555-051-1)

King of Thieves by Shea Godfrey. When art thief Casey Marinos meets bounty hunter Finnegan Starkweather, the crimes of the past just might set the stage for a payoff worth more than she ever dreamed possible. (978-1-63555-007-8)

Lucy's Chance by Jackie D. As a serial killer haunts the streets, Lucy tries to stitch up old wounds with her first love in the wake of a small town's rapid descent into chaos. (978-1-63555-027-6)

Right Here, Right Now by Georgia Beers. When Alicia Wright moves into the office next door to Lacey Chamberlain's accounting firm, Lacey is about to find out that sometimes the last person you want is exactly the person you need. (978-1-63555-154-9)

Strictly Need to Know by MB Austin. Covert operator Maji Rios will do whatever she must to complete her mission, but saving a gorgeous stranger from Russian mobsters was not in her plans. (978-1-63555-114-3)

Tailor-Made by Yolanda Wallace. Tailor Grace Henderson doesn't date clients, but when she meets gender-bending model Dakota Lane, she's tempted to throw all the rules out the window. (978-1-63555-081-8)

Time Will Tell by M. Ullrich. With the ability to time travel, Eva Caldwell will have to decide between having it all and erasing it all. (978-1-63555-088-7)

Change in Time by Robyn Nyx. Working in the past is hell on your future. The Extractor series: Book Two. (978-1-62639-880-1)

Love After Hours by Radclyffe. When Gina Antonelli agrees to renovate Carrie Longmire's new house, she doesn't welcome Carrie's overtures at friendship or her own unexpected attraction. A Rivers Community Novel. (978-1-63555-090-0)

Nantucket Rose by CF Frizzell. Maggie Jordan can't wait to convert a historic Nantucket home into a B&B, but doesn't expect to fall for mariner Ellis Chilton, who has more claim to the house than Maggie realizes. (978-1-63555-056-6)

Picture Perfect by Lisa Moreau. Falling in love wasn't supposed to be part of the stakes for Olive and Gabby, rival photographers in the competition of a lifetime. (978-1-62639-975-4)

Set the Stage by Karis Walsh. Actress Emilie Danvers takes the stage again in Ashland, Oregon, little realizing that landscaper Arden Philips is about to offer her a very personal romantic lead role. (978-1-63555-087-0)

Strike a Match by Fiona Riley. When their attempts at matchmaking fizzle out, firefighter Sasha and reluctant millionairess Abby find themselves turning to each other to strike a perfect match. (978-1-62639-999-0)

The Price of Cash by Ashley Bartlett. Cash Braddock is doing her best to keep her business afloat, stay out of jail, and avoid Detective Kallen. It's not working. (978-1-62639-708-8)

Captured Soul by Laydin Michaels. Can Kadence Munroe save the woman she loves from a twisted killer, or will she lose her to a collector of souls? (978-1-62639-915-0)

Under Her Wing by Ronica Black. At Angel's Wings Rescue, dogs are usually the ones saved, but when quiet Kassandra Haden meets outspoken owner Jayden Beaumont, the two stubborn women just might end up saving each other. (978-1-63555-077-1)

Underwater Vibes by Mickey Brent. When Hélène, a translator in Brussels, Belgium, meets Sylvie, a young Greek photographer and swim coach, unsettling feelings hijack Hélène's mind and body—even her poems. (978-1-63555-002-3)

A Date to Die by Anne Laughlin. Someone is killing people close to Detective Kay Adler, who must look to her own troubled past for a suspect. There she finds more than one person seeking revenge against her. (978-1-63555-023-8)

Dawn's New Day by TJ Thomas. Can Dawn Oliver and Cam Cooper, two women who have loved and lost, open their hearts to love again? (978-1-63555-072-6)

Definite Possibility by Maggie Cummings. Sam Miller is just out for good times, but Lucy Weston makes her realize happily ever after is a definite possibility. (978-1-62639-909-9)

Eyes Like Those by Melissa Brayden. Isabel Chase and Taylor Andrews struggle between love and ambition from the writers' room on one of Hollywood's hottest TV shows. (978-1-63555-012-2)

Heart's Orders by Jaycie Morrison. Helen Tucker and Tee Owens escape hardscrabble lives to careers in the Women's Army Corps, but more than their hearts are at risk as friendship blossoms into love. (978-1-63555-073-3)

Hiding Out by Kay Bigelow. Treat Dandridge is unaware that her life is in danger from the murderer who is hunting the woman she's falling in love with, Mickey Heiden. (978-1-62639-983-9)

Omnipotence Enough by Sophia Kell Hagin. Can the tiny tool that abducted war veteran Jamie Gwynmorgan accidentally acquires help her escape an unknown enemy to reclaim her stolen life and the woman she deeply loves? (978-1-63555-037-5)